Illusions & Dreams

Z. ALLORA

Dreamspinner Press

Published by
DREAMSPINNER PRESS

5032 Capital Circle SW, Suite 2, PMB# 279, Tallahassee, FL 32305-7886 USA
http://www.dreamspinnerpress.com/

Illusions & Dreams
© 2014 Z. Allora.

Cover Art
© 2014 Paul Richmond.
http://www.paulrichmondstudio.com
Cover content is for illustrative purposes only and any person depicted on the cover is a model.

ISBN: 978-1-63216-274-8
Digital ISBN: 978-1-63216-275-5
Library of Congress Control Number: 2014948402
First Edition November 2014

Printed in the United States of America
∞
This paper meets the requirements of
ANSI/NISO Z39.48-1992 (Permanence of Paper).

To the lovelies I met in Bangkok. May you all have happily ever afters.

Author's Note

I STRUGGLED with the title of this series: *The Ladyboy Chronicles*.

In the West, many people would see the word "ladyboy" as fetishizing someone who is transgender. I promise you that isn't my intention.

During my travels I spent some time in Thailand, and in discussions with a number of club performers, I found the word doesn't have the same negative connotation for them. They embrace their unique energy and are proud they are part of the third sex.

It is my hope I am conveying their story with respect and dignity.

Acknowledgments

BIG THANKS to Derekica Snake, Johnny Williams, Danny Bruggemann, Carla VanGronigen Nilson, P.D. Singer, and Val Hughes—your feedback and recommendations were invaluable.

A special thanks to Eden Winters for reading the first six chapters eight times and working with me until she could smell the Thai food.

All my love to my husband, who traveled with me to all sorts of clubs in Bangkok (over several years) and taught some of the performers how to play *Angry Birds* as I listened to the stories of their lives. You mean the world to me.

Hugs to all my Pretties on Facebook.

Glossary

ah loy ma: —Very delicious.

baht: Thai money equivalent to three US cents or two cents in the European Union.

chan rak khoon maak leeuy: I love you so much.

di: Good.

dtem: Full.

farang keenok: An insult that roughly translates into "birdshit foreigner."

gaff: Used to contain male genitalia to give the appearance of a smooth line.

kathoey: A transgender woman or an effeminate gay male in Thailand. A significant number of Thai people perceive kathoey as belonging to a third gender, including many kathoey themselves, while others see them as either a kind of man or a kind of woman.

khaa: Yes.

khaawy hak jao: I love you.

khanom khrauk: Two mini pancakes top layer contains vegetables like corn or spring onion and the bottom layer is made of rice and coconut milk batter.

khun: More.

ladyboy: A performer in Thailand who has not had sexual affirmation surgery. The word kathoey is used interchangeably.

maak: More.

mai naa cheuua: You're amazing/unbelievable.

phee seuua: Butterfly.

Prologue

"I DON'T know. Where do you want to go, Jake?" Randy Camster asked his best friend, not wanting to make the decision himself. If left up to him, he'd spend this vacation like his last—on his back deck, drinking beer and listening to ball games. Not a bad way to spend a few weeks away from the fascinating world of software development.

"We could go to China," Jake suggested with a laugh. Randy could hear the jingle of Jake's silver earrings, which clanged together against the phone.

"Nah." Asia did sound exotic, though. "Maybe Southeast Asia." Randy'd have to get his ass off the couch first.

"Singapore?"

"You'd get caned." Randy chuckled at Jake's suggestion, switching his cell phone to his other hand as he kicked his legs up on the scarred coffee table in front of him.

"Yeah, but I'd like it. I could sell the pictures and make a fortune," Jake snarked.

"Cambodia? We could go to the ruins of Angkor Wat." If Jake wanted to throw out off-the-wall suggestions, so could Randy. He pulled his computer onto his lap.

"Happy pizza, baby!" Jake ignored Randy's groan. "You know the Khmer used pot as a spice, and you can still get herb on pizza there."

Randy wasn't ready to babysit a higher-than-a-kite Jake in Cambodia. Amsterdam had been bad enough. His best friend had dragged him to the Netherlands when pot smoking had been a major tourist attraction, before the residential restriction policy came into force. Though

Jake had assured him the police weren't enforcing the ban on selling marijuana to the tourists.

Traveling there right after Randy's divorce, Jake had attempted to cheer him up by trying to convince him to utilize the red-light district. Randy'd never had a prostitute, and he refused to start in the Netherlands. Though after smoking something called White Widow at a coffee house, Jake got overly horny on a dance floor, almost causing an international incident to hear him tell it; what he really did was cause a brawl.

Maybe getting the hell out of the country would do Randy some good. He had the vacation time coming. He clicked around the Internet for tourist destinations, and Thailand came up.

"How about Thailand? The photos look inviting."

The tourism board had pictures of magnificent Thai architecture, lovely people, exceptional food, and interesting adventures a couple of hours away from the main airport.

Randy clicked a link for "Exotic Thailand." His imagination wandered as he stared at images of temple spires and a golden statue. The pictures changed—a group of smiling women in traditional clothing putting plates loaded with food on a table. His mouth watered. He could almost smell the basil chicken, heavy with spices.

Jake broke into his food fantasy with his usual spiel. "Oh, yeah. Thailand. Bangkok. Ladyboys. Hot sex."

Randy rolled his eyes, though Jake wouldn't be able to see it through his cell phone. "I was thinking more of the Grand Palace, Ayutthaya, temples, monks…." *Ladyboys?* An unexpected shiver slid down Randy's spine.

"I'm sending you a link—"

Before Jake finished his sentence, a new e-mail link pinged in Randy's box.

Randy opened the blue link. A sidebar on the site provided links to cities. He clicked on Bangkok.

"And ladyboys," Jake said again as if repetition would help his cause.

"Isn't ladyboy a derogatory term?"

"Um, I think it is here, but in Thailand many of the performers are proud to be a part of the third sex."

A few clicks later, Randy landed on a site that captured his complete attention: Illusions & Dreams, a ladyboy club. Neon outlined the classically French building façade. The performers posed and waved at the camera. The tourist rating put the attraction at five stars.

He clicked on a tab labeled Cast. At least twenty thumbnail sketches popped up. Hot damn! He stared at a beautifully feminine face, long lashes framing a pair of incredibly soulful brown eyes. An arrow beckoned, and he clicked, paging through scenes from the club's shows.

Wow! Those were ladyboys? They were some of the most resplendent women he'd ever laid eyes on.

"So Thailand, Rand?" Jake practically begged. "We've only been on one vacation since your divorce. I'm worried about you." Randy heard his friend's thumb ring tap out a beat on the phone. "Thailand, Rand?" He cleared his voice and started singing the song by Murray Head, "One Night In Bangkok."

Randy cut in. "If I agree to think about going to Thailand, will you stop singing?" He chuckled at his nutty friend.

"For now. So Thailand?"

"I said I'd think about it. I'll see you tomorrow at Chucky's for a beer, and we can figure out what to do." Randy ended the cell call and touched the computer in front of him.

A vision stood onstage half a world away, dressed in traditional Thai garb. The bright gold dress left one shoulder bare. Her head thrown back, eyes closed, microphone in hand, the olive-skinned stunner exuded poise and beauty.

Another link promised more. The touch of an icon brought the vision to life, a mesmerizing contralto belting out "Memory," the song from *Cats.* Randy's mouth dropped open. Damn. Just damn.

Unfamiliar excitement barreled through him. Her voice touched him. The singer's movements were sensual and suggested constrained energy. There was a mischievous gleam in her eye, and he wanted to know why.

He'd never desired a stranger to this extent. Hell, he'd never wanted anyone like this before. The fact *she* happened to be a *he* genetically should've stalled his lust. Instead the knowledge didn't seem to register.

Unlike Jake, Randy'd never slept with another man—but she wasn't a man. He squinted at the computer screen. This gorgeous creature who sent all his blood downward was all woman. He shifted on the couch, scooting his laptop back to give his lengthening cock more room.

The song ended, and the figure on-screen froze. Randy wanted more of the charming songstress, so he selected another icon. She appeared again, wearing a form-fitting dress similar to the first one, but in jade green instead of gold. A jeweled clasp held her dark hair in a loose bun at the nape of her long neck.

The camera panned in for a close-up. The singer seemed to stare directly into Randy's eyes. He swallowed hard, heat raging through him as her sweet voice caressed his soul. Randy watched every one of the video clips she performed in, some more than once.

Randy took a look around his own room, a room unchanged in the five years since his divorce. His ex-wife's picture still sat on the desk, though the woman herself now lived across town, happily married to somebody else. Jake was right, Randy needed to pull himself out of the rut he'd fallen into, and a vacation seemed a great way to start.

He grabbed up his phone to text Jake: *Thailand.*

Chapter One

A HIGH-PITCHED shriek of pure frustration hurt Randy's ears.

"I know you dress up to play a girl on stage! But I dress as a woman because that's who I am!"

The scream ripped through the nearly empty club. Service staff scattered, leaving Randy and Jake standing alone at the entrance to the empty Illusions & Dreams club.

Randy peeked farther into the hallway. The air conditioning cooled his face while the heat of Bangkok still heated his back. Jake glanced over at him with a questioning look. Maybe this wasn't a first-rate idea.

Jake opened his mouth and shut it before any words came out. The red curtains covering one of the doorframes fluttered open.

A man dressed in a colorful skirt swirled around the bar area. His muscular chest was bare except for a coconut bikini top he was tying with a pink ribbon.

He froze when he saw them in the doorway and adjusted the two coconut halves into the proper location on his chest. "Oh, my."

The guy in front of them appeared to be in his late twenties or early thirties. His age was difficult to tell. Like most Thai men they'd met thus far, he was quite attractive and ageless. His large brown eyes were made up and his silky black hair twisted up with flowers. He had to be part of the show.

He turned toward where the shouting had come from and frowned. Sighing, he pasted on a forced smile and seemed to pretend nothing was wrong. "Hello, my dears."

Randy and Jake were early, but Randy hoped the guy would let them wait until the restaurant opened. He promised himself it was the last time he'd let Jake talk him into a cheaper fare. Changing planes once sucked, but three times over the last two days had left him dazed and confused.

After they'd finally landed in Bangkok, when Jake suggested a quick shower before heading straight to Illusions & Dreams for a show, he didn't argue. He wasn't in the mood to fight the traffic in a cab or climb the stairs to the Sky Train just to go back to their hotel to wait for the show, so he hoped the guy would have mercy on them.

Jake greeted the flowered man as they stepped fully into the cooled room. "Hey. Everything all right in here?"

The man appeared out of sorts. He glanced behind him at the curtain again, his false smile fading. He must have realized they'd heard at least part of the argument.

"So sorry you had to hear that." He gave them a shrug and a sad smile. "Finding one's soul mate is no guarantee of life and love being easy." His eyes widened as if he'd just realized they were clients and not his therapists.

He cleared his throat. "I'm Adirake, co-owner of this wonderful establishment. The show isn't for another two hours, and the restaurant and bar don't open for another thirty minutes."

Adirake stared at them for a moment as if he were waiting for them to leave. Randy had no intention of facing that hellish heat until he was forced to, so he stood his ground.

Adirake readjusted a drooping flower in his hair and sighed. "Wait one minute."

Jake crooked his head at Randy and gave him a questioning, wide-eyed look.

Adirake turned in the direction of a red door and bellowed, "Tong!"

A distant indistinct grumble rolled through the club.

"Tong!" Adirake wailed loudly as he smoothed down his skirt with a quick flick of his hand.

"What?" A disembodied, annoyed voice asked before a lovely woman appeared, encased in a sheer black gown with layers of silk that hid her full charms. "You shrieked, Adirake?" The woman batted her eyes coyly at him.

Adirake jerked his head toward Randy and Jake. The beauty had her hair smoothed into a light brown chignon. She followed Adirake's pointing finger and noticed them as customers.

Not missing a beat, she raised her voice up into the female range. "Well, hello. You two are early." She glared over at the co-owner and jerked her head toward the door. "Areva is upset. Go deal and I'll take care of these lovely men." She fairly purred as she pointed to them with her exceptionally long red nails.

Jake mumbled something, but Randy ignored him, captivated by the drama as it took place in front of him. Jake got his attention by elbowing him, grinning with mirth at the compliment.

"She thinks we're lovely."

Rolling his eyes, Randy griped, "Jake, grow up." He couldn't have gotten through the past few years without his best friend, but sometimes he prayed maturity would rain all over Jake. But alas, there had been a drought.

Jake made a face at him. Usually Randy didn't mind Jake making light of any situation, but not now. Randy was in the club where the singer he craved sang. He wiped his hands on his pants and glanced around.

Ever since their first conversation about Thailand months ago, Randy had been researching the terms *kathoey* and ladyboys. He had discovered that the Thai people considered *kathoey* to be a third sex. *Kathoey* were popular in the entertainment industries—all types of amusements—but he didn't want to think of his singer in those terms. Unlike the transgender community in America, who mostly wanted to live their lives quietly and not be noticed for being different, Thai ladyboys seemed to want to shine for those differences.

Randy's singer did more than glimmer—she practically sparkled when she sang. He couldn't wait to watch her perform in person.

Tong's wiggle drew his attention to the present as she made her way around the bar in a soft sway. "My name is Tong. We aren't open yet, but let me get you settled. It's too hot to send you back outside. Right this way." Her hips had a nice roll, made more evident by the way her black dress clung to her round bottom.

She settled them at a corner table, where the smell of basil wafted through the air, and handed them drink and food menus. "Will you boys stay for the show?" she asked, smiling prettily at both men.

"Yeah!" Randy fairly shouted. He flushed, and he added more quietly, "I mean, yes."

He couldn't help his excitement; Randy'd waited so long to see his singer. Finally, he'd see her show in person.

He'd lost hours to YouTube watching documentaries exploring the ladyboy culture and shows from all over Thailand, but it was the impressive Illusions & Dreams performance that mesmerized him the most. Those pictures and video clips he'd seen online remained with him, especially of one performer in particular. Meeting her was probably a long shot, but he had to try.

Randy noticed Jake studying him with interest as if trying to figure him out. Good luck with that.

In the span of their ten-year friendship, Jake had made it his mission to hook Randy up and get him laid. He'd dragged him to strip clubs for lap dances, which Randy found unappealing. Jake, comfortably pansexual, had even coerced Randy into going to an all-male revue to see if he could get a rise out of him, but failed. Randy drew the line at a new BDSM club Jake wanted to check out. Jake's determination to help Randy find some "temporary happiness" seemed to top his agenda. Randy found it sad that "temporary happiness" was the only thing Jake claimed to trust.

Illusions & Dreams seemed to be the classiest ladyboy club in Bangkok. Most clubs appeared to be a thin veil for prostitution. This club, according to TripAdvisor, provided real honest-to-goodness talent. The performers weren't prostitutes, but entertainers, or so the past clientele had claimed in their reviews.

"I'll be back to take your order in a bit when the kitchen opens."

Tong slowly undulated away. Randy stared at the menu as the kitchen door swung open, allowing the smell of garlic and mint to hit his nose. The scent made his stomach growl.

"'Kay," Randy shook his head. It hit Randy. They were in Thailand.

"She's a 'ladyboy.'"

Jake apparently felt the need to inform Randy, like he was a remedial student. As if Randy could've missed her unique energy.

"No kidding." His gaze tracked across the room to ensure he didn't miss anyone who happened to wander in. He shifted in his seat and caught Jake gawking at him.

"Never seen you"—Jake gestured toward Randy—"all aflutter."

"I am not all *aflutter*." Randy sighed, and a big grin lit up his face. "Okay, I am a bit." Jake's rude laughter made him add, "A bit, damn it."

Jake thumbed the trail of silver rings around his ear, making them click together. "Dude, I'm glad to see something interests you. We've been friends for what? Ten years? And you've never looked with interest at another person."

Choosing not to correct his false assumption, Randy went for a slam. "Yeah, well, maybe if you'd have better conversation skills…."

"Fuck you," Jake tossed back with no malice as he leaned his chair back onto two legs.

"Not my type," Randy teased.

Randy froze as the enticing creature he'd watched via the Internet floated in. In the flesh, the object of all his recent fantasies, Lalana Dulyarat appeared. Her shiny hair flowed to the middle of her back in a silken waterfall. A few strands were artfully arranged over her full breasts. Her kissable lips pursed. She was feminine, but something in her energy told the truth of her genetics. She was breathtaking.

"She more your type?" Jake goaded as he put his chair back on all fours.

The online images barely did her justice. "Ah. Um. Yeah." Randy was completely entranced by the vision, close enough to reach out and touch. He started to wonder if he might be a pervert. He'd gone hard from gawking at her smile at someone else.

Behind the tall beauty followed a young, adorable little waif, who giggled at something the singer said. They stopped in their tracks when they unexpectedly spotted the two men sitting at the table.

The waif whispered to the other and wiggled her way over to their table. Randy's fantasy, Lalana Dulyarat, reached out to stop her friend's forward motion but missed, so Lalana quickly trailed after her, trying to slow the pace. But Lalana's determined friend kept ducking out of reach of her hand.

Randy's singer glared at her friend with a touch of censure when they reached the table. The waif seemed paralyzed as she stared at Jake with her mouth open. Lalana held out her delicate hand to Randy, purposefully bumping into the little one next to her as if to knock her out of the Jake-induced trance she'd fallen under.

As he clumsily stood, Randy wondered if he should kiss the petal-soft hand proffered to him, but decided on a light shake.

"Greetings, sir," a melodic voice chimed.

Randy gazed into Lalana's eyes, getting lost in their depth until Jake cleared his throat.

"Oh. Hello. I just… you are…." He wasn't making a goddamned bit of sense, and he should probably let go of the gorgeous lady's hand. But he couldn't. "I'm Randy Camster."

"An American." She said "American" like his nationality wasn't a question, but Randy nodded anyway. She arched one perfectly manicured eyebrow and gently drew her hand back. "You're too early for dinner."

Jake reached out to take the smaller girl's hand and bought it to his lips smoothly. The twentysomething barely held in her squeal. "I'm Jake O'Neil. I'm very pleased to meet you."

Randy wished he had his best friend's flair with other people. Instead he just stood there, mute, as the younger girl appeared near to a swoon.

She leaned into Lalana, who pursed her lips and shook her head. Glancing back up to Randy and Jake, she said in a silky voice, "I am Lalana Dulyarat. And this is Ms. Boon-nam Rattanawong."

Randy finally found his voice. "I know. I, um, found you on the club's website, Ms. Dulyarat. You're even more lovely in person."

Did that sound stalkerish? He probably shouldn't mention he knew she was single. He'd conversed with a number of bloggers on travel websites as recent as last week to confirm. Not that he'd even the slightest shot in the dark to get a date with her, but he'd at least ask.

"Oh, how very nice of you to say so. Please call me Lalana."

Lalana uttered the words with such practice, Randy could tell it wasn't the first time she'd heard compliments from a panting male fan.

Jake grinned at Boon-nam, who seemed focused on him. "Are you ladies in the show?"

Boon-nam's eyes remained glued to Jake. She nodded absently and said something in Thai.

Lalana tsked and answered, "Yes, we are." Lalana nudged Boon-nam. "English, Boon-boon." Turning back to the men, she asked, "Will you be staying for the performance?"

"Yes. Oh, yes. We wouldn't miss it, right, Jake?" Randy answered immediately, smiling at the vision who haunted his dreams.

Boon-nam tugged Lalana down so she could whisper while her brown eyes remained focused on Jake. After hearing what her friend said, Lalana exhaled. She glared down at Boon-nam, who looked away from Jake to give the taller woman pleading puppy eyes.

Sighing, Lalana said, "Good, maybe we will see you afterward?" She dragged Boon-nam gently toward the door to the left of the stage.

Randy panicked, hoping for Jake's intervention. He had to ensure he would see her again. This couldn't be their only exchange.

He knew he could count on Jake's experience. "Drinks?" Jake called out.

Boon-nam answered happily. "Yes. Meet us at the bar at ten o'clock."

Lalana must have yanked her a bit roughly through the red door because Boon-nam vanished instantly.

After the ladies disappeared behind the door, Randy turned to Jake. "Thanks."

"No problem." Jake grinned at Randy and stifled a yawn. "Drinks at ten."

Randy nodded as if he were trying to snap himself back to reality. "That's like a date, right?"

"Indeed. Just like." Jake rocked back in his chair, twisting his silver thumb ring as he assessed Randy a little too closely.

Oh, shit! "I haven't had a date in… hell, forever."

"Then it's long overdue." Jake slapped him on the back.

Randy drew in a long inhale.

The ambience changed, and Randy waited for the warning. He knew Jake didn't want to pop his bubble, but he was going to say what he felt he needed to.

"You do understand those girls used to be boys? And they might still have their twigs and berries." *Why did Jake find it necessary to hammer home this fact?* Jake continued. "I'm fine with it. I mean, a hole's a hole."

What the hell? "Do you always have to be so crass?"

Leaning forward, Jake shrugged. "Just a realist, my friend. I don't dress up sex with emotion."

This was a discussion for another time. "Your point?"

"Just that." He actually appeared uncomfortable. "I don't want you getting a surprise."

To be fair, Jake didn't know of Randy's research. He'd been well versed in the facts, and if he were honest, maybe it accounted for a little of the appeal. While he found other transgender people attractive, he didn't have the same response as he did to Lalana.

Lalana pulsed with vibrant energy, drawing Randy to her. Whatever she had or didn't have under her dress didn't matter all that much to him. As insane as it sounded, he felt a connection with her. A nonstalkerish connection, he amended.

Jake sat back hard in the chair and waved his hands in defense. "Hey, man. No issue for me. You know my cock is all about equal opportunity. I'm nondiscriminatory when it comes to fucking. Cock, pussy, mouth, or ass, it's all good."

"It's not always about sex." Randy's hands itched to shake some sense into Jake, but he didn't have that kind of time.

Jake chuckled. "Yeah, actually it is. Love is a fairy tale people convince themselves exists, so they can fuck like bunnies without the guilt society would heap on them. I say just fuck whoever you want and leave emotion out."

Randy snorted. "Like a furred hole in the wall."

Jake slapped his hand against the table. "Come on. I'd been drinking, was drunk perhaps. It was that one time… I think."

Randy laughed harder at Jake's confession. "You've no shame. You had relations, literally, with a hole in the wall."

Jake grinned as he leaned across the table to grab the saltshaker and spin it around. "I'm sure one of the guys purposely lined it with fur. Whatever, man. I was hornier than fuck, and it was tight."

"What does that even mean?" Jake exasperated Randy, but he'd gotten used to the idiot.

Jake cracked up. "Does it matter?"

"Probably not," Randy glanced toward the door Lalana had disappeared through.

"I'm an 'any port in a storm' kind of guy."

Jake pretended he was totally nonselective in his choice of partners and that "safe, sane, and consensual" were his only standards. But Randy had never bought his line of bullshit.

"Only requirements are hot and tight. I guess I didn't know you were ready to swing in other directions."

Randy shook his head. "Chances are neither one of us will be swinging anything."

Jake's laugh barked out. "This is Bangkok, baby, Bangkok! Why do you think they call it Bang Cock?" Jake's face was an open book, which displayed each and every one of his obscene thoughts.

"You're crazy, you know that?" Randy cracked up, but was glad the ladies weren't there to witness Jake being uncouth.

"Yeah, I know. But you love me anyway. You can't help yourself."

True, but Randy didn't have to admit it. Jake was a great friend and always made him laugh at life. Even when life had been dismal, Jake had always been quick with a joke to make him smile.

"Okay, back to the situation at hand. Didn't know you had a hobby."

What was he talking about now? "Huh?"

Jake laughed. "You know, the whole Internet-stalking thing?"

Randy dropped his voice, not wanting to be overheard. "Screw you. I did a little research and watched the clips of Ms. Dulyarat singing." When Jake clearly wasn't buying his watered-down version of reality, Randy added, "A couple of times."

"Ha! Couple of hundred, maybe." Jake saw he was right when Randy felt his face go red. "Whatever, man, no worries." Slapping him on the back, Jake asked seriously, "You like her?"

"No. Yeah. I mean, I know I don't know her, but there's a vibe, a connection between us or something." He rubbed his forehead, which started to hurt.

Jake's expression spoke his disbelief so Randy simply tuned out his words. Sighing, he rambled on, "Shut up. I know it's crazy. But now I'm seeing her at ten."

Holy hell, he was meeting her in less than four hours! "What do I say? I mean, she's way out of my league. What do I talk about with her?" In comparison to the glamorous and talented performer, Randy's life was a snore. "How can they speak English perfectly?"

Jake grinned as if he enjoyed Randy's spin of crazy rapidly turning into panic. "See. There you go. Your first topic of conversation."

Before Randy could smack his ex-best friend in the head, Tong reappeared. "What can I get for you?"

Jake ordered the pad Thai with a Thai beer. Randy ordered the same, because he couldn't form thoughts beyond the gorgeous creature he'd be seeing at ten.

Tong turned and almost slammed right into a muscular man behind her. "Oh, sorry, Jaidee."

Randy was struck by how satiny and soft her voice could be. She was probably a singer too.

This Jaidee's hands went around her waist to ensure she didn't stumble. "No problem."

Tong seemed almost to swoon from the sound of his voice. The drama unfolding before them riveted Randy. The guy's hands lingered longer than necessary, and his eyes held Tong's for several heartbeats as if he were going to say something.

Tong cleared her throat and stared at the floor before she confessed, "While you were away, I, um, I missed you."

Jake was busy checking his phone and completely unaware, but Randy watched Tong melt like ice on a scorching-hot day.

Randy wondered if Jaidee was that toned from hours of dance and performing or if he was a gym rat. Hell, Randy should've hit the gym if that's what surrounded Lalana all day.

"Did everything work out as Adirake planned?"

The transformation in Tong's demeanor surprised the hell out of Randy.

"Yes, the brother and sister are over at Thai Haven. The restaurant owner is a friend of Areva. He'll be teaching them how to wait tables and give them a job."

When Jaidee turned to go, he hesitated. "I missed you too," he said before he hurried down the hallway toward the stage door.

Aw, that's sweet.

Tong didn't move until Jaidee was out of sight. Then she must have noticed she had a captivated audience of one, because she turned to Randy and shrugged. "I'll place your order with the boys in the kitchen, and I'll get the beers for my two early birds."

When she brought the two beers to the table, her sympathetic expression told Randy she'd overheard him obsessing over their upcoming date.

"So, I mean, what else do I talk to her about? She's lovely. What is she looking for?"

"You're winding yourself into a ball of anxiety. Just calm the fuck down." Jake grimaced. "What do they want? It's not even a date, for Christ's sake. You just pay for their drinks. That's what they want."

Tong cleared her throat to get Randy's attention. "Romance." She sat down at their table with their beers. "Even though my love life is nonexistent, at least I can give some unsolicited advice."

"What?" Jake questioned her.

Randy knew Jake well enough to know that he clearly didn't like her sitting her ass anywhere she pleased. But Tong was secure in her place. She'd been here before Jake had arrived, and she would be here long after he left. Her posture almost dared them not to appreciate her crossed legs. Jake leered at them and relaxed back into his chair.

She smiled at him. "Romance. These girls crave romance. Their dreams are like those cheap happily-ever-after romance novels. They want a knight in shining armor to love them. To sweep away the miseries of the past and help them enjoy the sunshine of the future."

Not one to kiss anyone's ass, Jake chuckled. "Yeah, I'm sure a nice little bauble taking a chunk out of your bank account would suffice as romance."

Tong frowned.

What the hell is wrong with him? Usually he could ignore Jake's twisted view of love, sex, and relationships, but Tong knew Lalana, and Randy didn't want her to blow him off because his friend was a jackass. Randy kicked Jake under the table.

"Ow! Randy! What? It's true." Staring at Tong, Jake asked, "Aren't a few expensive trinkets excellent substitutes for true love?" The way he said *love* made the word sound tawdry and dirty.

"What do you mean?" Tong's tone suggested she was daring Jake to say exactly what she clearly expected him to say.

"Come on. Who do you think you're talking to? I mean, these places have the reputation of being high-class brothels," Jake stated as if it were a matter of fact.

Randy'd read that most clubs tried to get clients to fall in "like" with the performers and convince them to buy expensive gifts and trinkets. Sometimes the performers would even ask for money outright for their supposed families still in the countryside.

Embarrassment flashed across Tong's face before she regrouped. "Actually, that's not what Illusions & Dreams is about at all. Our girls and boys are well paid, get their educations, and are well taken care of. We aren't looking for a man to do it for us." Sniffing in annoyance, she appeared to want to punch the knucklehead in the teeth.

Jake snorted. Randy shook his head and made the toe of his shoe find Jake's shin again. Tong grinned at Jake's yelp of pain right before Randy apologized.

"Please don't be offended. My friend can be an ass sometimes. He was dropped as a baby." Randy smiled and held out his hand. "I'm Randy, by the way."

"Pleased to meet you. I am Tong." She smiled at Randy and delicately grasped his hand to shake. "The girls here are looking for love and romance." Standing, she said, "At least, until they grow up and realize it doesn't exist."

Randy stood up politely. "Oh, but it does." He grabbed her hand back as if he were going to convince her. "Truly it does," he told her adamantly.

Tong took the time to examine his sincerity. "Ah, you poor naïve thing. You still believe in happily ever afters. I really hope you're right."

As she hurried back to the bar, out of the corner of his eye, Randy witnessed Jaidee's head duck back behind the stage door.

Chapter Two

AFTER A delicious meal of pad Thai, Randy and Jake took another Thai beer into the cabaret-style club. Lights and mirrors covered the walls, so it was nearly impossible to gauge the actual dimensions of the theater. Their early arrival got them a bistro table for two in front of the stage.

The tables and plush velvet chairs slowly filled with a mix of middle-aged Japanese men and quite a few women, but also a lot of couples. How many were there strictly in hopes of getting lucky with a ladyboy? Before Randy could question his own motives again, the lights dimmed.

The level of anticipation cranked up ten notches. It seemed like the entire population of ladyboys in Bangkok flooded the stage in elegant, shimmery gold and silver costumes. Feathered headpieces balanced precariously on their perfect coiffures. Their makeup was flawless, but the grace with which they carried themselves made them splendid. After the stunning parade of loveliness exited the stage, Adirake took the center in a tuxedo.

He strutted to the edge of the stage and paced across, making his words seem like he was speaking directly to each audience member. Monitors on the left and the right of the stage translated his deep booming English into Chinese, Japanese, and French. "Greetings everyone. Hello! Bonjour! Hola! Konnichi wa! Privet! Ni hao! Ciao! And for the two Icelandic beauties in the back, hallo! I am Adirake, and I welcome you to Illusions & Dreams."

After a dramatic pause, he continued, "Illusions & Dreams is a place where we make illusions possibilities and dreams a reality. Our performers are not strictly ladyboys, though we have some lovely girls who are proud to consider themselves *kathoey*."

Randy's breath caught as Lalana appeared. She led a group of fifteen stunning women in sequined, jewel-toned, clinging gowns that skimmed along the floor. Every color of the rainbow sparkled as they fanned out across the stage like dazzling ornaments.

Adirake took a moment to admire the performers. "At Illusions & Dreams we have taken back the *kathoey* and ladyboy terms. We are not less here… we are more."

After a round of applause followed his statement, Adirake swept his hand toward stage right, where a group of ten men in tuxes danced onto the stage. They tapped into lines, canes twirling, until they came to a final spin, ending in a razor-straight line.

Adirake, as the MC, rolled off his top hat in a fancy move and tossed it like a Frisbee to a waiting performer, who caught it behind his back before disappearing with a bow behind the curtain. Adirake's long hair cascaded over his shoulders as he shook it out.

"Some of our men like to perform as women." With quick tugs three-fourths of the penguin suits came off, revealing grass skirts and coconut bras. "And some don't."

The performers remaining in tuxedos shrugged and leered at the lovelies in skirts next to them for a laugh from the audience. Lalana's group gracefully snagged the tuxedos from the performers holding them and glided offstage. The performers in drag and those remaining in tuxes backed up. Adirake introduced the next group. "And we have some lovely women taking the stage with us."

Jake's date Boon-nam was third in a line of ten women who came cartwheeling out, ending in a split. Each had on a glittery rainbow-colored bodysuit, tights, and ballet slippers. They held their hands high over their heads as they beamed out at the audience.

The skirted and tuxedoed performers in the back stepped forward. One by one, they twirled the ladies off the floor, up their bodies and onto their shoulders. The tuxedoed men carried the girls off the stage, posing with their arms out to the side.

"So I ask you to enjoy the talents our performers share with you. Without further ado, Ms. Lalana Dulyarat."

The announcer hustled off the stage. Lalana, in a short sequined red dress, took the stage. Within a minute she had taken Randy's breath away with her song. Her sexy, throaty rendition of "At Last" would have made Etta James jealous.

Her silky voice touched him everywhere. Fine, it also turned him on in an insane way. Jake chuckled as Randy found he needed to cross and recross his legs in the hope of adjusting the contents of his pants into a more comfortable position. The notes she hit gave him chills.

The sexy, bluesy tones faded into the rapid beat of Lady Gaga's "Born This Way." The song began with Lalana sitting at a vanity, singing. When the beat changed, all the women of Illusions & Dreams danced out onto the stage, wearing everything from work uniforms to glitzy glamour wear. Each sang a line of the popular song.

Boon-nam, wearing a baby pink sundress and cowboy hat, eagerly grabbed the mic. She proudly sang how God had made no mistakes before passing it to the next performer. She spun with a flourish and fell into perfect step with the other dancers.

After the curtains closed for a set change, Randy overheard the worried man at the table next to theirs whisper to the woman seated at his table, "I don't know which ones are the *real* women."

The reasonably attractive Western woman in her midforties snorted. "That's the point. They're all women, and they were born that way. Whether by genetics or they had surgery or they didn't, they are all women." She realized Randy had probably overheard their conversation and winked at him.

"Yeah, but...." The guy's words trailed off when the curtain swung open.

A low-hanging light resembling the moon lit the darkened stage. A singer sang a traditional Thai song as dancers acted out the words, which were translated on the monitors flanking the stage. The soft Asian strains of wind instruments gave way to a powerful high-energy mash-up of popular songs and dances. There were so many costume changes, Randy couldn't imagine how they kept them all straight.

Maybe his jet-lag-addled mind added a glow to his opinion, but the performance seemed full of one surprise after another. The show flowed from rock into Shania Twain's country hit "Man! I Feel Like A Woman."

A very masculine-appearing male tromped heavily onto the stage in work boots, looking like he had just come from a construction site. As he sang the song, off came the work clothes and on went the purple evening dress. Three makeup artists swirled around him to change his appearance into that of a lovely female. As the lyrics went on, he altered his voice to match his more feminine appearance. The physical metamorphosis was incredible to watch.

The butterfly emerged from her cocoon of attendants to stalk and flutter around the front of the stage. She was stunning. She finished the last line of the song in a deep bass voice, bringing the crowd to their feet.

Some songs included lighthearted campy sketches. Other times the club attempted to educate the audience. After a scorching execution of Aerosmith's "Dude Looks Like A Lady," the macho male singer unwrapped into a stunning woman. She finished by talking to the audience. "Remember, you can't judge a book by its cover. Gender identity can be different than what's down there. It's what's in your heart that counts. Respect the individual."

The entire production showcased the talent of the performers. Sure, sometimes the cast wore bikinis with their manhood clearly outlined in the clingy fabric, or sometimes the girls seemed to take pleasure in showing off their bodies in tight spandex while doing high kicks and splits, but for the most part, the show was superior entertainment.

"Damn, this show could go toe-to-toe with any I've seen in the last five years in New York."

Coming from Jake the Broadway Snob, this was an impressive statement of the performers' talent and the scale of the show.

Lalana was onstage for a majority of the numbers. Each time she electrified the audience with the range of her rich voice, so full of emotions. She wasn't doing any lip-synching. Wow, the girl had pipes and wasn't afraid to use them. The Internet clips of her voice didn't come close to how incredible she sounded. Several times during the songs, Lalana settled her gaze on Randy, and it seemed, at least to him, that she sang only for him.

In awe of her gift, her exquisiteness, and her grace, Randy's heart tripped over itself trying to keep up with his flights of fancy. He'd never wanted anyone the way he desired Lalana. He wanted to watch her forever. But even forever didn't seem long enough.

Jake kicked his foot during Lalana's next song. "Hey, lover boy."

"What?" Randy growled, not wanting to miss a note.

"Remember what I said. Watch yourself."

Jake was trying to rein him in, but Randy wasn't allowing the words of wisdom to dampen his starstruck fantasies.

"Yeah, now shh!" Randy hadn't even spared his friend a glance, too enraptured by Lalana's voice, style, and languid movements.

A bit later in the show, Boon-nam appeared in a dance number wearing a skimpy white bodysuit. The shimmery material highlighted her body to its best advantage. Randy noticed that Jake tried not to drool.

"Hey, lover boy." Randy nudged Jake's foot under the table, taking his turn to mock.

"What?" Jake's voice had more annoyance than Randy'd ever heard, and it made him smile.

"Just remember what you said to me," Randy reminded.

"Whatever." Jake dismissed the warning as easily as he had.

"You've never appeared this fascinated," Randy whispered loud enough for Jake to hear over the music.

"It's a marvelous show."

Was Jake trying to justify his interest in Boon-nam while getting Randy to shut up? "I think you like her," Randy teased in a singsong voice.

"Who wouldn't? She's smoking hot up on the stage."

"Yeah, it's all about her dance moves." Randy chuckled, but even he'd been impressed with the complex twists and turns Boon-nam made as she pranced across the stage.

Jake spared him a look of irritation before returning his attention to her. She did a high kick with a twirl and landed in a split. The audience applauded.

The finale followed, which involved every performer onstage in a big song-and-dance routine of "One Night In Bangkok," encouraging audience participation. What a perfect ending to the show. Even patrons who appeared shy got up and shook their asses while the performers sang a rousing rendition of the song. Unfortunately Lalana and Boon-nam were stage left, so another member of the show danced over to Jake and Randy's table to get them on their feet.

The performers sang the song twice, much to the delight of most of the audience. Eventually, as with even the best shows, the lights came on. The staff ushered everyone out of the performance area and into the bar. The stage area would be reopened a bit later for quieter conversations.

Randy dragged Jake directly to the bar. He ordered them each a beer and waited impatiently.

"So do you think they'll show?" *What if they don't?*

It would just be his luck to be dumped by his fantasy girl before he even got a chance to know her. She probably imagined him to be a stalker. Okay, she'd be right. But that wasn't a reason not to get know him, was it?

Jake laughed. "Of course they will. Boon invited us."

Randy admired the fact the guy had confidence to spare, probably from the attention both sexes lavished on him. Randy kept an eye on all the entrances, unsure which one Lalana would enter through. He didn't want to miss her.

Jake complained when Randy's elbow jab connected with his ribs. "There they are!" He'd never been so excited to speak to someone. Damn, he'd better not blow this golden opportunity.

Lalana spotted them and crossed the room with such elegance and grace, Randy wondered if she floated. Boon-nam bounced happily along behind her.

Once the ladies reached the bar, both men stood.

"Shall I get us a table?" Lalana asked in a soft voice.

"Yes, please," Boon-nam answered excitedly for everyone.

Randy beamed as Boon-nam completely ignored the glare of warning in Lalana's eyes. He wished he could reassure Lalana that he and Jake were nice guys, but he was sure the words would be wasted.

Settling into a seat, Boon-nam pushed her chair close to Jake while smiling at him. "So, did you see me? Did you like the show? I haven't been dancing long, but Tong says I'm getting better. I practice for hours every day. What did you think of all the splits toward the end of my last number?"

Jake pursed his lips, clearly enjoying Boon's enthusiasm. "How could I miss the way you lit up the stage? You were impressive. You're a wonderful dancer—and singer, I might add. I could tell you must work hard to do those complicated steps. Those kick splits were fantastic!"

Boon glanced down as a blush raced across her cheeks. She nervously pressed her lips together and patted her hair. Randy tried to figure out if the shyness was an act, the outgoing vivaciousness part was pretend, or maybe she was just that young. It didn't matter because Jake seemed to find the mix enchanting.

Randy needed to stop staring at Lalana, but it was impossible. He should be on guard, but he found he'd already lost his heart via the Internet. It was insane. All these years he imagined he wasn't normal because he couldn't find anyone who appealed to him. But half a world away, in Lalana's presence, Randy discovered the "one". He knew from the depths of his soul she was "it" for him. Jake was going to kill him.

"Lalana, you were magnificent." Randy wished he had the gift of words.

She batted her eyelashes coyly. "I am sure you say candied words to all the performers after the show."

"No, really." Randy took the bait she teasingly held out, but he didn't care. He'd gush because she was wonderful.

Lalana smiled and turned toward Boon-nam. "You did very well tonight, Boon-boon."

Boon beamed. "You think? I tried." Her gaze darted to Jake's as if seeking his approval.

"All your extra work has paid off," Lalana said. "Boon is working with some of the more experienced dancers to improve her skill set."

Jake and Randy nodded their agreement.

Randy filled the silence with a question. "How come everyone speaks English so well?"

Boon leaned forward. "The owners of Illusions & Dreams, Areva and Adirake, make sure everyone has finished high school and learns English."

"Why?" Jake asked, head cocked.

"Education is important. As for speaking English, it lets us work as tour guides, or in hotels and better restaurants, allowing us to obtain higher salaries if we decide we don't want to perform anymore," Lalana answered.

Randy watched Boon's eyes light up with heat as Jake ran his fingers through his shoulder-length hair. In the past the bastard had told Randy he knew both men and women found the move sexy. He'd used it to his advantage often enough to make the move a habit. Poor Boon-nam fell prey to a practiced gesture. Randy wished he had some trademark Lalana would find sexy.

Jake snorted. "Yeah, but what's in it for them?"

Apparently Jake had stepped on a land mine.

"The owners want what is best for us and help us so we don't have to work in the tourist bars," Lalana snapped. "Or in *other places* to earn a living." Her emphasis on *other places* suggested the disreputable establishments associated with Thailand's sex industry.

Randy skimmed his hand over the back of Lalana's hand, which she tightened into a fist. "The owners must be kind and decent people."

"They are." Lalana glared at Jake for a moment before turning her attention to Randy. "They have an English teacher come in twice a week and encourage all of us to speak English. English is the global language of business."

"Our last teacher taught us a bunch of Western slang," Boon-nam smirked.

"Which is why he was replaced." Lalana added with an arched eyebrow. "The club even gives us training on various jobs here in the club."

Boon-nam giggled, covering her mouth with her slender hand. "Yes, I even trained in the kitchen." She rolled her eyes and giggled again. "Though everyone was happy when I finished my rotation in the kitchen and learned how to do nails."

"Relieved," Lalana added as she patted Boon-nam on the shoulder. "You did have a little problem with timing all the dishes to be done in the right order, and the whole setting the kitchen on fire was another strike against you in your quest to be a chef."

"Did you have to touch raw chicken?" Jake asked and appeared on edge for her answer.

"Ew! No, chicken is disgusting to touch."

Jake's expression of horror echoed Boon-nam's. "I know. It's all slimy."

Boon-nam shivered. "Gross."

"I only buy precooked chicken. I'll take the processing and preserving chemicals over that mess any day."

Boon-nam nodded and then confessed, "Plus, I didn't like getting my hands dirty all the time."

"But you do nails very well, Boon!" Lalana showed off her perfectly manicured nails. "She even puts designs on them freehand," she said, showing Randy the tiny artistic flowers decorating all ten digits.

Boon-nam ignored the compliment and beamed at Jake with big doe eyes. "You must have a girlfriend."

Randy snorted. Jake shrugged and twisted his thumb ring. "No one special."

"But there is someone?" Lalana glared at him, possibly trying to point out any flaws to Boon-nam.

Jake grinned. "There have been many *someones,* but no man or woman in particular... currently."

Boon-nam and Lalana's mouths were agape at the reference to his open sexuality. Jake never bothered to hide who he was for anyone. Jake expected everyone to take him as he was, or they could go fuck themselves.

Jake smiled. He enjoyed saying things for shock value. "How old are you, Boon-nam?"

"Ladies don't answer such questions," Lalana bit out.

Her dislike of Jake was reestablished in her tone. Randy knew she'd seen Jake's type before and wasn't happy to see his attentions directed at her friend.

Shrugging her shoulders, Boon-nam cupped a hand over her mouth and adorably stage-whispered to Jake, "I'm twenty-three. How old are you?"

"Old enough to know better than to answer." Jake smirked and touched her cheek.

Boon-nam giggled harmoniously. Jake howled with laughter. Randy joined in because he couldn't help it—the guy was a jackass, but a lovable one. Even Lalana chuckled as she shook her head, probably trying to figure out the Americans sitting across from her.

"I'm twenty-nine," Jake said.

Randy decided to fess up. "I'm twenty-eight." He cast his eyes downward. Randy didn't want Lalana feeling pressure to answer.

With an exaggerated sigh, she confessed, "Fine, I'm twenty-seven."

After a pause, Boon-nam put a hand over her mouth and grinned behind it. "I guess I'm the baby here."

Jake tucked an escaped piece of hair back into her elaborate hair comb. "You are indeed, little one."

Boon-nam leaned into his hand, and her eyes fluttered closed as if she were inviting more of his touch.

Lalana must have kicked her under the table because Boon-nam jumped upright and yelped. She frowned, but Lalana pointedly ignored the nonverbal rebuke and asked, "What do you do for a living?"

"We work for a software development company. I write code." Jake always enjoyed busting the myth of what a computer geek should look like.

"You must be smart." Boon-nam gave him another dreamy smile.

Randy cracked up, and Jake's glare only made him laugh harder.

Boon-nam didn't seem to notice and asked, "What are your plans for your vacation?"

"Well, I don't know. I guess we're going to see the sights around Bangkok, go to Ayutthaya for the day, and maybe the Tiger Temple."

"Oh! You like animals too?" Boon-nam purred.

"Of course. I love them. I try to have as many experiences with them as I can."

Boon-nam blushed and confessed, "I have a list of all the places I want to visit with animals."

Jake pulled out his phone. He clicked up something and handed the device to Boon-nam. "My list."

"Oh my! Yes! Koalas at Lone Pine Koala Sanctuary, pandas at Bi Feng… sad about Wolong…." Her mouth moved as she silently read his list. "I never heard of this ostrich farm or the wild horses of Cumberland Island."

"Oh, add them to your list for sure."

Jake had never showed Randy this mystery list. Randy knew Jake liked animals but not to this extent. Though if he thought about it, most of Jake's trips included some type of animal interaction.

"I know a lot of people have issues with zoos because all animals should be free. While I agree with that, having animal ambassadors is the best way to educate." Jake sighed.

Boon-nam nodded. "Yes, zoos and reserves that take good care of them help people understand that by overdeveloping they are destroying habitats."

"Exactly." Jake leaned toward her.

Once she handed Jake back his phone, Boon gushed, "Did you hear the Tiger Temple had eight baby tigers this year?"

Jake nodded with the enthusiasm Randy knew he usually reserved for discussions involving sex clubs. "They did. Now I did read some controversy about whether it was right to keep the animals at the temple and their treatment, but you can't argue with those numbers."

"What do you mean?" Lalana asked with frustration, probably at not following their conversation.

"Tigers don't mate unless they are happy," Jake replied.

Boon-nam giggled hysterically. "Neither do I." She batted her long eyelashes for effect.

Jake's laughter barked out. Randy wasn't stupid, so he hid his smile behind his hand while Lalana dropped her head into her hands. "What am I going to do with you, Boon-nam?"

"Nothing, I hope! That would be weird, La-la!" Boon-nam cracked up; even her laughter was musical. Even Lalana gave in and smiled at her. Boon-nam turned to Jake and stroked the earrings running from his lobe to the top of his ear. "I like the way they jangle."

The bastard smirked but didn't say anything. He knew women were drawn to his bad boy image.

The ladies stayed for a round of drinks, and after much laughter, Lalana tried to convince Boon-nam it was time to say good night.

"Oh, Lalana," Boon-nam pleaded, with an exasperated sigh. She cut her gaze to Jake, who tried to hide a yawn. Jet lag had finally caught up with him. "You're sleepy."

Jake shrugged. "A bit. The time difference kicked in. It took over a day to get here."

No! Randy didn't want their time to end. "Would you ladies like to join us tomorrow? We're going to Ayutthaya." Hey! He didn't freeze up while asking, and the day trip was a great plan to see the ladies again. Go, him!

"Where?" Boon-nam didn't seem to have any idea what Randy had just tried to say.

Jake supplied the answer. "The old capital. About seventy kilometers from here."

Boon-nam's pink-lipsticked mouth curved up as she pronounced the name one syllable at a time. "I-U-tie-ya."

Randy tried the name again. "Thanks."

Boon-nam beamed. "Anytime."

"Can you make it?" Randy addressed the question to Lalana.

Boon-nam answered. "Yes, we would love to. Wouldn't we, La-la?" She put her manicured hand on Lalana's arm, giving her friend a Morse-code-type squeeze that left nail indentations in her flesh.

Lalana's expression said she didn't believe the trip sounded like a good idea at all, but apparently she couldn't say no to Boon. She smiled at Randy. "Sounds lovely."

Dare Randy hope maybe she might want to spend a little more time with him? He ignored his inner voice that said maybe it was just getting out of Bangkok that appealed to her. Either way it would allow Randy more Lalana.

"Great! We'll pick you up at eight."

Jake glanced at his watch and groaned. "Well, if that's the case, we need to get some sleep." They all stood and made their way to the exit. Once outside, the warm humid air of Bangkok surrounded them like a damp wool blanket.

Boon-nam bounced in front of Jake and smiled up at him. Not the usual stage smile or the practiced smile someone might have given Jake back home, but an honest smile filled with warmth and good feelings. "I'll have my phone, so I can show you my animal list."

Pulling his attention back from the other couple, Randy glanced down at the beauty by his side to study her. Her beautiful voice enamored him, but his heart told him this was no crush. She glued her gaze onto Boon-nam as if she could communicate through telepathy.

Randy was startled to hear Jake ask, "May I give you a kiss?"

Who is this person? Jake took what he wanted, and if the person didn't like it, he stopped. Granted, they always liked it, but Jake never asked.

"Please," Boon-nam whispered as she tilted her face up toward him, eyes fluttering closed.

Randy witnessed Jake draw the girl into his arms and back up a few steps into the alley, but he and Lalana could still see them. He felt like a voyeur, but Lalana wouldn't take her eyes off them. Her eyes narrowed like she wanted to put a stop to this immediately.

Sighing, Randy wished he had Jake's confidence. He watched as Jake slipped a hand under Boon-nam's hair on the delicate nape of her neck to tip her head gently back. The gesture seemed to show her Jake had skilled hands and caused a little whimper of surrender to escape her mouth.

JAKE PRESSED in tight against Boon-nam's feminine little curves. He didn't even try to hide his arousal. He wanted to let her know she'd caused him to harden.

She moaned as he brushed against her. He wasn't used to having someone affect him. He'd watched her interactions all evening, and her pure essence shone like a beacon. But Boon-nam's surrender intoxicated him.

He touched his lips to hers, briefly grazing over them before another small sound of appreciation came from Boon. He took the invitation and gave her a hot, wet, open-mouthed kiss. She melted into his arms, nearly swooning. This trembling little sprite amplified Jake's alpha nature.

Emotions he'd always avoided came erupting to the surface with the kiss. *Insanity.* He had to remind himself this was Thailand, where the only happy endings came with the massages.

"Oh my. Stop, Boon-boon, before someone sees you," Lalana whispered, tugging Boon-nam's arm.

Fuck! What a spoilsport Lalana was! But she was right; they shouldn't have been doing this on the street. They should do it in bed.

"Oh…." Boon-nam allowed herself to be slowly tugged away from Jake with a groan. The club lights highlighted the blush on her cheeks and the naughty grin on her face as Lalana hauled her back to the sidewalk.

Lalana shook her head and hesitated but leaned up into Randy. Jake knew Randy hoped she'd kiss him, but instead she put her nose on his neck and sniffed.

"*Mm-mm.*" Lalana sighed.

Randy kept his arms to his sides as if he didn't know what to do. But then he leaned into her sexy nuzzle, and Lalana the Ice Queen seemed to melt. *Go, Rand!*

Her actions seemed to bemuse Randy. He did nothing but smile at her. Jake's cough helped wake him from the spell she cast, and Randy reconfirmed their date. "Eight tomorrow?"

Lalana sighed with what sounded like regret. Hell, yeah. Lalana had cockblocked him. He'd simply returned the favor. Score.

Lalana smiled a bit shyly and nodded before dragging Boon-nam, who was still making eyes at him, into the side door of the club. Boon-nam kept turning around to smile slyly and wave.

Damn, she was captivating. Even after Lalana pulled her inside, she poked her head out and waved one more time. She made him laugh and feel… what? Fuck, happy.

Jake never sat around reflecting on his navel lint. He prided himself on not overthinking. Determination didn't seem to stop him from analyzing why he missed her already. She disturbed his peace of mind, so he turned his focus onto his buddy and slapped Randy on the back.

"I do believe you were just hommed."

"I was what?" Randy asked in total confusion.

"The Thai people don't kiss in public." He was probably grinning like a big old cat, but he couldn't help it. "Except for Boon-nam."

Randy slugged him in the arm before Jake continued his lecture. "The first kiss on Thai television was only in 2005, and they're still worried the actress isn't fit to play the good-girl roles. Instead of kissing in public, Thai people snuffle each other."

"Snuffle?"

"She sniffed you, right? That's homming."

"Yeah." Randy's smile turned into a grin, and he rubbed his neck with all the reverence of a groupie never planning to wash where the rocker had signed their skin. "I was definitely hommed."

Even after midnight the streets were filled with tourists shopping for souvenirs, or a companion for the night, hour, or their next orgasm. Hanging out in bar doorways, in front of dance clubs, or congregating in small groups, scantily clad women, men, and ladyboys searched for a friend for the evening. For some reason they held no appeal for Jake. And he didn't think it was because they seemed far too young to be plying such a trade. What had Boon-nam done to him?

Randy asked as they trudged up the million stairs to the Sky Train, "If you knew they don't customarily kiss, why did you kiss Boon-nam?"

"Wanted to give her a thrill." He shrugged. Fuck if he was going to admit he needed to taste Boon-nam's sweetness before leaving her, because that would be weak. He ignored the emotions that skidded around the edges of his heart.

Jake O'Neil didn't require anything from anyone. To do so was to set himself up for disappointment. He'd learned early on he wasn't meant to be someone's boyfriend. He wasn't the type of man to bring home to Mama.

"Yeah, I guess you certainly did." Randy chuckled. "I don't think I've ever seen you date someone twice in a row."

"It wasn't really a date." He grimaced at the noise in his head, trying to define what he'd done with Boon-nam and why it was different. "What? No sex."

Randy's groan turned into a loud exhale. "Dates don't always involve sex."

Ah, the simple joy of bugging the guy.

"Maybe your dates don't…." Jake shoved his arm playfully.

"Must you sexualize everything?"

"It's the safest thing to do. You get pleasure and avoid pain that way." Damn, he was tired.

"You also avoid joy and true happiness."

Fuck that. Jake scoffed. Randy kicked a piece of trash off to the side of the road. They sidestepped a woman washing a dish in the runoff water in the gutter before hurrying back to her food stall and setting it back with the *clean* ones. Sanitary. Thankfully Randy didn't notice.

"I'm just glad you don't mind seeing them tomorrow."

"Not at all. You *like* Lalana." He switched gears to tease Randy and had the added bonus of keeping his mind off disturbing too-young-to-know-better imps that were a danger to his way of life.

"I do," Randy confirmed. "She's wonderful."

Jake wanted his best friend to be happy. Randy'd had a tough time when he realized his marriage was over. Jake had to give him credit; though the divorce had come as a surprise, Randy had still parted on congenial terms with his ex. But he never seemed excited by life. Hell, Jake did his very best to introduce Randy to all manner of interests. Until they started planning the trip to Thailand, Randy was always somber. He'd shown no interest. But tonight he seemed enthralled by Lalana.

Jake might be harping a little, but it wouldn't hurt to remember the facts. "Just be careful, man. I know this is the first person you've been interested in since your divorce, but—"

"I think you should be taking your own advice."

"What?" Fuck, he just liked Boon-nam. Okay, maybe more than just liked her, but he wasn't stupid. They'd only met tonight, and he didn't believe in love, let alone love at first sight.

"Boon-nam seems way too innocent for the games you normally play. Try not to hurt her, man."

"I know, Rand, I know." Jake sighed. "Eight a.m. tomorrow, date two."

Chapter Three

IT WAS bright and early when Lalana chased Boon-nam downstairs for breakfast. All she'd talked about long into the night was Jake. Lalana had seen his type before. He'd take everything and leave Boon-nam with a broken heart. He was nothing like his kind friend. She attempted to push down her own excitement at seeing Randy Camster again.

As with most days, the family of Illusions & Dreams usually ate breakfast and a late lunch together in the back corner of the club. The owners acted as house parents, ensuring their "children" were happy. The ritual created a feeling of home that Lalana had never experienced in her own family.

Boon-nam hesitated at the bottom of the stairs when they heard Tong's voice in the dining room. She was so naughty, stopping to retie her tied sneaker lace in the hopes of hearing some juicy gossip. Boon-nam shouldn't spy, but they were already on the steps, so Lalana couldn't help if she heard something. The stairway had a mirror at the bottom that reflected the dining room mirror, and their position gave them a fly-on-the-wall view of where everyone took their meals.

"Areva, he's too damned gorgeous. His body's as hard as a rock, and his damned black T-shirt seemed way too tight. Did you see how the material barely stretched across his chest? How am I supposed to think?" Tong complained to her long-time best friend as they studied themselves in one of the mirrors.

Lalana didn't have all the details, but Areva and Tong had been through a mess when they were younger and now helped others avoid their pain.

"Tong, deep breath. I don't know why you don't have him. He wants you." Reflected in the mirror angled around the room, Lalana watched as Areva pulled at the short cap sleeves of her Jackie O navy dress.

"He doesn't. We were in the kitchen, and he didn't say one word to me."

Areva arched a perfectly sculptured brow. "Did you say anything to him?"

Tong sighed dramatically. "Impossible. I just wish he didn't look edible this early in the day. Isn't there some rule? No gorgeousness until noontime. I need time to build my defenses."

Areva giggled softly and caught Boon-nam as she stood up from her pretend sneaker crisis, catching the pair's attention. "Oh, good morning." Areva turned away from the mirror to smile at Lalana and Boon-nam.

"Where are you ladies off to, looking so cute?" Areva asked, sitting down at one of the two chairs at the head of the table.

"On a day date to Ayutthaya!" Boon-nam pranced back and forth from foot to foot in her girlie pink sneakers—with freshly tied pink laces—and studied her reflection. Her face scrunched up. "Are you sure I shouldn't have worn heels? I'm short!"

Lalana rolled her eyes. "Not to Ayutthaya, Boon-boon. You'd look like an uneducated ladyboy!" Lalana petted a hand down Boon-nam's face to soothe her fragile young ego.

Areva covered her chuckle at the stricken expression on Boon's face and inspected the outfit in question. "You look positively adorable, Boon-boon."

Boon had borrowed a pair of denim pedal pushers, long enough not to cause a problem at the religious ruins. A pink T-shirt matched the pink-cotton-candy-colored girlie sneakers. She wore the gold chain that Adirake and Areva had given the staff last year at the holidays.

Boon-nam twirled around as if to make sure Areva took in everything. "You sure?"

"Yes, I am," Areva replied with complete authority.

When Boon-nam stopped obsessing, Lalana decided she needed to learn that trick.

Tong stopped staring at the kitchen door long enough to join the conversation. "Now who are these princes who have you ladies smiling?"

Lalana hadn't realized she'd been grinning, but knew nothing got past Areva and Tong.

Areva pointed to two chairs and said, "Sit and eat."

Lalana did as she was told before speaking up. "We met them last night. They appear to be lovely. At least Randy did. The court is still out on Jake."

Boon-nam gave a huff of disapproval. "The jury is not still out. Jake is great! He's sexy, and he loves animals." She reinforced her bold declaration by sticking her tongue out at Lalana.

Lalana leaned toward Areva to stage-whisper, "I think Boon has fallen head over heels for this bad boy."

"I think I met them. Two Americans?" Tong asked in a tone that suggested she knew the answer.

Areva steepled her hands in front of her deep-red lips and stared at Boon-nam with worry. She shot a quick glance at Lalana as if to say "you should know better."

Tong shook her head. "Oh, honey. Be careful! You know how men are. The Westerners come here on vacation, hoping for a good time, not looking for a wife."

Boon-nam shrugged and tried to carry off nonchalance but failed miserably. Her "I know" came out rather like a pout.

Other performers came down to sit around the table for the first meal of their day. "Thank you," Boon-nam and Lalana said to the kitchen staff who brought out their breakfast of rice porridge, *khanom khrauk*, and fruit.

Boon-nam focused on cutting a piece of the vegetable pancake and dipping the triangle into sugar before putting it in her mouth. Her tea was cool enough to drink. She looked up and waited for the lecture to continue.

Tong sat in her usual chair on the opposite side of the table and continued to throw in her two *bahts'* worth of advice. "Men are no good. It's plain and simple. Remember, they will use you if they can before they abandon you." She sipped her milk tea and added, "You will get what you settle for."

Lalana watched in amusement as Tong pretended not to notice Jaidee, who'd raised an eyebrow at the comment as he joined them at the table. She'd rarely heard him speak.

"Well, not all men," Tong amended, sparing a glance for the handsome man next to her. Lalana took note of Jaidee's small grin, which appeared a little like victory. "But most are nothing but creeps who are trying to get off on you." Without looking at Jaidee, she continued, "Just protect yourself and your heart. You're too young and too open." Frowning, Tong dropped her voice. "You are new and too easily broken."

Lalana knew Tong referred to Boon's recent sex-affirmation surgery.

"I know." Boon-nam picked the carrots out of her pancake to eat them separately.

Lalana put her arm around Boon-nam, afraid Boon's bright happiness would disappear. "We just don't want you to get hurt."

Adirake entered the room with a groan of disagreement. If Areva filled the mother-figure role at Illusions & Dreams, Adirake played the father. "Why must you ladies scare the young ones?" Adirake asked, patting Lalana and Boon-nam on the shoulder in passing before sitting at the head of the table, acting like the grumbly father figure Lalana believed him to be. "Men are not all evil."

Lalana wasn't sure she agreed with his assessment, but she owed Adirake and Areva, so she kept her mouth shut. They weren't like other club owners. Some of the heartless bastards kicked out the girls who transitioned completely with full surgery like Boon-nam had done. Usually the performers had to keep their male parts to continue their roles in the ladyboy productions. Most clubs traded on the ladyboy fetish of their customer base, so retaining one's male parts was essential.

Lalana, unfortunately, had found out there was a fine line between a man appreciating and accepting her special energy as part of her and a man only wanting her because she was a ladyboy. She'd never be someone's chick with a dick again. Never!

She'd always be grateful Boon-nam didn't have to make the excruciating decision to be true to herself or to have gainful employment. Too many times the only employment available for the ex-ladyboys who were no longer allowed to perform was prostitution. Even though Thailand was a Buddhist country, the government didn't acknowledge sex-affirmation surgery for its own people, so prejudice limited options.

Areva moved closer to Adirake and placed a hand on his. "Not everyone is as admirable as you are," she said without hesitation, leaning in to place a soft kiss on his cheek.

Adirake didn't hide his shock. Everyone went still and turned to stare at the couple. Lalana prayed peace and happiness would return to their relationship permanently.

"You're speaking to me again?"

Lalana realized weeks had gone by since they'd done anything but yell at each other. The last three days there had been deafening silence between them, with small, periodic eruptions.

Areva rolled her eyes. "Sometimes my silence is about not saying things that will just upset us further and has nothing to do with speaking to you or not speaking to you." She lifted his hand and kissed the palm gently.

Tong snorted. "Areva, you know everything you do is all about him."

Adirake growled but for the most part ignored Tong. He pulled Areva onto his lap, kissing her soundly for a long moment before jumping up with her in his arms.

He glanced over at Boon-nam and Lalana. "Be careful, you two." He trained a stern gaze at the other performers sitting around the table and said, "Have a great day. Study. And be happy. If there's an issue, go to Tong."

He must have decided nothing further needed saying, because he hurried out the door, carrying Areva into their private living space like a new bride.

Boon-nam watched them disappear with a dreamy expression on her face. "See! See, that's what I want!" she exclaimed, pointing toward the door where the loving couple destined to remake their bed had escaped through.

Tong glanced at Lalana before shaking her head at Boon-nam. "Oh, honey, you don't know the half of it."

"I know I want love. Just like that!"

Lalana didn't miss the fact Jaidee's eyes rested hungrily on Tong, whose gaze crept over to meet his. When they seemed to notice they were gazing into each other's eyes, they quickly found the floor interesting.

Love was everywhere, and Lalana was tired of pretending she didn't want her fair share. She did! But her Boon-nam ran headfirst into disaster.

JAKE IGNORED the happy feeling he got when Boon-nam bounced into his arms for a brief hug when she jumped into the van. She thrust her phone at him.

"See! I added the ostriches and the wild horses on Cumberland Island to my list."

He examined her impressive list. "You even have web links and the best times of year to go. That's a good idea."

"You might want to add the snow monkeys of Nagano. You know, the ones in Japan that sit in the hot springs?"

What an idiot. He pulled out his phone to add some excellent suggestions to his own list. "How could I have forgotten the reserve? I saw a YouTube video of a man enticing the monkey into his ryokan room."

"Oh, my goodness. I saw that too. The ranger of the reserve was yelling at him, but the owner of the hotel just laughed and laughed."

Boon-nam opened the link on her phone and handed over the device for Lalana and Randy to watch as they headed toward Ayutthaya. Everyone laughed. Even though Jake couldn't see the video, the exasperated Japanese man yelling never failed to give him a chuckle.

Jake never thought the one-hour van trip would fly by, but it did, with talk, laughter, and song. But maybe all it proved was that Thai women were as skilled as geisha at giving men what they wanted.

"That's lovely. What's the name of that song?" Randy asked.

"It's an old Thai song." Lalana reached out to touch Randy's hand briefly.

He brought her hand to his lips and pressed a kiss to her knuckles. Go, Randy! For a brief moment, Jake thought the Ice Queen might thaw, but she took back her hand with only a flickering smile.

Boon-nam bounced in her seat, drawing Jake's attention. "The title is 'For My Love.'" She batted her eyelashes. "Did you like the song too, Jake?"

A little too much, and that worried him. He needed to take his own advice. "I did." Saved by the Wat Phanan Choeng sign. "Looks like we're here."

Randy helped Lalana out of the van they'd rented.

Jake landed his hands on Boon's hips to guide her as she scooted out of the backseat. His palm might have skimmed her rounded ass by accident. Boon-nam didn't complain. She gave him a wink and a tiny giggle.

Their first stop was Wat Na Phra. Boon-nam explained, "Wat Na Phra is part of the old capital." She toed off her sneakers.

Lalana whispered, "You need to remove your shoes before we enter the temple."

Jake nodded. "So this whole area is the old capital?" He bent over to untie the laces on his sneakers.

Boon-nam nodded. "Yes, and there are many complexes and temples. I spoke to the driver, and he'll take us to the best ones. I'm sorry I can't hold your hand." She giggled, causing Jake's insides to dance.

He sighed. "I know. No public displays of affection. After all, this is a working monastery."

Oddly enough he'd rather enjoyed chastely holding hands with Boon-nam during the entire van trip. Oh hell. He wasn't typically a handholding type of guy, but with Boon-nam he wanted to be in contact. But even such a tiny show of affection was a no-no here.

"So this is the wat with the large golden Buddha?" Jake asked. He liked doing his research and understanding the places he traveled to on vacation.

"Yes. How did you know?" Boon-nam demanded, seeming pleased.

"I read about it."

RANDY CHUCKLED and busied himself with untying his shoes. Lalana appeared lovely in her sporty outfit of brown calf-length pants and a fitted button-up blouse in a tropical pattern. White sneakers had graced her tiny feet. They strolled up the carpeted path, past the images of Buddha with peeling gold-leaf paint and up a small flight of stairs leading to a giant Buddha statue.

"Wow!" Randy stopped dead to take in the enormous figure. He lowered his voice and strained his neck to see all the way to the top of the statue. "That is stunning."

Lalana's lips turned up at the corners. "It is," she said, but she studied Randy and not the Buddha.

Was she flirting with him?

"Let's walk around him." Randy didn't bother to hide his awe. "Look up. That's not wallpaper. Those designs are hand painted, aren't they?"

Lalana appeared pleased he'd noticed the delicate details of the intricate gold pattern on the red walls and ceiling. Hundreds of smaller Buddha figures sat in niches along the walls. "Rarely have I met anyone," she told him, "Thai or foreign, with such an appreciation for the detail. You seem to take everything in."

"I try." He turned to her, and she pinned him with her curious inspection. He desperately wanted to set himself apart from the countless men who'd wanted something more than Lalana gave.

She sighed. "What worries me is you might actually succeed."

"Would that be so tragic?" He got the distinct impression Lalana avoided entanglements any way she could.

"I want to say yes, but... your eyes are very gentle." Shaking her head, Lalana spun on her heel to exit the temple.

Randy trailed after her, walking on air mixed with a little bit of hope.

JAKE AND Boon-nam trailed a distance behind the other couple. "Have you ever been here?"

Boon-nam shook her head, "No." A group of chanting young monks in saffron-colored robes passed them. Her lips twisted. "My father wanted me to be a monk."

Jake couldn't imagine Boon-nam as a monk. "Really?"

Boon nodded, causing wisps of her coal black hair to brush across her cheeks. "You know being a monk isn't like being a priest or something. You don't have to make a lifelong commitment. But each Buddhist man, if they are able, should become a monk. Sometimes for as little as three days or a week. Others join and never want to leave the peace and tranquility."

"Their lives seem to be led without much hassle. Prayers, meditation, work a bit, more meditation. Food and shelter is provided. What else is there?" Jake mused out loud.

Jake turned to Boon-nam and found her staring up at him with the answer shining in her eyes. "Love, Jake. There is love. Without love, life is empty."

Fuck! She turned away before Jake could respond, though what could he have said? Love didn't exist? She'd not believe him anymore than Randy did.

They meandered out onto the temple grounds and explored the newer, ornately carved colorful altars housed in buildings the size of a one-room apartment.

Jake pointed to the dragons circling the pillars that decorated either side of the small structure. "These look almost Chinese."

"No one knows who built them. But I love how the Chinese style has been influenced by the Thai." She pointed out several carvings of Thai mythological creatures not belonging to the Chinese. "Some believe an explorer from China came. Many believe he fixed the Buddha's face in 1902."

"Maybe he made these," Jake said, leading her to another intricate building.

One vividly colored structure appeared lovelier than the next, but none could compare to his companion. He wanted to throw her up against a wall and take her where they stood, but another part of him wanted to protect her from his baser self. His need to shield her confused him.

After fully appreciating this temple complex, they jumped into the van and headed to their next stop, Wat Mahathat.

"The ruins here look Cambodian," Jake said, peering past the ticket booth to Wat Mahathat grounds.

Lalana nodded with approval and murmured to Boon-nam, "Hmm, Jake's not just a pretty face."

Boon-nam giggled and playfully slapped Lalana's arm. Good. Maybe he was scoring points with her.

THANK GOD! Lalana had started to warm up to Jake. Now if Randy could just get them to ease up on the tension when they got into each other's space, he'd be set.

Lalana stopped at the restroom, and Boon-nam ran ahead to get the entrance tickets. Her treating them was a thoughtful gesture, and he could tell Jake appreciated it.

"She's very appealing." Randy gestured to Boon-nam. "Angelic even."

Jake grunted. "You're telling me! Ha! I know."

Randy slapped Jake on the back. "Methinks you are fucked, my friend."

"God, I hope so!"

Randy smacked him in the back of the head.

"What? She's the most amazing woman I've ever met." Jake shook his head. "I mean…."

Randy froze and stared at Jake. Damn, who was this man, and where was his jackass of a buddy from home?

Jake took a breath and huffed the air out. "Look, I have this thing in perspective, but man, look at her."

As if on cue, Boon-nam turned around to smile and wave with a little kick of her pink sneakers.

"Fuck me. But she's more than just an adorable bouncy little bit of fluff. I just want to keep making her smile. Though I think you're right, as usual. I am completely fucked."

Lalana stepped up behind them. "Gentlemen, shall we?"

"Of course, my dear." Randy held out an arm for her, which she hooked hers into until they were reminded at the entrance gate that touching was prohibited.

Jake leaned over to mock them. "See, I knew you were a perv, touching at a temple."

They meandered among the ruins, taking pictures of the various Buddha statues housed in the burnt-out temples. Though ruins now housed these relics, they still received their alms and flowers daily from the observant. Farther along the path, they came upon the stunning highlight of the site: a Buddha head, caressed and held in place by a bodhi tree.

Boon-nam kneeled in the sandy dirt and stared at the imbedded head. She didn't say anything, but her mouth dropped open as she studied the serene statue and the tree twining around it. Jake snapped a couple of pictures.

Lalana stayed off to the side, observing Jake's fascination with Boon-nam. Maybe her opinion of Jake had begun to reform. Wanting to help tip the scales, Randy whispered, "He really is a stand-up guy. I know he comes across wrong sometimes, but he is a good man."

Lalana nodded. "As are you." She gazed up through her lashes. "You are a good man. I almost wish you weren't."

WHEN THEY drove past a Häagen-Dazs parlor, Boon-nam yelled, "Oh hey! Let's stop for ice cream!"

"Mm-mm, sounds fabulous," Randy called out.

Lalana shook her head. "You too?" She laughed. "Boon-nam can't pass a sweets parlor without stopping."

Jake chuckled. Somehow that didn't surprise him.

"That's not true." Boon-nam seemed to consider Lalana's observation. "Okay, fine. It is true, but they have a new flavor."

Randy nodded, and at the same time, he and Boon shouted, "Dark chocolate orange!"

"How do you two know this?" Jake asked.

"E-mail." Boon-nam and Randy shrugged. Boon-nam reached over the seat to high-five Randy.

That's ridiculous. "You two get Häagen-Dazs mail?"

The guilty simply chose not to answer.

Their van driver was on the ice cream dream team. "I can circle around the block. In this afternoon traffic, you'd have time to enjoy your dessert."

Lalana arched an eyebrow at Jake. "Shall we get the kids some ice cream?"

Jake laughed with her. "We don't have a choice."

Boon-nam wasted no time in telling the driver they would jump out from their van immediately for ice cream. "What flavor can we bring you back?"

The driver licked his lips. "Not necessary, but if you insist, I will try this new flavor."

Randy and Boon-nam led the charge through the food court to Häagen-Dazs. Lalana and Jake shared a smile.

"Two medium dark chocolate orange in a cone, please," Boon-nam excitedly ordered. She turned to Randy for confirmation.

"Oh absolutely, Boon-nam."

Jake couldn't help but tease his friend. "Randy, I'm surprised. I thought you were a vanilla kind of a guy."

He shrugged. "Usually I am."

Lalana ordered. "A small vanilla cone." She winked at Randy and said, "I'm really into vanilla."

Not quite believing the Ice Queen was putting the moves on Randy, Jake studied Randy's response. Giving credit where credit was due, Randy nodded once and said, "Good, 'cause even though it's underrated, it always satisfies."

Restraining his instinct to high-five his friend, Jake ordered a small vanilla cone and ran his fingers through his hair. "Only time I go vanilla is with ice cream."

Boon-nam squealed. "You're perfect."

Jake wasn't sure what she meant, but he wasn't stupid enough to ask for clarification with the Ice Queen's laser beams pointed in his direction.

Once they'd gotten their ice cream, he said, "Look, a table opened up over there."

They nabbed the space before someone else snatched it.

Boon-nam wiped her seat with a napkin before taking a lick of ice cream. "Mm-mm, that's delicious." She swiped her tongue out almost sensually to gather the cold treat.

Jake set a bag of dry ice, keeping the driver's ice cream cool, on their table. He found it impossible to focus on anything other than Boon-nam consuming her treat. He'd never seen anyone eat an ice cream cone in such an erotic manner. He remembered hearing an old rerun of sex therapist Dr. Ruth Westheimer's radio show, instructing her audience that to give a proper blowjob they needed to pretend the penis was an ice cream cone melting.

Boon-nam placed long, slow licks around the base of the cone, then licked up, up, up to the very top of it. She moaned with bliss every time she brought the dark chocolate orange into her mouth and swallowed. Was she doing it on purpose?

Jake felt like a pervert when she noticed his stare. "Er, do you want some?"

God, yes!

She held out her ice cream cone. *Oh.* "Um, no thanks."

When Boon-nam returned to the task at hand, Jake imagined every lick she gave the cone right on his dick. Her wicked little pink tongue kept snaking out to take the yummy goodness into her mouth. He watched her throat work as she swallowed. Jake would melt immediately if he were ever in her mouth.

Lalana coughed at Boon-nam as if trying to get her to stop her unconsciously arousing display. "She doesn't even know," she mouthed to Jake when Boon-nam's eyes closed.

Boon-nam perked up and looked between the three of them. "What?"

Jake wanted to smack Randy for laughing at him. He couldn't help drooling over every swipe of Boon-nam's tongue, but that would require energy. Randy took his grin down a notch when Lalana gave him the evil eye, but the bastard had the nerve to kick Jake under the table.

Jake coughed to cover up the "ouch." Fucker. He rubbed his soon-to-be-bruised shin. As if it were his fault Boon-nam's ice cream lust was more sensual than most porn.

Boon-nam stared at him questioningly but didn't say anything.

He filled in the silence with a question. "So, um, ladies, we're all having such a great time. I don't want to be forward, but would you be free for a short trip after tonight's show?"

Jake probably should have asked Randy first, but he was positive his friend would be onboard with his idea, especially since Randy'd get to spend more time with Lalana.

When she asked, "Where?" Lalana's tone let him know she was suspicious of his motives. Queen of Ice didn't trust him. Hell, he didn't trust himself.

"The Tiger Temple. Rand and I were planning to go. I do believe your theater is dark after tomorrow night's show." Jake had researched the show online last night before bed. Never hurt to be prepared.

"It is," Boon-nam exclaimed, bouncing in her seat. "We're free." Her gaze glued onto Jake as if she were trying to ignore Lalana's look of chastisement.

"We could leave after your show tonight. The Temple's about three hours from Bangkok, which means we would arrive about one in the morning. We could get some sleep and be ready to give alms to the temple monks at sevenish."

"And then play with the tigers, right?" Boon-nam grabbed Lalana's knee. "Jaidee is from that area."

Jake was pleased when Randy jumped on the bandwagon and tried to reassure Lalana. "We'd have separate rooms."

Boon-nam vibrated excitedly.

Jake took Boon's hand, and he spoke only to her. "I really want to share this experience with you."

Boon-nam almost crawled into his lap. "I say we should go. Right, La-la?"

Lalana glanced away from Boon-nam and stared directly at Jake. "I don't know." She exhaled loudly as she seemed to catch Randy's eye before studying Boon-nam. "Aren't you working with Jaidee and Adirake on a new number? And I'm supposed to help Tong with restocking the bar."

"Argh! Tigers! Lalana! Baby tigers!" Boon-nam nearly shouted. "Come on!"

Jake and Randy joined in with the peer pressure. The three of them started chanting, "Tigers! Tigers! Tigers!"

"Okay. Okay!" Lalana gave in with a strained smile.

"That's grr-eat!" Jake teased, but only Randy laughed.

Boon-nam and Lalana likely never had Tony the Tiger cereal for breakfast. The advertisement wouldn't translate, but they had dates to the Tiger Temple. Jake let it rest.

JAKE AND Randy enjoyed the show for a second night. This time Boon-nam had them seated backstage. The intense experience allowed them to witness the unseen dramas unfold: the costume quick changes, the warm-ups, the disasters averted, and how the expression of pure terror vanished as the performer's feet hit the stage—the dynamic change was fascinating to observe.

A man in a tux and top hat ambled over to them. "Hello. We met the day before yesterday. You were early. I'm one of the owners. Name's Adirake."

"Of course, we remember. Hey, I'm Jake, and this is Randy. We're friends with Lalana and Boon-nam." They stood up to exchange handshakes with Adirake.

"Enjoying the show?" Adirake asked while taking a cane from a prop person.

"Yes, it's great." Randy said enthusiastically.

Adirake pursed his lips and pinned them with his eyes. "Seriously, boys, if you're only after a hot time, go to Patpong. You two will find a nice ladyboy bar called King's. They'll see to your needs."

"What? No. It's not like that," Randy denied.

Jake, who wasn't going to justify himself to anyone, remained silent. Who the hell was this guy? Last time he checked, he didn't have to answer to some stranger. Boss or no boss, Jake didn't report to this man. Thailand happened to be a free country, so the girls could do as they pleased. They were adults.

"What's it like, then?" Adirake practically snarled. "You're taking two of our ladies on an overnight trip." The accusation rang clear.

Areva strutted off the stage in a floor-length sequined blue dress. "What's the problem, love?"

Assessing the situation by inspecting each of the three men in turn and catching Boon-nam gently biting her nails as she waited for her stage cue, Areva didn't have to be a genius to figure out the situation.

"Baby love, we mustn't scare off all the men. Our boys and girls are not children, and they make their own decisions. We'll be there to guide them and support them."

Boon-nam sighed deeply and gave a little wave to Jake before skipping off to take the stage.

Areva shifted closer to Adirake's side to grab his hand. When she turned back to Jake and Randy, her lovely smile vanished into a mask of anger. Her melodious voice dropped away.

"And if you hurt one of our boys or girls, I will personally hack off your dick and force-feed it to you until you choke." She paused to ensure her updo had remained perfectly smooth before she added, "Tong and I know where bodies can be hidden and never found in this city."

Her expression changed to serene as she lifted Adirake's hand to kiss it. She tilted her head, batted her long eyelashes, and her ultrafeminine voice returned. "I imagine we understand each other?"

Randy's eyes widened. Jake nodded and told them, "Not our intentions to hurt anyone. We're all just getting to know each other."

"Yeah, well, they're family, and you hurt them, we bleed."

"Understood," Randy choked out. "We really lo—like them."

Adirake appeared skeptical, but he and Areva nodded their blessing before moving off to answer a performer's question.

Chapter Four

PRIOR TO the show, Lalana and Boon-nam packed for their overnight adventure. Boon-nam tried to be reasonable, but a lady had to be prepared for whatever, which meant she and Lalana had a large suitcase and smaller case—each.

The guys smiled at their luggage, but neither said a word about the size of their suitcases. Boon-nam knew they had won points in their favor with Lalana. La-la's last boyfriend had plagued her about the amount of clothing she would take on trips, and it was one of the many reasons she let him go. No one could judge Lalana or tell her what to do for very long.

During the three-hour drive, when conversation lagged, Randy quietly asked Lalana, "Could you sing something to us in Thai?"

Her angelic voice filled the van. The proximity gave Boon-nam chills from the intensity of the pure notes.

Jake wiped away the tears Boon-nam didn't know she'd shed. Whispering in her ear, he asked, "What's she singing?"

His deep manly voice turned Boon's insides to a fluttery nervousness. "A sweet-sounding but mournful song about love." She sniffed and rummaged in her pocketbook until she found a tissue. When Jake tucked her into his side, she couldn't stop herself from cuddling into his warmth.

Randy appeared to hang on every word Lalana sang. When the final words almost ripped a hole in Boon-nam's chest, Randy said, "Thank you, Lalana. You sing marvelously. The song sounded so sad. What was it about?"

"A girl who falls in love with a boy who never loves her in return. He leaves her to go back home to his village."

Boon-nam blew her nose as delicately as she could before she added, "She can't live with the pain and throws herself in the river."

Jake and Randy frowned at each other as if they didn't know what to say.

Jake shrugged. "Well, that's a shitty idea! No one looks attractive dead."

There was a pause before Boon-nam and Lalana lost control of their laughter. Boon-nam hated her laugh because it sounded too masculine, but the unexpected comment made her erupt. She hoped the tissue muffled the noise a little. But it was wonderful to take something sad and to twist until you found something silly.

She adored Jake. He had her kind of humor.

Randy played the straight man. "What? A water death is just unsightly!" He gave Boon-nam a look of faux innocence, making her giggle even more.

When they arrived Boon-nam hated that they needed to wake up the hotel night staff to check in, but it couldn't be helped. She'd never admit this to Lalana, but she'd been disappointed the men had kept their promise of separate rooms, though the two rooms were on the same floor and just down the hall from each other.

Jake slung his arm around her as he guided her and her suitcases toward her door. A peek down the hallway showed Lalana busy murmuring quietly and exchanging kisses with Randy.

Boon-nam turned her attention back to Jake, who'd maneuvered in close, pressing against her. Mm-mm, and the way his strong chest pressed against her breasts felt marvelous. A wave of arousal washed through her as she gazed up at him. Between them no space remained.

"May I kiss you, sweetheart?" Jake asked in a deep, dark voice that made her heart race. He was such a gentleman. Lalana was wrong about him.

Boon-nam's eyes fluttered closed, and she tilted her face up. She parted her carefully made-up, pretty pink lips, hoping to give him a clear invitation. But just in case, she answered with the release of a breathy little moan. "Please."

His fingers slipped under the nape of her neck to grasp her hair. The action screamed dominance as he tipped her back farther. Oh, yes! Her insides liquefied in excitement as his lips touched hers.

Fireworks! Ahh, the kiss couldn't have been written better if it had come straight from a romance novel. Explosions of happiness went through her as his lips grazed over hers. His kisses made her toes curl.

"Oh." She groaned, opening her mouth farther, wanting more of him. He licked her lower lip before sliding his tongue into her mouth. His tongue danced as she melted with his teasing probes. She wantonly rubbed herself against his erection.

Her new body was almost out of her control with desire. Boon-nam barely contained her moan of lustful need. *He wants me… the real me.*

A big laugh that came from the general area of Randy and Lalana startled her, causing her to jump away from Jake. They weren't looking in her direction, but the wicked spell had been broken. Boon-nam swallowed and tried to dismiss the loss as Jake's hands dropped away from the small of her back.

Jake's stare burned down into her. He was perfect: he loved animals as much as she did, he was funny and smart, and not to mention gorgeous with a little edge of something dangerous. She loved the silver hoops that decorated his ear and the bangles clanging about his wrist. She was sure he'd be exactly what she dreamed of in bed. His sexy lips were moving, forming something other than kisses.

Oops, he spoke, meaning she should pay attention. She wanted to listen to him forever.

"Well, beautiful, we should say good night before *it* gets any harder."

His cock rubbed across her belly, reminding her of his excitement. Did he mean—? Seeing the gleam in his eyes, she knew he did! Wow. Boon-nam covered her mouth to hide her giggle. He was naughty but very delicious. She could eat him up.

Lalana came strolling down the hallway with Randy holding her hand, appearing happy, which burst any idea of Jake and eating or sucking or…. What a shame.

Jake leaned into her, allowing her to take a deep inhale before saying, "Good night, Boon-nam. Sleep well." He placed one last lingering, titillating kiss on her lips before leaving her side.

Randy kissed Lalana's cheek and whispered something in her ear that made her blush before he headed down the hallway.

Lalana fumbled with the key and the door as the men watched at a safe distance. They all waved once their respective doors were open. "Meet you at six thirty," Boon-nam said to them.

When the door shut, she leaned against the wood and gushed, "Oh, Lalana, the morning can't come soon enough!"

After both women completed their evening routines, Lalana said, "I'm exhausted, Boon-boon."

She collapsed into one of the twin beds, and Boon-nam pulled up the thin blanket around Lalana's shoulders.

"Me too. But I have to do my dilation." Sometimes the necessary postoperative care annoyed her.

"You should be happy the surgeon cut you down to two dilations a day."

"Tsk, I know. He said he wants me to continue for the full eighteen months. When I complained, he asked if I wanted his lovely work to close up like an earring hole you don't use."

"Boon!" Lalana pretended to be horrified, but it didn't stop her infectious laughter.

"He did say if I fall asleep with the stint in me, I could count it as my first dilation of the next day." Yawning, she realized that might happen.

"Night, Boon-boon. Love you," Lalana said tiredly as she rolled over on her twin bed facing the window to give Boon privacy.

"Love you, La-la." Getting her supplies out of her bag, Boon-nam opened up the vanilla-scented oil she used as a lubricant. She applied a liberal amount of the oily substance to the vaginal stint before she lay down on her bed. She arranged the pillows and the covers into a wall, giving herself an increased sense of privacy.

Boon-nam gently touched herself, fingers exploring her recent modification. Even after all these months, each time she found no awful appendage sticking out of her, relief swamped her. She might complain about the dilations, but she was grateful that the fleshy shaft she'd been born with—which had never belonged to her—was gone. In its place was a physical confirmation of who she was in her head.

She parted the folds of skin, adding more slippery gel as she slowly inserted her largest stint to the right depth.

Each day she felt more sexual. She lay for a moment with her knees bent, staring at the ceiling, before remembering to note the time on the digital clock. She began her hour of insertion. Too bad sex didn't count as dilation. She could ask Jake to—*mmm, Jake.*

Her toes curled as she pictured him, recalling his wet sexy kisses and his hard erection. He'd dilate her. Ah, she was positive he'd be a skilled lover. The way he strutted across a room like he owned it and the knowledge he could make her scream heated her.

Her mind flashed a vision of Jake slowly undressing, watching her with his sleepy, bedroom eyes. Yum. She was definitely having what her doctor had called "warm arousal." Prior to surgery, the part not belonging to her would have been disgustingly erect and pulsing, ready to make a mess. But now as she touched herself, she was exactly as she was meant to be.

Glancing at the clock revealed only fifteen minutes had passed. Lalana snored softly in the other bed a few feet away. The doctor told Boon-nam to let her largest sex organ—her brain—wander free when she was feeling turned on. He suggested she fantasize about anything she wanted.

Jake's muscular body flashed through her mind. Yes, he should be on the bed next to her. She could almost imagine his mouth on her skin. His sinful lips made her want to part her legs for him.

Well, her thighs were open, allowing her hand to press down on her Venus mound. *Mm-mm.* Little stars flashed past her eyes. She rubbed in a slow circle, which gave her delightful sparks. Her other hand found the base of the vaginal stint, which looked like a dildo, and she tapped it.

"Oh," she inhaled. Her head turned toward the other bed, Boon-nam worried Lalana had heard her. Thankfully, La-la slept like the dead.

Moving her hips against the bed, Boon-nam shifted the stint enough to redirect all her attention to the heat igniting between her legs. Her body had started to function the way she'd hoped it would a few weeks ago, and now with Jake in her mind, she was hyperstimulated and ready.

She skimmed her hands up to her enhanced breasts. She teased the fabric of her pink lace nightie, which made her nipples harden. She cupped her ample breasts, happy she'd not lost the sensitivity of the tips with the enhancement surgery. She circled and scraped her fingernails over her pointed nipples before she squeezed them. Release. Pinch. Release.

She ground her butt down into the bed as her lower body screamed out for her attention. *Mm-mm,* her fingers set off amazing feelings as she toyed with her feminine curves. Thoughts of Jake passed through her head—a shirtless Jake with pants tight enough she could see his erection straining.

She cast Jake in the starring role of her own personal love story. *Oh, my.* He stalked over to her bed. Almost miraculously her mind conjured up the image of her hands bound to the headboard. His large hands landed on her thighs, and with one quick move, he spread her legs wide before he crawled between. *Jake!*

Whispered words and soft lips erased her worries of being nonorgasmic. She shifted the vaginal stint, pretending the pressure was the slow slide of his cock as he entered her. She locked her mouth shut to stop the whimpers threatening to escape.

His hot wet kisses covered her face as she tapped the stint, pushing it a little deeper, simulating steady thrusts of her fantasy Jake's hardened shaft impaling her. She couldn't quiet her breathing as she built on the longings her fingers generated. Jake was shifting inside her in perfect precision.

Her body coiled tighter as she got closer to flying apart. She massaged her fingers in places to increase her sensation as Jake kissed, stroked, and whispered words of love.

"Jake."

Closer. In and out, stroking her new body.

Inhaling, she could almost smell his distinctive scent of leather and spice. She held her breath as she teetered on the razor's edge. Pushing down into the bed, she swiveled her hips back and forth, adding to the sensation of fullness inside.

"Oh." Groaning softly in frustration, she couldn't seem to get enough of what she needed. She trembled on the cusp of release. Relief was so close, but she couldn't cross over.

Her pretend Jake unbound her wrists to turn her over and mount her from behind. She flipped over onto her stomach and shoved a pillow between her legs, hoping the stuffed soft cotton square would help her regain her momentum in her quest for satisfaction.

She rode the pillow, rubbing and pumping her hips against its softness. He'd like seeing her, watching her come. She could almost feel him wrap his long fingers into her hair and tug to control her motions. She could almost hear him demand her surrender to him.

She lost control and came. Hard.

"Yes. Oh. Jaaake!" Her hoarse voice croaked out in a loud whisper. "Oh. Yeah."

The pleasure rolled over her as intense sensation swept through her entire being from head to toe. She rubbed and pressed against the pillow as the orgasm flowered and bloomed, then collapsed in a satisfied puddle.

Ahh, that was flawless. The orgasms her new body had gifted her with were nothing like the ones before, quick and over in a flash. No, her real orgasms touched every part of her, giving her more exquisite satisfaction than she'd never known. She shivered with the aftershocks.

"Mmm...." Boon-nam moaned happily to herself as she pretended Jake cuddled her into his chest.

She would definitely sleep tonight. She pulled the pillow out from between her legs and tucked it behind her. She snuggled down into a Zen sense of completeness and let sleep take her.

ACCORDING TO the weather report on television, the sun was shining brightly, but the temperature hadn't soared as of yet. It would be a delightful day for the Tiger Temple.

Boon-nam was glad she only had to remove the stint this morning to be done. She had neither the time nor the patience to wait to do the dilation. Cleaning the stint carefully, she couldn't help but smile, thinking about last night.

"So, I won't ask if everything is working for you." Lalana grinned at Boon-nam.

"Huh?" Boon-nam applied her eye makeup carefully while standing before the bathroom mirror in frilly pink boy shorts and bra. She loved the mirror now and couldn't help but stare at the reflection she'd always wanted to see looking back at her. This was the real Boon-nam.

"Oh. Oh. Yes. Oh. Jaaake!" Lalana mimicked what she'd obviously heard hours earlier.

Boon-nam opened her mouth and closed her lips into a frown, watching as a deep shade of red colored her face. "I believed you were asleep," she grumbled.

"I was until 'Jaaake.' Ha, like anyone could sleep through that." Lalana sniggered. "Oh, my sweet butterfly, don't look horrified."

Boon-nam tried not to die of embarrassment. She thought she'd been quiet.

Lalana came up behind her and gave her a warm hug. "Sweetie, I'm pleased everything is in working order now."

Boon-nam's surgery had been difficult. She'd dealt with a postop infection, which had made the dilations—which she needed to do several times daily to maintain the shape of her vagina—painful. Lalana had held her more than once as she sobbed about her nonworking, painful, and mostly numb parts.

She'd been terrified that after doing all this, she'd be in the small group of people who never experienced the pleasure of orgasm once they had surgery. But over time the numbness and pain dissipated, and Boon's excitement and arousal had returned little by little.

Boon-nam rolled her eyes. "The doctor said my body would heal. I guess I needed time." It had taken longer than she'd hoped to relearn how to orgasm, but now everything appeared to be in working order. Since meeting Jake, her libido had soared off the charts.

"Boon-boon, I know what the doctor said. I was scared. Even he warned you not everyone's surgery is successful... as yours is now." Lalana chuckled. "And it sounded like you were successful last night." The word *successful* had never sounded obscene before to Boon-nam's ears. "Was last night the first time since the surgery that things... um, worked?"

"No. I've been able to, um, *you know*, for about a few weeks. But this time was much better." She felt the blood rush to her cheeks again.

"Better?" Lalana's eyebrows shot up toward her hairline. "Geez, if *it* gets any *better,* we're going to have to call an ambulance for you." Lalana smoothed down Boon-nam's hair. "Honey, a huge weight has been lifted off my shoulders, knowing my little Boon-nam can be happy in a physical way."

"Hush, La-la!" Boon-nam applied her lip gloss, still talking. "You know I've heard you too."

Lalana turned toward her suitcase, pulling out her chosen outfit to visit the Tiger Temple. "I don't know what you're talking about."

Her voice rose to a higher octave than normal. *Got you!*

"Oh, really? For you, it's more like thwack, thwack, thwack... ahh!" Boon-nam laughed, taking the upper hand from Lalana. "Three strokes and you spurt! Maybe a grunt thrown in."

Boon-nam cackled at her best friend's horrified expression. They'd shared a room now for years, and if you weren't deaf, you heard things in the dark not meant to be heard. "What? I heard you go at *it* in the shower this morning."

Lalana sighed with exasperation. "Yeah, well, whatever," she groused, trying to use a phrase the American English teacher had taught them for fun.

Boon pressed on with a smirk. "It must have been dire."

Lalana rolled her eyes before pulling on the top she'd been holding. "So Boon-boon, you aren't planning to, you know...."

"What?" Dear Buddha, she hoped Lalana wasn't going to talk to her about sex. Any discussions in the past had always ended in awkward silences and embarrassment.

"You know, give yourself to him."

Lalana would've fit perfectly into a Victorian novel. It was only a matter of time before she went into vapors. "Is that any of your business?"

Tapping a pretty pink nail against her chin, Lalana replied, "Umm, yes, I do believe anything involving you is my business."

Boon-nam sighed and then shot back, "You know the answer. Why do you ask?"

"Because you shouldn't!" Lalana pulled on her pants. "You should wait."

Boon-nam rolled her eyes. She'd been waiting her entire life. "Wait for what?"

Lalana frowned at her, grasping at straws as she said, "You aren't healed yet."

"The doctor disagrees with you. He said my body is more than ready. On the last visit, he asked if I was seeing anyone."

"Oh, he checked for himself. I told you he wanted you."

Gross. He would never let her explore her naughty side, and she didn't go through all this to ignore her kinkier tastes. "Stop! Argh! How am I going to face him next visit?"

Lalana smiled sadly at Boon-nam. "Oh, baby." She grabbed Boon-nam up into a hug, rocking her back and forth. "I'm terrified the sparkle will go out of your lovely brown eyes."

Boon-nam hugged Lalana tightly. "I love you, La-la. You always watch out for me." She inhaled deeply of Lalana's flowery perfume, mixed with her hair products, before stepping away.

"I try to, but you make my job difficult." She sighed and shook her head. "I don't want you to get hurt."

"And you think Jake is going to hurt me, don't you?"

"He's going to break your heart into a million pieces." She huffed, "And there isn't a thing I can do about it. Is there?" Lalana stared at Boon in the mirror and saw deep inside her, just like La-la always did. "It's too late for caution, isn't it?"

"Shh! It'll be okay. I'll be fine. I just…." Boon-nam gathered her thoughts. "I need to love him. I can't help how I feel, and even if I could, I don't want to."

"Sweetie! You are too young! I can see you're setting yourself up for a fall. He's only here for two weeks."

"Two weeks of love is better than none." Boon-nam smiled at Lalana. She wanted to be brave, but a big fat tear rolled down her face, defeating her efforts.

Boon-nam turned from the mirror to let Lalana hug her. Lalana gently rocked her back and forth exactly as she used to when Boon-nam had been much younger. "I just hope you feel the same way when he's gone."

Boon-nam closed her eyes, trying to block out the stabbing loss that pierced her heart at the notion of not seeing Jake again. But their relationship had an expiration date. She opened her eyes to watch in the mirror as another tear slipped past the rim of her eyelashes and traced down her face. Love wasn't what she had expected at all.

Lalana wiped the tear. "Don't smudge your makeup, Boon-boon." She tightened the hug. "It's okay. We'll get through this together."

Chapter Five

THE SUN shined brightly, and the sky was blue. The day was ideal, but it was only seven a.m. Jake wasn't fooled. The temperature would rise to hellacious for an Upstate New Yorker in a couple of hours.

Once everyone had piled into the rented van, Lalana spoke to the driver. "Excuse me, sir. Could you stop at a gas station with a market attached?"

"Yes, ma'am, one is up ahead."

"Good. Thank you." Lalana explained to Randy, "We need to pick up some food to give as alms to the monks who live at the Tiger Temple."

"I understood alms meant money." Randy seemed puzzled.

"It can, but food shows you went the extra mile," Jake chimed in. Hey, he'd done his research, and if he earned points with Lalana, it would translate into her letting him get closer to Boon-nam, so he'd use what he had.

Once the vehicle came to a stop, Lalana and Boon-nam hopped out of the van. His little cutie turned and gave him a wink before following Lalana into the store. Oh, he needed to get control of himself.

Randy faced Jake and gave him a love-struck expression. Jake rolled his eyes. His friend could be tagged a goner. "There's no hope for you, is there, Rand?" A piece of him wanted to be happy for his friend, but he feared Randy was falling too fast.

"Nope." The corner of Randy's mouth turned up. "As if you can talk."

Exhaling loudly, Jake chose to ignore him. He tried not to dwell on it, but he chastised himself for developing affection for a particular Thai beauty. Feelings? What the fuck? Jake didn't want someone to have power over him. What was next? Love?

He stopped his thoughts from going any further.

Jake never lacked a bed partner. Male, female, and a few lovers who were transgender all looked good tangled in his sheets. He'd become friends with some of them, but they knew he didn't do the whole happily ever after. The whole idea of love was simply ridiculous. But the concept kept bouncing around his head like an annoying little rubber ball in bright neon pink from a gumball machine. *Boing! Boing! Boing!*

He'd never gone for adorable but found something alluring about Boon-nam that called to him. She loved animals as much as he did and didn't think it was weird that he wanted to interact with as many as he could. Boon-nam was someone who could get into his "scratch and sniff" vacation plans as much as he did. Most people liked cats or dogs, but few were crazy about getting into enclosures with exotic animals. Hell, even Randy had needed a bit of convincing when it came to the Tiger Temple.

Jake knew he'd lost his grip on reality when Boon-nam came springing back to the car with a huge grin on her face. He didn't give a fuck about reality. It was usually smoke and mirrors anyway, so fuck it.

Boon-nam handed him a bag before she climbed into the van. Lalana did the same, accepting Randy's help getting in the vehicle.

Jake reached into the bag and pulled out the first item his fingers touched. "Wait a second! Coke? Dried soup. Chocolate? I imagined you would be picking up vegetables."

"You're right. Vegetables and rice are a monk's main diet, but these things don't go bad."

Boon-nam snorted. "And who doesn't like chocolate?"

True. Jake chuckled. He took her hand and kissed her delicate knuckles soundly. Monks and chocolate, go figure.

ONCE THEY arrived at the Tiger Temple, they took their place with the other tourists in line along the dusty path to give alms. As they were waiting, a volunteer handed them a waiver to sign, releasing the temple of responsibility for any injury up to and including death resulting from interactions with the tigers. Shit!

Randy grimaced at Jake. "Well, that's a bit off-putting."

"Shut up and sign on the dotted line," Jake advised, not wanting to dwell on the damage a free-roaming tiger could inflict on any of them, because if he thought about it, good sense might talk him out of the experience.

The weather wasn't as humid as Bangkok had been yesterday, but the sun started to beat down on them. Geez, it was only seven thirty in the morning. What would the temperature be like in this valley at high noon?

Giving the monks alms didn't come close to the spiritual experience Jake had imagined. None of the monks chanted as they scuttled past, and none seemed particularly at peace. It appeared to be a parade. The saffron-robed men trailed past the tourists, one after the other, with their bowls and sacks, allowing each tourist to place an offering inside before continuing to the next.

A group of volunteers herded the tourists together in a group. "Good morning. Is everyone excited to see tigers?"

"Yes!" Boon-nam shouted, shifting from side to side as if unable to contain her excitement. She glanced up at Jake through her long lashes and blushed.

Her enthusiasm exhilarated him. He hoped the good reviews of this place were accurate and the bad a matter of opinion.

The volunteer droned on. "First we'll be going to the main building, where you can bottle feed a tiger. The babies will be in the middle of the floor. Directly after morning prayers, breakfast will be held. After prayers we will split up those who want to go to the tiger kindergarten and those who want to see the big cats up close. Any questions?" Without pausing for more than a second, the tour guide proclaimed, "Aces. Let's go."

Another man in a different-colored volunteer's shirt gathered them up like cattle and marched them to the main building.

A roar cut through the group's chatter, followed by another. Boon-nam clapped her hands. Jake made a grab for her hand before Lalana stepped between them.

"We're on temple grounds. Public displays of affection aren't allowed."

Damn. Forgot about that. Jake would respect the rule, but he didn't want to accept the general concept. Would monks see him holding Boon-nam's hand and cast off their saffron robes to have an orgy? Wait. There was a movie in there somewhere.

Damn it. He needed to touch Boon-nam. She shyly glanced over at him with those big brown eyes, and he wanted to scoop her up to kiss her senseless. He played the good boy and reined in the desire. He'd wait. The group stopped on the steps of a building and could see very large tigers peering down at them.

Jake whispered to Boon-nam, "I hope they're well fed."

Boon-nam gazed over her shoulder and said, "We're here for breakfast. The question is, are we theirs?" Jake chuckled as he watched Boon-nam's eyes go wide as if she wondered about the validity of her own tease.

The next volunteer introduced himself as Michael and said he was from Canada before asking everyone their country of origin.

Once the ice was deemed officially broken, he clapped. "Let me tell you a little bit about the history of Wat Pha Luang Ta Bua. It was founded twenty years ago as a forest monastery and sanctuary for wild animals. Five years after it opened, the villagers began to bring injured or orphaned tigers to the abbot."

"Didn't the first one die?" a tourist standing close to the volunteer asked.

"Sadly, yes. But more came. In the early years, it was difficult. Tigers eat a lot. Does anyone know how much tigers eat?"

"About forty to sixty pounds a night," a tall guy with red hair called out.

"Correct, and you said 'a night.' That leads me to the next fact I want to explain to you. Tigers are nocturnal. If you see a sleeping or relaxed tiger, they have not been drugged." Michael pointed to a tourist to the left.

"Tsk, so, then, shouldn't they be, like, sleeping?" one teenager asked.

Michael shrugged. "We have a large number of tigers now. So each tiger's schedule is interrupted only a few times a month for a couple of hours. Usually we try to respect the tigers' wishes and allow nature to take its course, which is the Buddhist tradition. And why we seem to have so many tiger babies."

Michael seemed grateful for the sympathy laugh the crowd gave him.

At the front a tourist in a baseball cap raised his hand briefly before speaking. "But that's good, isn't it?"

The volunteer nodded. "Yes. Even so there are only two hundred and fifty wild tigers in Thailand. According to National Geographic, there's only an estimated three thousand two hundred in the wild worldwide."

The crowd murmured. Someone called out from the back, "Why?"

"The tigers' habitat and their prey's habitat is vanishing due to Asia's population explosion, expansion of cities, and poaching. In the last eighty years, three out of the nine species of tiger have become extinct. We'd like to prevent this from happening to the rest." The volunteer from Canada frowned.

"Isn't that what our entry fee is going for?" a woman in a straw hat and sunglasses pointed out.

"Yes. It's our hope that we can raise enough money to expand the Tiger Temple. We are currently reforesting the nearby area, and it is believed we can possibly release some of our animals back into a protected area. We also want to expand where the tigers are kept currently."

Boon-nam leaned into him to whisper. "And by employing people from the local area, they give the people a different way to make money instead of poaching. If businesses see an increase in sales, they are less likely to allow their family members to practice poaching."

"But it's big business." Chinese medicine used every part of the tiger for various treatments and to obtain the vigor of the creature itself.

Boon-nam pointed out the Japanese and Chinese tourists. "And by letting people see the beauty of these animals and allowing them to experience a connection with them, maybe this generation will be less likely to use medicines made from tiger product."

Jake sighed. That was the hope. But he wasn't naïve enough to believe, even with these gorgeous animal ambassadors, the Asian attitude toward tigers here would simply vanish overnight. Aw, but he wanted to hug Boon-nam for her more Western view.

Michael cleared his throat to get their attention. "So follow the rules you were given, eh, listen to the volunteers and staff, and keep your hands out of the tiger's mouth, eh?" He laughed as if he'd told an amusing joke.

Jake arched an eyebrow at Randy, who shrugged. Jake watched Boon-nam shove her hands into her pockets. She appeared as if she might vibrate up the steps. A few more people prattled on about rules, but it all came down to "listen to the volunteers, don't touch the monks, and keep your body parts out of the tigers' mouths." The group was led to an elevated white tiled structure. The second floor was open, but a rail encircled it.

The staff chuckled as several tourists jumped at the loud welcome roar several of the orange-and-black faces gave them. "You can leave your shoes on the steps."

They toed off their shoes and headed up the stairs to the tigers. Boon-nam ran up the stairs, leading their group. "Come on. Tigers! Jake, tigers!"

Babies were in the middle and adolescents were tied up on the sides of the open air balcony. A volunteer grabbed Jake's hand and led him over to the tiger equivalent of a teenager. The tiger was more like a small pony. Immediately a staff person shoved a bottle into his hand. The volunteer pointed over to the tiger before grabbing his camera to snap pictures.

Jake started feeding the hungry one-year-old tiger. Since Jake had never fed anything with a bottle, the creature immediately repositioned it properly with his paw. The hungry creature wasn't willing to depend on Jake to give him the milk right. The tiger started sucking and staring at Jake. Jake wasn't sure if the thoughtful expression meant gratitude for the milk or if he was being sized up for the main course.

"Wow!" Randy exclaimed with a big grin on his face, feeding the tiger right next to Jake.

"Pet head. Look me," the volunteer demanded in an Asian accent. Jake did as directed and the staff continuously snapped pictures. The routine continued until the tiger emptied the bottle.

Jake glanced over at Boon-nam. She glowed with what appeared to be pure happiness. Since Jake's hungry tiger had finished his bottle and therefore had no further use for him, Jake started snapping pictures of everyone else's feeding sessions. He ended up really pleased as he got some great pictures of Boon-nam with the tiger. *Gorgeous!*

A staff member gathered up their group, ushered them to the middle of the enclosure, and told them to sit down. Their volunteer pulled a baby tiger out of a makeshift playpen. "Play," she told them as she set a tiger the size of a large housecat between the four of them.

The baby tiger strolled over and batted Jake's leg. Aww. The second swipe was a bit stronger. Ow, damn. He was glad he'd worn jeans, but he'd have a scratch mark. "The little tyke is strong! He's built like a baby bear!" Jake stated as he petted the tiger. Soon the tiger shifted away from him to go to Boon-nam.

Boon-nam squealed as the baby batted at her blue-painted toenails. When the tiger tried teeth on them, a staffer scolded the tiger and Boon-nam. "No. Bad tiger." She yelled at Boon-nam, "And you, teach him no bite. No."

"Sorry." Boon-nam bit her lower lip.

After the overly harsh staffer left, Jake bent to her and whispered, "Hey, not your fault your toes are tasty. I want to nibble on them too."

Randy must have heard because he pushed his head toward them to add, "Tasty tiger treats," making Boon smile and chortle a little.

Jake couldn't miss the true affection in Lalana's eyes when she glanced over at Randy.

"Bite-size tasty tiger treats," Jake said as he grabbed a blue-nailed piggy.

The chastised baby tiger decided Lalana made a perfect place to nap and curled up on her lap. Randy and she talked to the little guy and petted him right to sleep. Jake snapped pictures until a volunteer dropped a tiger in Boon-nam's lap. "Play. But monks start soon."

A group of English-speaking ladies nearby explained that the monks would say their morning prayers before food passed their lips.

The new baby tiger wasn't interested in petting. The little thing was very active, wanting to play, and decided to use Jake and Boon-nam as a personal jungle gym.

As the orange-and-black ball of energy crawled up Jake's shirt, he couldn't help saying "Ow." He grimaced in Boon-nam's direction to warn her. "Be careful, his nails are like needles. Definitely time for this small fry to get a manicure."

The animal finished with Jake and must've decided Boon-nam might provide more fun. The mini tiger jumped from Jake to her, landing on her shoulder. The baby froze for a moment, gaining his balance before swatting at her earrings.

Lalana glanced up. "Boon, you better take those off."

Just as the baby tiger opened his mouth to taste the dangling jewelry, Jake slipped the earring out of her ear to put in his pocket for safekeeping.

Randy snapped pictures of them. "These are great pictures," he proclaimed, eyes riveted on the view screen of his camera.

A volunteer smacked Jake on the shoulder to point out that the monks had started to pray. Oops, Jake hadn't even heard the soft chanting. Their group fell respectably silent, more silent than the restless tigers chained along the walls waiting for their morning playtime to restart.

These adolescents appeared to possess the same impatience human teenagers displayed. They tested the boundaries of their chains, made irritated noises, and did everything except roll their eyes.

The tigers took turns roaring their displeasure at not having the attention of their caretaking monks. Once the prayers ended, the monks invited the visitors to breakfast with the volunteers and staff. The saffron-clothed monks stayed in the circle and ate without interacting with the guests, though several younger monks ran back to pet and talk to their spoiled charges before eating their own breakfasts.

Jake's group was too excited to eat. They stayed in the middle of the area to have more baby-tiger time. "This is amazing!" Randy exclaimed. "Super choice, Jake."

"Oh, Jake chose this?" Lalana asked, not hiding her surprise.

Jake wished for something he could do to prove to Lalana he wasn't a bad guy. It wasn't his fault he didn't believe in love. Maybe he hadn't met anyone like Boon-nam before….

Shit! Where did that come from?

"Yeah, Jake did most of the research. I'm the *lazy* travel partner," Randy confessed.

"Hey, dude. You made calls and did the transfers," Jake replied, not willing to take all the credit.

"Oh!" Boon-nam cried out.

The baby tiger lapped at her face with a sandpaper tongue. Randy still had the camera in his hand and snapped the picture.

"You need to send us those," Lalana said. "Let me get the two of you with a baby tiger."

Once she did, Jake took a picture of Boon-nam and Lalana with a tiny creature in the middle. The babies started wiggling anxiously as if their patience had come to an end. He quickly snapped pictures with the tiger tot and Randy and Lalana. Randy snatched the camera to get a final picture with Jake, Boon-nam, and the baby tiger.

The volunteers scooped up the babies and called everyone back into the group. "Okay, folks, let's head downstairs. Now you'll have a choice. You can go see the kindergarten with the babies again or spend time with the big cats."

Everyone seemed to want to go spend time with the large cats. Jake whispered to the other three, "According to TripAdvisor, we want the kindergarten."

He didn't want to let on the others were making a mistake. Everyone would get an opportunity to spend time with the larger animals to have pictures taken, but for safety reasons people couldn't play with them. The crowd would sit on the sidelines and watch the monks play. A successful trip was all about the research.

"So whoever wants the big cats, come over here and you'll go with Monique and Jason." The assembly went en masse over to the two of them, except for Jake and his entourage. "We'll meet up with you later." The Canadian volunteer grinned at their small group. "Who wants to walk a baby tiger to kindergarten?"

Boon-nam's hand went up. She squealed. "Oh, me! Me! Please!"

The volunteer handed her the baby he held. "Actually, since there's only four of you, each of you can carry a baby if you want."

"Definitely," Jake said, swapping his camera for a squirming, whining ball of fur. "Hey, there, big guy." The tiger stopped moving and cocked his head forward to sniff Jake. "That's a boy."

"Oh." Lalana cooed down at her female bundle of baby tiger. "Oh, you are a darling. Such a well-behaved baby girl." The volunteer put Lalana and Boon-nam together for a picture of them each holding a baby.

Randy simply beamed at his orange-striped cargo as they made their way to the tiger kindergarten about a quarter of a mile away. "I can't believe I'm walking a baby tiger to kindergarten."

"It's a proud day," Jake said, grinning at his munchkin kitty, who'd apparently decided squirming and whining about being held was the best way to cover the distance. He spoke directly to baby tiger. "You complain now, but you'll have fun. Go play nice with the other little tigers."

The tiger kindergarten consisted of a large room with a cement floor to allow for easy hose downs. Floor-to-ceiling bars opened to the outdoors, making it less like a cage. Scattered across the floor were tiger toys: tires on ropes, tires tied together to form a tunnel, mop heads, swatches of saffron fabric, and a couple of balls. But Jake quickly realized people were a baby tiger's favorite toy.

"You play with them much like you would a big dog." Michael demonstrated by swinging the mop head around. A mini tiger pounced and held on, then backed off when the stringy mop went still, to bat at it with its large paws.

Everyone got the hang of playing with the tigers. Lalana dragged the two babies across the floor on a saffron cloth while they hung on for dear life. Randy sat in the corner, taking pictures of Lalana while a baby climbed him like a tree. He played with the mop head, whooshing the strings back and forth across the floor. The babies took turns pouncing on it.

Boon-nam tossed a ball against the wall while one of the tigers chased after the bouncing toy. She seemed to be having a great time playing with the baby tigers until one decided she was delicious. The little demon attached himself to Boon-nam's shoulder with his teeth and clamped down.

"Ouch!"

Tears rolled down Boon's face before the volunteer managed to get the demonic baby off.

"Ow!"

The volunteer finally unlatched the bad baby tiger and turned to Boon-nam, but Jake was already there.

What the hell?

"Are you okay, honey?" Jake checked the injury. The puncture wounds weren't deep, but the surrounding skin had already begun to bruise.

"It hurt so much, and the pain was sudden," she cried out. "I didn't even know why I started crying. Everything hurt." She took the tissue Lalana handed her.

"Tsk, my little baby girl. Here, let me see." Jake carefully pulled her top off her shoulder.

Lalana crowded in around them, speaking in quick Thai. Boon-nam nodded.

The volunteer came over with the first aid kit. Jake took medical supplies out of his hands.

"I got this. Thanks," he said, dismissing the younger man. No one would be touching Boon-nam but him.

Jake cleaned the wound with an alcohol wipe and put an antibiotic cream on the tooth marks, which marred her flawless flesh with thin lines of blood. He wanted to hug her close, but he couldn't.

"I'm fine. Really." She sniffled a bit.

Randy got his first look at the bite and whistled. "Wow, it's already turning black and blue." He touched her face in a kindly gesture as Lalana helped her straighten her shirt.

Jake added, "Though I have to say not many people can claim they were attacked by a tiger and survived." He pulled out his camera. "Let me get a picture. You'll have proof you survived a tiger attack."

Boon-nam cackled and started posing for pictures to display her bite.

Jake hurried over to the staff, who appeared to oversee everything. "Any need for rabies shots or follow-up?"

"Nah, the animals are given all their shots and never roam beyond our temple's preserve. It should be fine."

Boon-nam didn't demand to leave. She simply sat right back down and continued playing with the babies as if one hadn't used her as a chew toy. The volunteer flew across the enclosure to scold the baby monster. "No. Bad."

The tiny tiger that had tasted blood was starting to stalk Boon-nam again.

When the staff member reprimanded it, the damn thing rolled over onto its back as if he were trying to appear deceptively cute and innocent for the staff.

Boon-nam was a terrific sport and took her injury in stride. She joked, "I can almost hear your thoughts, you tiny devil. Come on, man. She's delicious. Just one more bite!"

Everyone laughed, including the volunteer and staff.

Jake inspected her shoulder again and whispered, "Well, I do have some sympathy for the tiny tot. I know how delicious you taste." He lowered his voice so only Boon-nam could hear him. "And I want to taste more, my little tiger."

Her eyes fluttered shut as if she were savoring his words. Jake had never been with anyone inexperienced. He'd never wanted someone this much. He couldn't decide if he wanted to protect her or ravish her, though it might be more a question of which order rather than a choice.

Lalana's high-pitched voice cut through Jake's inner turmoil. "Eww!"

When all eyes were on her, she grimaced and said, "I stepped in tiger pee."

She stood daintily, shaking off her foot. Everyone cracked up as she sat down to wipe it off with a wet towelette. Randy grabbed another from a volunteer, while another baby tiger paraded by Lalana, peeing as it marched over to the mop head.

"Eww! I didn't think that it was possible to piddle while walking."

A pungent ammonia smell wafted past, making Jake wrinkle his nose and step back.

After a few more minutes of playing with the cubs, they rejoined the larger tourist group and took pictures with very large, full-grown tigers. First they took individual pictures with the big adult tigers as they stroked the huge animal firmly, exactly as the staff had told them to. Then the helpful staff member gathered them and took pictures of the entire group.

Jake couldn't help himself—he examined the animal for signs of being drugged up. He wasn't a vet, but all he saw was a relaxed animal used to people. The tiger perked up when his caretaker came and jumped up to nudge the man until he was cuddled a bit.

It wasn't until the monks escorted the huge animals down to the waterfall canyon that Jake realized how amazing and scary what they were experiencing was.

The sun beat down from directly overhead. He mumbled to no one in particular, "Getting hot." As if nature disagreed, a gentle breeze blew past. Randy wiped his brow and nodded.

Once in the canyon, the tourists gathered in a protected, fenced-in area. The fragile fence dividing the tourists from the tigers didn't appear to be able to keep out a small dog, let alone six to seven hundred pounds of animal that might decide humans were dinner. Tigers weren't supposed to be man-eaters, though there had been some cases. In front of the flimsy fence crouched four men with four-foot wooden dowels about an inch wide. Someone called out in Thai, and a whoosh of air rushed by as seven adult tigers ran past the enclosure and jumped into the water.

Boon-nam stared up at Jake with nervous eyes. "They're big and fast."

Jake leaned down to whisper in her ear, "You don't have to be fast, little tiger, just faster than the person next to you."

They glanced over at an older Japanese woman standing next to Boon-nam with a big camera whirring and clicking.

"I think we should do okay." Boon-nam grinned up at him.

Jake swallowed his chuckle and nodded his approval of her assessment. "But it's still a bit scary."

Boon-nam leaned closer to Jake's side but didn't say anything.

Jake believed they were safe, but all his dormant protective instincts came out on full alert. He stood a bit in front of her as one of the adult tigers stalked over to the enclosure, surveying the gathering of tourists as if they were a box lunch.

The smell of wet animal flesh accompanied by the scent of the tiger marking his territory was overwhelming even in the open air. Jake understood why so many animal repellants used tiger urine. The stench made it hurt to inhale.

"*No!*" the men with wooden dowels shouted, along with some words in Thai. They whacked their hands with the dowels, hard. If the wood hadn't been so smooth, the men would have gotten deep splinters. The enormous animal flattened its ears back in annoyance but backed away. Eventually the giant feline went splashing into the water after his friends as if he were an overgrown kitten.

"It's amazing to watch them. They're magnificent," Jake said, remembering he held a camera. He started snapping pictures of tigers flying through the air to get into the water, splashing and playing with each other.

Randy snapped some pictures as well, but kept teasing Lalana. "We can outrun at least nine of these people. Since there's only seven tigers and fifteen including us, we should be fine."

She snickered at his silliness. Randy beamed with happiness at making her laugh. *Good. Randy deserves to be happy.*

Finally the tigers were called back, and the monks guided the big cats out of the canyon. The volunteers led the people out of their pitiful gated "safety area" and directed them to the exit. They meandered for a bathroom pit stop to clean up and get all traces of tiger off them, which took them past woefully small enclosures for some of the other animals.

"So what did you think?" Jake asked Randy as they waited outside the ladies' room.

"I thought in general it was good. I hated to see some of the other animals' crowded enclosures. I just don't understand not putting down sick animals."

"It's not the Buddhist way. They do not kill. Period and end of story."

"Yeah, but a couple of those animals seemed to be suffering," Randy pointed out.

"I'm not going to disagree. It's upsetting, but this is their temple and Buddhism doesn't allow euthanasia. But I will say the volunteers and staff were kind to those animals." He could see one staffer still sitting with an injured gibbon across the way. He was chatting with the creature as he helped him eat. Jake sighed.

"Acceptance of suffering is part of life, I guess." Randy mumbled. "But other than a few rude staff, everyone was good to the tigers."

"It's not a perfect place, and maybe it's grown too fast, but I think it does much more positive than negative." Sometimes that's all you could expect. In a perfect world, animals would roam free, but then where would all the people live?

The van ride was quiet as the late night and early morning caught up with everyone. Boon-nam didn't even wait for the van to begin moving before curling up in Jake's lap like a baby tiger. Within minutes she was snoring.

Jake stared down at her, petting her face and watching her as she slept, trying to ignore the pure burst of affection that raced through him. Even her snore was adorable. Fuck!

He distracted himself by focusing on the other couple. He took mental notes on what he'd say to bust on Randy later. Jake observed Randy go through the process of pulling Lalana to him. The drama took Randy twenty minutes before he gathered Lalana against him. But once they were finally cozy, they did look sweet from the glimpses Jake caught reflected in one of the driver's many rearview mirrors.

Randy rubbed Lalana's back until she appeared to sag against him in sleep. Randy didn't say anything, but glanced back at Jake and sighed with contentment. Without saying a word, Randy closed his eyes.

Jake's attention refocused on the sleeping woman in his lap. Too many emotions seemed to vie for attention. He'd never been in love before, but….

Everyone started waking up when traffic stalled the van's progress outside Bangkok's city limits. A loud blare of a horn caused Boon-nam to lift her head out of Jake's lap and peek around. Wiping a bit of drool from her mouth, she glanced up at him with utter devotion, which made his insides flip.

"Where would you ladies like to go for lunch? Or early dinner?" Randy asked, breaking Jake out of Boon-nam's stare of adoration.

"Oh, I know the perfect place," Lalana said.

Jake couldn't help the nasty intuition they'd be paying through the nose for a fancy meal. He knew plenty of women and men back home who'd have taken advantage of such an offer. Lalana would probably pick someplace super expensive, making them break the bank on the meal.

Would Boon-nam do the same thing, given the opportunity? It would serve him right. Jake reminded himself to keep his feet on the ground.

He was glad he'd kept his big mouth shut when they headed to the basement food court of the Siam Paragon Mall. Granted the shops were upscale, but the restaurants were as cheap as fast food in the good ole US of A. Jake didn't know what felt worse, thinking like a jackass or having those distance-provoking thoughts proven wrong. All the walls he tried to build between him and Boon-nam kept crumbling to dust.

"Wow! Great choice. This is delicious. Try this," Randy exclaimed, holding out some pad Thai on chopsticks for Lalana.

Boon-nam smiled hopefully at Jake. "Do you like it too?"

"Yes, very much." His answer had nothing to do with the question and more to do with her. He'd never experienced anything like he did when he was with her. Other than Randy, he wasn't used to liking someone this much.

After they enjoyed a leisurely dinner, they did some shopping before they trudged their way back to their hotel. They zigzagged a path through the streets, still bustling with activity even this late at night. Bangkok never slept.

Randy shocked the hell out of him when he asked Lalana, "Would you like to come upstairs for a bit?"

Jake whispered in Boon-nam's ear, "Would my little tiger like to come?"

His double entendre received a heated moan and a long, hard swallow. Boon-nam's eyes shot to Lalana, imploring her to agree.

Lalana glanced back at Boon-nam with a small frown, which turned into a smile when she faced Randy. "Yes, for a bit."

Jake put his arm around Boon and escorted her to the elevator. When Randy pushed a different floor number than Jake, Lalana said, "I guessed you shared a room."

"No," the men replied in unison, shaking their heads. Damn, he hoped this wasn't a deal breaker. He didn't want Boon-nam to leave.

"Oh." Lalana bit her lip as if she were going to call an end to this party. But Boon-nam touched her hand and said something in Thai to her. The pleading in her gesture was universal; Jake didn't need a translation.

Lalana gave Boon-nam a long stare and a big hug. As she hugged her, Lalana took the opportunity to glare at Jake over Boon-nam's shoulder and mouth, "Don't hurt her!"

Jake gave a slight nod of understanding as he led Boon-nam out of the elevator. He wouldn't hurt her—but no one promised she wouldn't break his heart.

Chapter Six

RANDY PUT his arm around Lalana to support her. She deflated a little when Boon-nam stepped off the elevator with Jake. When the elevators doors closed to ascend two floors, Randy tried to reassure her. "Jake's really a nice guy. He'd never hurt Boon-nam."

"I know. He wouldn't hurt her on purpose. But this is a first for her." She paused to let the meaning sink in to Randy's head. "Jake will be going home in less than two weeks. Both of you will be leaving." Turning away from his eyes, she added, "She is going to be devastated."

The implication in her tone said what she wouldn't allow herself to say. Though her face told Randy she already mourned the loss.

"Really?" Hot damn! Randy tried not to sound happy.

"Yes, my sweet little butterfly already fancies herself in love for the first time." Lalana paused before finishing her thought. "And he is going to break my Boon-boon's little heart." Lalana sniffed. "Sorry."

Randy reached out and squeezed her hand. He had the same concern about Jake. Though this time his best friend seemed rather smitten with Boon-nam. Relationships were risky, and no one got any guarantees.

Once inside the hotel room, Randy was drenched. His nerves got to him. It wasn't like he hadn't had sex, though it'd been a while. But almost every time he had sex, or tried to, the experience usually didn't end well.

Why did I invite Lalana up here? Usually he'd lose his erection, and at other times he didn't even get one. He'd taken care of his wife with his fingers or tongue. Talk about upsetting and embarrassing. He was only in his late twenties, and far too young for erectile dysfunction.

Lalana seemed to sense his reluctance as she sat down on the love seat in the corner of his room. Patting the place next to her, she said, "Come here, Randy."

He shoved his hands in his pockets and meandered over to her. His dick swelled a little as if his cock was pleased she was taking the lead. Biting his lower lip, he took a deep breath and sat down. His inhale allowed him to smell her delicate perfume.

Would he keep his erection? Would he be able to satisfy her? What should he do if she had male genitals? Did he want her to ignore her boy parts? Did she want him to ignore any of her parts? Would she love him back? 'Cause he was certain he was in love with her. Hell, he'd been half in love with her before even leaving the States. His mind swirled faster than a whirling dervish.

She reached out to comb her fingers through his hair, erasing some of the stress and anxiety. Ever so slowly she pulled him toward her. She tilted her head to place her lips on his mouth. Her perfectly formed pink lips captured his in a soulful kiss.

Randy opened his mouth, letting the kiss deepen naturally. Her tongue traced over his lower lip, making him groan from the sensuous slide before she dived in.

Kissing her made him dizzy with want. He let her stay in control, loving the result. Her fingers dug into the short hairs at the back of his neck as if to secure him. She slid her lips over his mouth again and again as her tongue danced with his. Breathlessly, he pressed closer to her shapely body, invading her space. He kissed her back with such passion, he wondered if they would catch fire.

All Randy's nervousness evaporated in her arms. His doubts vanished as he reached up to pull out the gadget that kept her hair knotted in a bun. Her long, dark brown hair cascaded over her shoulders, calling to his fingers to touch the strands. He caressed the long waves of chocolate silk and deepened the kiss, letting her know how much he wanted her.

This was what kissing an angel must be like… a hot, dirty angel who set him on fire. In truth, he'd never been kissed like this before. Lalana seemed to put everything she had into kissing him, making his blood boil. She held nothing back. He grunted at the loss of her talented mouth when she tilted her head back but wreathed her arms around him tighter.

Instinct kicked in as he took her up on the invitation to devour her neck. He bit and kissed his way down to where her neck met her shoulders. He placed a small nip here and there and followed the edge of her blouse with his tongue.

"Oh, Randy."

Her eyes closed as she groaned for more. He would gladly give her anything she needed. He wanted to give her everything.

Tracing the skin exposed by her top, he tried to decide if he should pop open a button. He didn't want to advance too quickly. Randy smiled to himself as he noticed the clock. They'd been kissing for at least half an hour, making out like horny teenagers, kissing the same places, only getting hotter each time. An unfamiliar desire built past his control. He needed something more than kisses to satisfy this urgent compulsion.

As if reading his mind, Lalana slipped a hand down the front of his pants. She moaned happily when she reached her destination to find his erection waiting for her. She massaged his cock through the material of his cotton briefs, her grip firm and not tentative like his past lovers' touch had been. She didn't appear intimidated by his size.

He needed to maintain control. But having the object of his fantasy touch and handle him with such confidence, even through fabric, aroused him further. He bit his lip, trying to hold back the floodgate of his excitement, knowing he needed her to slow down. He actually trembled with lust as she started to unzip his pants.

Shit! Suddenly panic ripped through him. He'd embarrass himself by spending immediately. "No, Lalana. Don't." He attempted to struggle away from her as he tried to stop her. "Augh! Lalana!"

But his attempted escape didn't work; she was a girl on a mission. She put her hand through his open zipper and worked past the cotton to touch his naked flesh. Lalana stroked him firmly.

"No...." He whimpered pathetically. His release immediately followed. When Lalana realized what was happening, she squeezed around him and firmly stroked him through the rest of his orgasm, making it his strongest ever. He came too quick.

"Oh, God. I'm sorry." Mortification ripped through him. Now she'd figure out he was a loser.

Premature ejaculation had never happened to him. Usually he had the opposite problem of trying to keep his lower region interested. But with Lalana that wasn't even a consideration. He seemed to be constantly hard around her. Maybe it was understandable that her first touch made him shoot like a fire hose.

Groaning again, he couldn't even meet her eyes. "Oh, I apologize."

Was she disgusted with him? Would she leave his sorry ass alone?

"Shh! It's okay, baby. You were excited." She kissed him on the mouth before standing up. "Let me get you a warm cloth."

Lalana returned from the bathroom with a warm wet washcloth, and much to his surprise, she cleaned him up. Lalana told him, with a sparkle in her eye, "Liked that I turned you on to the point you lost control." A small smile played on her lips. "You make me feel ravishing." She wiggled a little to emphasize her point and gave him another peck on the lips.

"Oh, Lalana, you are. Still, I am sorry. It's just that… well, I haven't been with anyone in a long, long time."

"How long?"

"Since my wife… and even then it had been a couple of years." Randy wound his hands around in the waves of her hair. "You are truly stunning. I couldn't hold back."

She gave him another kiss as she dropped her hand to zip up his khakis. "That's okay, Randy." She started to gather her bag as if she were preparing to leave.

He was desperate for her to stay. "Please don't go." Maybe he was a loser, but he wanted to return the pleasure. "I want to make you happy too." Randy had never been a selfish lover and had no intentions of starting with his dream girl.

"No, that's okay. I'm happy. I liked pleasing you." Lalana propelled herself toward the door.

"Please, Lalana." He didn't know what he pleaded for, but he didn't want her to leave. He followed her to the door and placed a kiss on her palm.

"Randy, I'm…." She frowned and turned away. "I haven't…." Sighing with what sounded like irritation, she went on. "I'm not like Boon-nam. I haven't had the surgery." She resumed her trek toward the door, but he still held her hand.

He hugged her. "Okay."

He wasn't sure what the proper response should be to this information. He'd never touched anyone else's penis in his life, but he knew he wanted to touch anything of Lalana's to please her. "Please."

She stiffened in his arms. "And, well, I don't want the surgery," she said as if daring him to cease his bid for her attention. "I happen to love that part of me, and just like the rest of me has transitioned into a female form, my male parts have become my clitoris."

Randy only nodded and took her hand again. He relocated them a few feet in front of the bed.

"No surgery, ever. Seriously, Randy, I will never be a *real* lady."

"You're a real lady. A truly lovely woman, who I find enchanting," he reiterated.

"No, I want you to be clear. I used to be confused, but after a lot of… what do you call it?" She stared at him as if she could find the words she wanted to say in his face. "Soul-searching. I did a lot of soul-searching, and I accept who I am."

She stared at him, radiating a boatload of defiance. Had someone questioned her right to decide such things for herself?

She raised her voice, and she waved her hands around, becoming more animated than he'd ever seen her. "I am a lady with some parts that resemble male parts. But I'm staying intact. So if you are expecting a proper lady, look elsewhere. I'm keeping my clit."

Randy leaned toward her, needing to be closer. Her misplaced anger saddened him, but he wasn't going to let it detour him. "And what is a 'proper' lady?"

He then did something he'd never envisioned doing.

"Oh!" she called out as he swept her up in his arms ready to carry her the short distance to the bed.

Mine. He planted his lips on hers, hoping to keep her fury at bay. The press of their lips scorched him from the inside out. He stumbled over to the bed to set her in the middle. Her confession gave him more confidence than he'd ever had in this situation.

After following her onto the bed, he slid in close to her. Her chocolate eyes were wide as he studied her. She desired him. This gorgeous creature desired Randy Camster. Randy's lips found hers in long, slow kisses, trying to lace them with heat.

She stiffened when his hand skimmed up her legs. "You really don't have to do this," she told him as he reached the undergarment that kept her parts hidden from the world.

"If you want me to stop, I will, but I really want to touch you." He was determined. Randy ran his hand over the tight restrictive undergarment that ensured her parts didn't broadcast her arousal. Since she didn't tell him to stop, he kept trying to find a way in, but the wrap proved too secure.

Breaking from another kiss, he skated his lips over her chin. "Take this thing off, please. I want to touch you."

She frowned as she examined his face as if trying to understand what his motives were.

Then with quick, practiced movements, she sighed with relief as she released the gaff within seconds.

Damn, that thing has to be uncomfortable.

She tossed it to the floor and smoothed down her little skirt as if she were trying to hide parts of her. The way her skirt puffed out, Randy could see she was rock hard. "Randy, really, it's okay. I know you aren't gay or anything."

His face heated up. He wasn't gay. But for the last few months, he'd been crushing on her via the video clips, and here she was in his arms. He couldn't ignore the opportunity. "You're right, I'm not gay. But you're the most elegant woman I've ever seen, and I'd like to do this with you."

Oh, hell, please don't let me screw this up.

"But…."

"Gender isn't based on what's down there." Randy quoted Jake, stunned to be repeating lines from Jake's repertoire, but it was appropriate. *Go figure.*

Randy traced a hand down her cheek. *God, her skin's soft.* He'd read some transgender women didn't like to be touched in certain ways, or they wanted their lovers to avoid the intimate area. Did Lalana feel like that?

Randy didn't want to make her uncomfortable, but he whispered to her, "Please. Let me appreciate how gorgeous you are." His tone must have convinced her to give him a chance.

She lay back flat and squeezed her eyes shut. Was she afraid she would see disgust on his face when he saw her body?

"Here." She pulled up her skirt and held her breath as if she were waiting for his rejection.

Lalana was appealing everywhere. She had finely toned legs that went for miles. From this angle, the side swell of her ass created a lush curve. Her cock—no, her clit, as she'd called it—might have been small, but it was pretty. Edible.

Finally she cracked one eye open and peeked at him. He stared at her. He watched as she struggled with her arousal. Randy wondered if the poor girl had been hard for hours like he'd been.

"May I?" he asked as if it were a simple question and not something completely beyond his realm of experience.

She whimpered. "Yes."

Randy hoped she saw not only his acceptance of her body but his desire to worship her.

She groaned and pushed her hips forward, begging for his attention. "Oh. Please, Randy. Touch me."

This was better than any dream he'd ever had. "Mmm, yes."

Randy teased his fingers across her sac and ran up and down the straining length of her clitoris. He recaptured her mouth as he took her erection in his hand, much like he would his own. The medications she took to live female might have shrunk her male member, but it was very responsive and seemed to pulsate for his attention as he kissed her.

Randy separated their lips to take a deep breath, giving him time to think. He lost his breath as he wrapped his hand around her. He kept waiting for something other than his excitement, but as he stroked her, everything else was overshadowed.

Randy used his free hand to unbutton her blouse and push the silk aside. He froze, faced with her rounded, perfect breasts. They might have been surgically enhanced, but her nipples beckoned his mouth. Randy licked lightly at her aroused tips until they hardened into tight points. He teased until her body arched toward his mouth as if she begged him to bite. He bit down lightly, causing her to arch off the bed. He sucked her, making her cry out.

She must have been as keyed up as he had been because within a few strokes Lalana thrust her hips in time with Randy's fist and painted herself in sticky spurts. Randy continued to suck at her breast, deepening her moan of ecstasy.

"Oh, Randy." Her body rippled with her orgasm. "Mmm, good." She shivered as he squeezed the last of her release out of her.

She closed her eyes and smiled. He slipped out of bed and returned to clean her up with a warm towel. Randy returned to the bed to lie down next to her and pull the blanket up around them. Cuddling her close, he fell asleep to her soft snores with a grin on his face.

LALANA WOKE from the most amazing sleep. Mmm, refreshed and happy. She realized she wasn't alone… and this wasn't Boon-nam. Damn, a large male pressed up against her. Mm, Randy.

She turned over to get a better view of her lover and couldn't suppress a smile. This was the first time she'd woken up with someone other than Boon-nam. Growing up, Boon-nam had terrible nightmares. Lalana would try to soothe them away with soft words and hugs. But Randy had been the one to cuddle her to sleep. Damn, it shouldn't feel so good.

Randy was still out cold. Jet lag must be ruling him because he didn't wake when Lalana slipped into the bathroom to freshen up. She took a quick shower and, thankfully, her well-stocked pocketbook helped her fix her face.

The driver had left her bags at the front desk with Boon-nam's, as she hadn't intended on spending the night. But to bring them up would've been an admission she hadn't been ready to make. She'd had everything she needed to maintain her image: razors, makeup, fresh underwear, a different T-shirt, hair products, her medications. You name it, she had it.

Slipping into the closet, Lalana borrowed one of Randy's shirts. She hoped he didn't mind, but she wanted to hide her parts without tying them up this early. The shirttails hung low enough to conceal her morning clit erection, which she refused to take the time to tend to in the shower. Pondering her erect clitoris poking up, trying to break out of her panties, maybe she should have.

The doctor had been right when he prescribed a lower dose of estrogen. The new dosage allowed her more enjoyment sexually. Even so, she rarely woke up so horny. She cupped a hand over her clit erection and gave it a long slow stroke. Mm-mm, staring at the sleeping Randy, she knew the cause of this particular problem. But now wasn't the time to worry about her wayward clit.

She crawled under the covers, found Randy's morning arousal, and slid her lips down over his dick. Lalana loved a cock in her mouth almost as much as something up her bottom. The act of giving oral sex and the act of receiving cock were pretty much tied as her favorites, and depending on the day, either one might be in first place. Meanwhile, she planned on showing this gentle man's cock her appreciation.

His cock was quite a beauty. She would never have guessed what he packed, but oh my, his endowments made her heart triple its beat. Boon-nam accused her of being a size queen, and admiring Randy's mammoth phallus, she could definitely become one. His shaft was a work of art.

Her cheeks hollowed as she sucked him in. Randy must have woken up, because she felt a hand resting on her head as she bobbed up and down on his cock. She made the tip of his shaft hit the back of her throat, causing her to gag around his dick. All men seemed to love that.

Instead of the usual moan of pleasure and pushing her head down farther, Randy threw off the covers.

"Are you okay? I'm sorry."

"Huh?" she asked around the mouthful of cock.

"I didn't mean to choke you. I must have thrust too much. Are you okay?" His face, so expressive and full of concern, twisted Lalana's emotions up tight.

His worry for her confused her. What man cared whether he choked the cocksucker on his dick? No one she'd ever sucked.

Lalana didn't want to care about him as much as she did. Maybe if he could stop being charming and gentle to her, she would find perspective.

She pulled her mouth off and rested a hand on his thigh. "No, it's fine. I pushed down on you. I expected you to enjoy that."

"I love being in your mouth, but I don't want you uncomfortable."

He caressed her face as she leaned into his palm.

She smiled to reassure him. "I'm not uncomfortable." She blew a stream of hot air across his dick.

"Oh!" He pushed his head into the pillow and groaned as if in pain.

Blowing air up and down his shaft again just to get the reaction, Lalana giggled. She ducked back down to tease him with her tongue.

"So sweet and talented," he said, right before his eyes closed.

"Are you safe for me to swallow?" Stupid time to ask, but Randy had said he hadn't been with anyone, and she believed him. Tong would have her head if she knew, but Lalana hadn't demanded paperwork.

"Yes. My doctor screens for all sexually transmitted diseases, and no issue." He inhaled as if he were struggling to keep it together as she took him back into her mouth.

She slowly deep-throated him, and once she had all of him where she wanted him, she swallowed. Strangling sounds echoed off the white walls; she knew this was the right track. She deep-throated several more times before she rode her throat up his cock. She licked and teased the crown as she admired him in the morning light streaming through the curtains.

He had a gorgeous dick. She'd appreciated the size last night, but in the light of day, she noticed how nicely he was veined. Staring at the ridges made her ass clench with emptiness. His whimper of need brought her back to the important activity of making him come.

She welcomed him back into her mouth and down to the root. Randy expanded and throbbed. Lalana swiped her tongue out to lick his sac before moving her head up and down in a nice steady rhythm sure to bring him off.

Lalana used every trick she knew to give him the hottest blowjob he'd ever had. Her head bobbed up and down, she dragged her lips over Randy's rod, sucking hard as she went. He tensed up as she got him closer to orgasm. His cock strained for release.

Sucking his dick made her throb. She pressed her body into the bed and tried to ignore the need to fuck herself to orgasm. Pushing aside her frustration, she redoubled her efforts and allowed herself the comfort of thrusting hard against the mattress.

When his balls tightened and his body froze, Randy called out a warning, "Lalana, honey. I'm going to…." Randy pushed up onto his elbows, trying to wiggle away from her, but she wasn't about to let him. She let her mouth fill with saliva and sucked hard. The noise of the increased suction appeared to be the final straw, and she watched as he lost the battle of restraint against her mouth.

"Lalana!" Randy shouted as he froze for a moment before his dick throbbed out his load into her mouth.

"Oh, Lalana!" Her name had never been howled like this before.

Eyes closed, he cried out in ecstasy as she caressed his shaft with her throat muscles. She'd been told getting deep-throated by a singer had its advantages. Again and again she swallowed his essence without stopping for breath until not even a single delicious drop remained. He collapsed onto the bed with a bemused expression on his face.

She licked him to ensure she got all his cream. "Yum." She said it quietly, hoping he wouldn't hear her.

Randy raised his head and said, "Beautiful one, come up here. Ah, you're amazing." He sighed with such contentment, she was sure she blushed.

She crawled up his toned body to reach his face. He pulled her down to kiss her, but she turned her face aside. "Let me go brush my teeth." He certainly wouldn't want to taste her mouth coated in come.

"Oh, sorry. I didn't think. I guess I don't taste good." He shied away from her as if ashamed.

"No. You must drink a lot of juice, you're almost sweet." She chortled, having never tasted delicious come before. "But I know you don't want to taste yourself."

"Well, if it's on your lips and you say my come is sweet...."

She snickered again, and he chuckled while he gathered her up in his arms to kiss her. Firmly Randy grabbed the damp hair at the nape of her neck to guide her to his mouth.

Lalana melted into his hot lips. Oh, he could kiss. His lips were pliant and soft. Oh, and he knew how to use his tongue. But seeing him become a little assertive made her almost orgasm, hands-free. She liked taking the lead, but she could also enjoy having someone else take control.

Randy must have felt her wayward cock at the same time her erection rubbed up against him. Lalana tried to scoot off him to hide the fact she'd tented her mint green panties. But he refused to let her go.

"Mm-mm, Lalana, what do we have here?" He shifted, putting her on his thighs, and flipped up the borrowed shirt to reveal her body begging for attention.

Casting her eyes downward, they stared at her arousal, which had escaped her tiny girlie pants to poke out of the top of the elastic band.

"Nothing." Lalana knew her cheeks had reddened as she tried to get off him, and again he held her still.

Glancing up at her, he asked nicely, "Can I see?"

After she choked out a yes, he lifted up the shirt to reveal her entire package. The mint green lacy panties only seemed to accent the boldness of her parts.

He gently traced a finger over the lace. "So delicate." His fingers grazed over her trapped and engorged clit. A tear of want escaped its tip. He swiped a single finger over the slit and brought the fluid to his mouth.

"No, you don't have to," she whispered, mesmerized by her cock getting closer and closer to his lips.

"I want to taste you. If that's okay?"

She was unclear. Was Randy asking if taking her in his mouth was safe, or did the question just ask her permission? Both would be okay. She tried to convince herself no one died from not getting head.

Lalana decided to answer the biggest question first. "I get tested like all the performers every three months. Whether we have sex or not." She shrugged. "Adirake makes getting tests a requirement of working. But the routine is a good practice, especially for the younger boys and girls. It helps them remember to always be safe."

Randy nodded with approval. "I like Adirake, but"—he licked his finger clean of Lalana's juice—"I don't want to talk about him."

Lalana giggled. She never remembered laughing as much as she did when with Randy. "What do you want to talk about?"

"Well, I have a delightful little girl in front of me, and she appears to be in need." He smiled with a handsome blush. "I've never done this, but I really want to share this wonderful experience with you. Can you be patient with me?"

"Oh, um. No. You don't have to do that, Randy."

Lalana's clitoris pulsated, not pleased she had offered to forego satisfaction, but her brain forced a quick backpedal from the emotions that already swirled around in her head. She tried to swing her leg over him to get off the bed.

He stopped her again. "Hey, I don't want to push you, but I want to do this." He smiled up at her. "Don't you want to be my first?"

Lalana strangled on her tongue. "You want to... for me... and never?"

She tried to make a full sentence, but her brain wouldn't comply. The sweet bastard appeared to be enjoying the situation to the point he even teased her.

Randy sighed. "I know you probably think I won't do it right."

Maybe his playful tone confused the translation, but Lalana got all flustered. "No. I mean... I don't know what I mean." She frowned in horny confusion.

Randy guided her up his body. When she straddled his shoulders, he said, "Teach me, Lalana. Teach me how to use my mouth on you."

An unfeminine groan escaped, proving how out of control Lalana truly was. She braced her hands on the padded headboard as his palms cupped her ass, pulling her forward. "I...." was the only word she got out before Randy took her clitoris in his velvety, wet mouth.

He seemed to be guiding her hips, making her thrust in and out. Lalana wasn't big enough to have to worry about choking him. She was barely a mouthful, and Randy didn't seem to mind.

Incredible. She wouldn't last long. Already her body climbed toward its peak. Had she ever experienced this kind of chemistry or connection before? She loved sucking him off. And now she was "teaching" him how to suck a cock.

"Oh!" The concept was almost enough to make her come. Desperate to prolong the pleasure a little longer, she tried to hold out. "Close." Her voice sounded rough and masculine, but as Randy sucked on her, she couldn't have cared less. Just a little more of his eager tongue and hot mouth would make her orgasm.

Randy didn't pull off as all the men before him had. He sucked deeper and bobbed his head a little faster. Lalana gripped the headboard as she was sucked off into heaven. She groaned as she pulsed out her essence right into Randy's mouth.

He didn't seem to mind getting a mouth full of Lalana's passion. Randy sucked and swallowed her until she was completely spent. He let her pull out of his mouth, but not before he licked her several more times.

"Mm-mm, Randy." She needed to catch her breath.

He swallowed to clear his throat before he asked, "Was that okay?"

Stunned by the question, she laughed. "I couldn't have faked that."

Randy chuckled. "I hope not." His expression changed. "I never want you to pretend with me. I want to make you happy. You just have to let me."

Speechless, she dissolved into his embrace.

Chapter Seven

Earlier the same evening

JAKE AND Boon-nam strolled into Jake's hotel room. Boon-nam checked her appearance as she passed a mirror, and a ghost of a smile appeared. Jake realized she checked frequently as if to make sure the outside still matched the inside. He couldn't envision the sensation of being born the wrong gender, but he was glad she lived in a time when surgery was possible.

Boon-nam pulled Jake over to the neutral-colored love seat. Immediately she started kissing him. Her eager kisses were appealing and a little awkward, but her obvious inexperience didn't lessen her passion. The innocent kisses incited his lust, which he tried his best to keep in check.

"Hey, let's talk." Jake was surprised to hear himself suggesting such an alien thing.

"About what?" Boon entwined her arms about him as he gently pushed back to sit a distance away.

"Tell me about yourself."

Boon-nam frowned. "Okay. What do you want to know?"

"The basics. What's it like growing up in Thailand?"

"Before my mother died it was wonderful, afterward not so much." She paused and forced a smile onto her face. "But it got better again when Lalana and I came to Bangkok and got terrific once Tong and Areva found us."

Before Jake could follow up with questions on what "not so much" meant, Boon-nam asked, "How about you?"

"I grew up in a small town. I have a sister. We used to be close but not anymore."

"How come you're not married?"

"Never found the right one." That sounded like a good excuse.

"What's the right one for you?"

You. Fuck! Where did that thought come from? "Um, I don't know. I guess I like smart, sexy, fun to be with, cute, funny."

Jake could almost see Boon-nam checking off those qualities in herself. Fuck if she wasn't the best candidate. He needed to get a grip.

"Do you like me, Jake?"

"So much." He shook his head at what his mouth spilled out and figured what the fuck. "I like you so much it scares me."

"Why?" She screwed up her face.

"We've only just met and…." He couldn't imagine his life without his little tiger in it.

"I like you too. A lot."

Fuck. A piece of him wanted to hide from the connection he had with her, and the other part of him demanded he man up and see where it went. But he was leaving in a couple of weeks. His indecision must have shown on his face, because she kissed him.

"Shh, Jake. Don't think so much. Kiss me." Her hands were in his hair, combing through the strands.

He could do nothing other than obey. He cupped her precious face to tip her chin to the left. Her lips were soft and wet as their mouths glided over each other's, making him want to kiss her forever.

Forever. He'd never wanted forever. But he wanted this connection he had with her to never end. The more impossible it seemed, the more desperate his kisses became.

Their necking session reminded him of ones he'd had in high school. All hot lust building toward a plateau. Unlike then, Jake didn't want to push past Boon-nam's comfort level. He needed to make sure everything was copacetic with her.

"Boon, sweetheart, is everything okay?"

When Boon didn't answer, Jake shifted away from her tempting curves and responsive body. "Sweetheart, we can say good night right now."

"No!" Boon-nam said quickly. "I don't want to…."

Jake smiled at her outburst. "We don't have to do anything more. Okay? I don't want you to feel pressured." He couldn't recall ever considering someone's feelings to this extent. Hell, not even his own seemed as important as Boon-nam's.

Boon appeared utterly miserable as she pulled back and sagged into the hard love seat. "It's just…."

Jake sat back and tucked her hair gently behind her ear. Boon sighed and leaned into the touch. "Just what, sweetheart?"

Boon's upset was more important than his cock trying to rip out of his pants. This truly was a first! His libido iced. Damn, his friends would laugh their asses off.

A blush stained her cheeks, and she twisted away from him. "I haven't…." Her refusal to look at him translated her broken sentence.

"You haven't?" *Fuck.* If he had gotten a new body, he would have definitely taken it out for a spin as soon as he could. But he was grateful Boon-nam was more selective than he would have been. Jake picked up her delicate hand and placed a chaste kiss on the knuckles.

She shook her head, tossing her waves of hair about her face, frowning in frustration.

"I see…." Jake wanted to be supportive and nonthreatening, but he wasn't sure what she needed from him. A virgin was new territory for him, but a transgender virgin who'd had affirmation surgery was beyond his experience.

"No. You don't." She moaned miserably into the palms of her hands, which covered her face from his perceptive eyes. "The doctor thinks I am healed." Very quietly she said, "Everything is in working order."

"Oh? Oh, um, good." Relief washed over him because the surgery could have varying degrees of success in terms of sexual pleasure. Jake didn't know how to ask Boon since she seemed embarrassed by the whole conversation, but he wanted to make sure. "So, um, then you've had sex?"

"No. No, I haven't…." She peeked up sadly at Jake, and he decided his first priority should be to kiss her happy. He kissed her frown until she whimpered.

Talking in half sentences confused his lust-addled mind. "Um, how do you know things are in working order?"

"Well, you know, I have done some things. But that was just…."

Jake tried to restrain the chuckle but failed as Boon's blush stained her face darker. "Oh, right. Masturbation?"

Batting her eyelashes, she glanced away, nodding. Why was her innocent mortification of admitting to solo play alluring? Jesus, he needed his head examined.

Her face got redder as she ignored his statement. She wouldn't meet his eyes, but she traced a finger along his earrings, making them jangle. "I like your earrings. Men in earrings are sexy. And you have... eight of them."

"So I'm eight times sexier than most men?"

Boon-nam giggled, covering her mouth as she nodded.

Jake hid his grin. *Damn, she's cute.* He pulled her into his arms. "Little tiger, were your solo adventures acceptable?" He used his "sexy" voice to ask.

"Is that nickname going to stick?" She tried to artfully change the subject.

"Do you mind if it does?"

She shook her head. "I like it."

"Good. Now back to my question. Was your alone time successful?"

A tiny smile played on Boon's mouth. "Oh, yeah."

Damn, she isn't going to make this easy on me.

"Was it different? Than before your surgery?" Jake didn't want to pry, but was hoping she would provide some details, giving him a clue to what she liked.

"Yes."

An expression of excitement washed over her face. She seemed to want to share the details with him.

"The feeling was more. I don't know how to describe it. The sensation comes in waves, and it's longer. Not just in one place. It felt right." After her confession she peeked up at Jake from under her lashes to study him.

Jake nodded. He wanted to understand. Most of the trans people he had met said the same thing. Their descriptions made his cock envious of the female orgasm.

His balls ached, but he reassured her, "We don't have to do anything you don't want to do."

"I know." She tried to sound confident, though Jake was starting to feel anything but his usual bravado. "But I want to, you know. There are so many things I want to do."

She played the aggressor by sliding back to him. The action caught Jake a bit off guard when her breast pressed against his chest. She wrapped her arms around his neck, pulling him down for more kisses.

"We could fool around a bit," he said between the kisses.

"Don't you want to… you know?" Boon-nam seemed to be struggling to put thoughts into words. She giggled a little and covered her mouth. Shrugging, she said, "Lalana and Tong always say 'if you can't talk about it, you shouldn't do it,' but I don't care. Don't you want to… *you know?*"

The concept made Jake smile, and her determination was admirable. "Yeah, of course I do. But it's your first time since the surgery. You're like a virgin again. This needs to be done right. Your first time should be special."

Wiggling as she twined her arms around him, she said, "I know. That's why I want you to be my very first."

Wait. What? Her very first… as in ever?

He bit back saying he wanted to be her last. Too soon for declarations, though he couldn't deny the seduction of her sweet innocence. But that couldn't be right. "You mean since your surgery? You have had sex the other way before your surgery."

"Ew! No!" She sounded as if the idea of sex with male parts had been completely repulsive to her.

"So you've never…." This was a little too farfetched for Jake to hope for, and it probably made him a real bastard, but he couldn't stop the possessive need of wanting her to be untouched. He wanted to be a primitive caveman and claim the position of first and only for Boon-nam's affections.

"Well, no. I wanted to wait until after the surgery. And my healing took forever, months and months." Becoming uncomfortable, she defended herself. "I have given yum-yum a couple of times."

"Yum-yum? Oh, okay." Jake hid his smile when he realized she referred to oral sex. Shit! His head spun as he contemplated having his first complete virgin.

"I am superior at yum-yum," Boon-nam said proudly and twirled a piece of her hair. "Do you like yum-yum?"

Is she planning on a demonstration? Save me from this siren! "Yes, of course." He put his hands out as if he could hold back her desire as well as his. He cleared his throat. "Um, did you ever receive yum-yum?"

Boon-nam bounced back on the sofa to collapse next to him. "Again, ick! No! That thing wasn't part of me. I didn't like having one of those. I'm a girl. I wasn't meant to have one of those *things*. I couldn't wait for my surgery!" She stood up as if to pace off the bad memories of having a male body.

"So you have never had oral sex before?"

Jake jumped and stalked toward Boon-nam, who backed up a step. When he witnessed the desire and need flash over her innocent face, he decided how he'd spend the next hour or so. Boon-nam stepped back again, sending the predator in Jake signals the hunt had begun.

"Um, well, no," Boon choked out, propelling herself farther, just out of Jake's reach.

"No one has ever loved on you with their mouth?"

Jake hated to admit it, but he was probably a bit below average in the cock department, which he tried to make up for by having skilled fingers and a talented tongue. He always prided himself on being quite adept at getting a partner off with his mouth. Playing his bed partners like instruments always gave him a thrill. He listened, became attuned to the music their moans made, and learned how to compose a concerto, bringing each to their own crescendo. He knew lots of tricks to get even the most difficult to orgasm.

When Boon-nam shook her head no, Jake fairly purred, "No one has ever licked you?"

He loomed over her as the thrill of possession ran through him. He would be her first.

Boon-nam squealed, giggled, and blushed, and she backed into the rolling desk chair. She pulled out the chair to create distance between them. Her eyes widened. She looked excitedly at Jake. Her breath came in pants as she waited for what was next.

"Do you want me to be first to kiss and lick your prettiness?" Jake dropped his voice an octave, and his tone predictably sent visible shivers through Boon-nam's body.

"Mm-mm, yes."

She seemed compelled to press closer to Jake. It was as if he were a magnet and she a piece of metal. Jake encircled her protectively in his arms.

"My tongue is going to touch you places no one else has." Jake intended on building a fire in her mind that would ignite her entire body when his tongue finally got involved.

Boon-nam groaned, and her eyelids fluttered. She glanced around the room at anything but Jake.

He surrounded her with his body. As he leaned down to kiss her neck, he asked, "You want me to, don't you? You want me to lick you to pleasure."

She melted into Jake. "Yes. Yes, so much."

He bent down to scoop her up in his arms and stalked over to the bed to gently lay her on it. He studied her, lying back with those big, trusting brown eyes. His heart tightened in an unfamiliar way. "You are too lovely, Boon-nam."

New emotions attacked him, and he didn't know what to make of them. Jake wanted her in the worst way, but more than anything, he wanted her happiness. His contentment took a backseat to hers. Staring down at her, he tried to understand these feelings of protection and affection.

He kicked off his shoes and reclined on the bed next to her, determined to take his time. Probably slower than he had ever gone in his life, but he wanted to make the experience satisfying for her.

Jake slowly kissed off her clothing, one piece at a time. He traced each button of her blouse, building her sensual tension before popping it open. When the buttons were all undone, he skimmed his hands over her clothed body before he slipped the cotton off her shoulders and down her arms. Her pretty shirt drifted to the floor amid her sighs.

Her lacy bra encased a lovely pair of breasts, but Jake trailed his fingers down to her pants. He grazed the soft skin above her capris before touching the zipper. He teased his fingers up and down the metal teeth until she squirmed.

He licked his way down to her belly, pausing to dip his tongue into her belly button until she arched into him with a whimper.

"Jake."

Jake kissed his way over her thin pants to the snap. He gripped the material with his teeth and tugged it open. Catching her gaze, he circled his tongue under the metal tab to flip it up so he could grasp it with his teeth and slowly slide it down.

She writhed under him. She tried to help but didn't understand that her desperate fumbling impeded his progress. Finally her zipper was open, and she eagerly pushed her pants past her hips. He helped guide her trousers off her legs.

Jake slid back up to her pink bra. Blooming lotus flowers created the cups holding her ample breasts. He spied her nipples pebbling under the lace. He breathed hot air and lapped his tongue over them until she begged him for everything he wanted to do next.

She brought her fingers to the front closure. He kissed her impatient hands away and toyed with the clasp until she moaned. With a twist and a flick, her bra separated, exposing her to his tongue. He fluttered tiny wet licks across her breasts until he reached her nipples.

"Jake." She whined as he wiggled the bra off her shoulders and shrugged her arms through the straps. He kept licking her skin until she pulled his head down onto her, all but demanding he do more.

He sucked one nipple into an excited peak before he slid his mouth across her skin to the other. She keened at the sensation. He skimmed his hand down slowly to her matching lace panties and trailed his fingers across the top of her waistband before dipping a finger inside to touch the skin hidden beneath the pink froth.

"Please, Jake." She clenched her fists and her eyes squinted shut as he slowly eased her panties off her hips and down her legs. The skimpy pink lace floated to the pile accumulating on the floor.

He sat back for a moment to appreciate her loveliness.

"Oh, I don't have on anything." Boon-nam opened her eyes and made the statement as if this fact would have gone unnoticed by Jake. In her momentary lapse into shyness, she tried to cover herself up. "You're the first person to see me other than my doctor and maybe Lalana."

He forced himself to stare at her eyes and not her comely form. "Shh, sweetheart. Let me see how spectacular you are."

Very slowly Boon-nam dropped her hands, which had covered her breasts and her new female parts from his view. She closed her eyes.

"You are breathtaking." Jake didn't touch her, he simply drank her in. Dance toned her body, but she was still delicate, fragile somehow. If an artist created a goddess of Thailand, Boon-nam would be the result.

She opened her eyes as if to check Jake's sincerity. The smile she gave him said she believed him, but she still asked, "Really?"

"Oh, yes. Really. You're a vision of perfection." He brushed a kiss over each of her eyelids, her nose, and finally across her lips. He hoped to engage every part of her to melt her inhibitions.

Boon-nam moaned as she opened her mouth. Her tongue swept across his lips to invite him in. Jake took control of the kiss, and in short order, Boon-nam writhed with passion again. Her thrust against him begged Jake to do more. But he opted to err on the side of caution, determined to protect her even against himself.

He settled into the idea of being the first to please her sexually, and a possessive nonfeminist part of him liked the fact way too much. He wanted this bond with her. Was this love or just lust?

He licked his tongue down to her neck. He teased and bit Boon-nam's breasts until he reached her nipples. The sensitive brownish-pink tips begged for the attention of Jake's tongue. As he laved them wet and blew them dry, Boon-nam whimpered. He filled his hands with her breasts and massaged them.

Boon-nam let out earthy moans, and restlessly pushed her lower half off the bed. She arched to present a light brown tip, and he couldn't resist. His mouth closed over one nipple before gently nipping the other.

"*Mai naa cheuua!*" Boon-nam started babbling in Thai, which was sexy as hell. "*Ah loy ma!*" Jake assumed by the tone of the words that she enjoyed his attentions.

Her hips were in constant motion as if she were doing a dance routine. She rocked restlessly. Jake kissed his way down her body, painting her in long licks, trying to excite her wherever his tongue lashed. He finally got to the junction of her thighs. He ran his tongue teasingly down one side and up the other. Slowly he traced his tongue in patterns.

The closer his tongue got to where she wanted him to be, the more she would arch up and try to maneuver his tongue to find her womanhood. Smiling, he purposefully restrained himself from giving her what she wanted.

He wanted her lust to build up more. Again and again he came within a quarter of an inch of where she desperately needed him to be and backed off in another direction. He teased her until he knew insane need took hold of her.

Finally she lost all patience and grabbed Jake's hair. Her fingers tugged his head to where she wanted him to be. She held him against her firmly.

Jake growled with appreciation of Boon-nam finally taking what she needed. As her confidence and experience grew, she'd make the perfect partner. He parted her with his fingers and gave her a nice long lick.

The doctor had done a lovely job. Jake understood only a little of the basics of her surgery, but viewing her chased all the medical knowledge out. All he could see was sexy. He gave her another long, slow lick where it counted.

"*Maak!*" She humped her body against his mouth. "*Maak*, Jake!"

He assumed she begged for more, and he never ignored the needs of someone in his bed, especially not someone as deliciously sweet as Boon-nam. He licked a couple of his fingers and gently inserted them into her. He used his tongue and fingers together to bring her maximum pleasure. Boon-nam trembled as pleasure rose quickly in her.

He wouldn't let her rush. He backed off, much to Boon-nam's frustration, before he built her right back up. The expected lubrication he used to gauge his female lovers' readiness to orgasm was absent, but her body sang to him in other ways. He stayed in synch with her through her breathy moans.

She'd gotten close again, and he eased back one more time. Boon-nam groaned in disappointment.

Poor needy thing, he'd take her to heaven this time. "Shh, sweetheart. Going to take you up there again. Breathe."

A little giggle escaped with the unsteady exhales of breath she'd been holding. "*Khaawy hak jao*, Jake."

She smiled at him with a whole lotta love. He didn't need to wonder if those words echoed the sentiment. And if her expression was any indication of how she felt, he wanted to tell her how much he cared about her too. How special she was to him even though they'd only known each other a short time. But he wanted to make promises he could keep. Instead of confessing what chased around his heart, he simply put his mouth back on her and went to work.

Jake caressed her with his tongue in maddening circles across her newly formed body. His licks grew firmer as she began the ascension. Jake held her suspended for a moment, allowing her to appreciate the tension before he pushed her over the edge by again adding gentle pressure from his fingers in combination with his tongue.

Her body was racked with erotic bliss as she cried out, filling the hotel room with his name. Boon-nam mumbled Thai words as she raced through the final stages of fulfillment. Small tremors ran the length of her as Jake licked her once more.

Fuck, he had never been this turned on in his life. Not even when he was fucking, let alone just going down on someone. Too amped up to wait for her to recover, he kneeled over her and unzipped.

Damn, he had to come. After only a few pulls, he shouted his relief. The creamy drops of his release rained down on her still quivering breasts, decorating her in ribbons of his come. He moaned in satisfaction.

"Mm, Jake." She trailed her fingers through his drizzled cream as if decorating herself with him. She swiped a finger through it, brought it to her mouth, and sucked it off.

Fuck! Was she trying to kill him? Jake's brain melted, and the vision coaxed one more spurt from him. He collapsed next to her, then pulled her to him so he could cuddle her softness close.

He forced himself to remind her, "You shouldn't swallow any fluids. But I've been tested, and I play safe, so no problem."

Duty done. This was what complete peace felt like. Giving her the ultimate pleasure and holding her in his arms satisfied him in a way nothing else had. She snuffled his neck a little before falling into a light sleep.

But all too soon, she woke and asked to go home.

"Jake, Lalana will send out the police to look for me."

Jake wasn't sure if she was serious or not, but decided if she wanted to go home he would meander along. The stroll back would get him a few more minutes with her.

Wow! Fuck Randy for being right, I've got it bad.

Refusing to dwell on his wayward thoughts and saying fuck it all to his feelings, he got dressed while she took a quick shower. Soon he watched her dart around the room, gathering up her clothing.

On the way back to Illusions & Dreams, they talked a little, but mostly they enjoyed the quiet of the side streets. He held her hand and didn't let it go once. He had the strangest need to keep her close.

Jake decided he wanted to make sure she'd see him again. Hell, he didn't want to separate from her now, but she did have a life. He settled on asking for another date. "So can I see you after the show tomorrow night?"

She jumped to an excited stop. "You still want to see me?"

Why would she ask that? "Of course, my little tiger."

Jake noticed they were already outside the side entrance to the apartments and rooms over the club. "Unless you don't want to see me?"

Insecurity wasn't something he suffered from—it sucked.

Boon-nam grinned quickly. "No. I want to. I didn't know. We didn't...." She put up her hand to stop Jake from discussing the matter further. "I should be done at the usual time. How should I dress?"

Not attempting to hide his probably wolflike grin, he teased her for the sole purpose of making her blush. "Clothing is optional."

She giggled. "Jake!"

She surveyed the surroundings as if to figure out if anyone had overheard him. Since no one was around, she allowed him to pull her into the shadows.

His fingers ran up her back and caused her to shiver. He pulled her to him and dipped her low, knowing she would love a romantic movie-like lip-lock. When she cried out in surprise, he kissed her open mouth thoroughly. Upon finishing he stood her up with a pat on her round little butt.

"I can't wait until tomorrow night."

"Oh, me either."

He waited until she was safely inside and blew her a kiss before trudging back to his hotel. Alone.

Fuck. He really cared about her. The idea of leaving her in less than two weeks scratched the inside of his brain raw, so he pushed the threat out of his mind. He wasn't sure if he'd have an opportunity, but he decided if he did, he would make all her first times special.

He glanced at his watch. He needed some advice. Damn, way too early to call Lalana without being incredibly rude. But he'd never get to sleep before speaking with her. Hm, maybe while he was waiting, he could get another tattoo.

Chapter Eight

"DUDE, SORRY to bug you this early…." Jake heard feminine giggling in the background. "Oops, really sorry. I shouldn't have called so late. I mean… early." He had no clue when Randy had last gotten laid, so he didn't want to impede his progress.

"No worries. What's wrong?"

Randy had to know something was up. Whether Jake's voice gave him away or the time of the call, he'd never know.

"I don't want to bug you if this is a bad time." Jake didn't want to cockblock his best buddy. "And by bad I mean you doing deliciously dirty things with a certain lovely lady in your bed."

Randy chuckled. "You're not calling at a bad time." He must have covered the phone because Lalana's laughter sounded muffled.

"Ah, you already knocked boots. Excellent." Jake laughed.

Randy tried to sound shocked and annoyed, but it came out as just plain happy. "Jake! Don't be crass." He chuckled.

"Okay. Look if this isn't a bad time, I called to find out Lalana's number." Jake hoped Randy wouldn't ask too many details about why Jake would want to speak to her.

"Um, okay. Hold on."

After a brief wait, Lalana's voice came on. "Randy said you wanted to speak to me?"

"Um, yeah. Could you come to my room? It's 374."

"Why?" Her voice got higher than usual.

"I want to talk to you about Boon-nam."

"What's wrong with her?"

"Nothing. I just… you know, never mind. Bad idea." The tat had started to sting a bit.

"No. I'll be at your room in five minutes."

Lalana didn't take no for an answer. She ended the call before Jake could argue with her.

Ow! Fuck. As he buttoned his shirt, the fabric brushed against his tattoo, making him cry out like a baby. Damn, maybe he'd put a bandage on it after Lalana left.

Within three minutes, a soft knock on the door woke him out of his stupor. He unlatched his hotel door to welcome Lalana in.

"Have a seat. You want something to drink?" Jake asked, stalling for time.

"No." Lalana sat on the coach. She crossed her legs primly and surveyed him for a moment before she broke their staring contest.

"So?" She tapped a nail against the arm of the sofa.

"Boon-nam—"

Nodding, Lalana snapped, "Yes? What about *my* little butterfly?"

Jake didn't miss Lalana's possessiveness when it came to Boon-nam. He resisted the urge to call Boon-nam *his* little tiger. Lalana had been nice enough to come—he didn't need to thank her by irritating her on purpose.

"Well, I, um…."

Damn, this is a shitty idea. He wasn't in high school begging advice from his crush's best friend. He shrugged and finished his musing because he needed to say something. "I like her. A lot."

"Outstanding. She's a sweetheart," Lalana stated, deadpan.

The woman seemed determined to not make this easy on him. Frowning, she shook her long brown hair. "And you are going to hurt her. I know you are."

No. He remained silent. She wouldn't believe him, but he shook his head.

She appeared sad and almost helpless as if she would cry. "You know you will."

Fuck. "Don't want to do that."

Jake ran his hands through his messed-up hair. He paced in front of the sofa. Fuck, truly breaking Boon-nam's heart was the last thing he wanted to do. Not wanting to contemplate the outcome, he changed the subject with a segue. "That's why I wanted to talk to you."

Lalana pursed her lips, sat back, crossed her legs, and folded her arms, then stared at him.

The best course of action was to get everything in the open. He'd always been a "rip off the fucking bandage" kind of guy.

"She wants to have sex. But she hasn't before, and, well, I've been with some transgender women, but I have never been first, you know?" His words tumbled out, and he hoped they made sense, but by the expression on Lalana's face, he couldn't be sure.

"You didn't have sex with her?" Lalana's mouth fell open.

"Supply your definition of sex." Jake stopped when he realized he sounded like Clinton and his misadventures. "We had oral sex."

"Oh, of course. I'm sure you enjoyed it."

He couldn't miss the disgust in her voice. "I did." It dawned on Jake what she had meant. Lalana really didn't know him at all. "She's delicious." He licked his lips to tease her.

"Oh, really?" Lalana's eyes widened. "I, I apologize. I assumed you would have…."

"You figured I would selfishly use her?" He tried to figure her out. "Jesus, what must you think of me?"

Lalana rolled her eyes. "Nothing personal, but I'm not naïve and neither are you. Quit with the games. We know why Thailand gets tourists. You get off the plane, and you want sex. You want kinky sex with a ladyboy."

"Not everyone's like that." He'd not give her the satisfaction of knowing that was his original reason for encouraging Randy to come to Thailand.

"I've known a few foreign men, and I know how they usually are." She unfolded her arms and dared him to deny it.

"Fine. In some cases, you're right. But just like all ladyboys aren't whores, all foreign men aren't the devil."

Her eyes flashed, but he could see she understood his meaning. Her tiny smile betrayed her understatement. "That is true. Your friend Randy is certainly not the devil."

Jake witnessed her going off on a little daydream. So the Ice Queen had feelings for Randy. "He's a good man."

She nodded. "Now let's get back to *my* Boon-boon."

"Look, I can't fuck this up. I haven't been with a virgin, let alone someone who has fairly recently had the sex-affirmation surgery."

Lalana made a face like she'd bitten into a lemon. "And you don't want to." Repugnance dripped from her voice.

"No! No, God, I want to. Of course, I want to. She's amazing. Stop jumping to the worst possible conclusions about me."

This wasn't going well. How could he make Lalana understand?

Lalana exhaled her impatience and swung her foot in annoyance while he gathered his scattered thoughts.

"I want her first time to be… I don't know… worthy of her." He hated being vulnerable with someone who kept assuming he would do the scummiest thing in the world, but she might be his only hope.

Lalana stopped, her mouth open and ready to say something, but she halted and stared at him. She chuckled a little. "I really want to hate you, but I can't." She exhaled in frustration. "Okay, the fact you haven't already taken Boon-boon up on her blatant offers wins you points."

Jake grinned at her without shame. He totally deserved some credit, because resisting Boon's charms had been a fucking accomplishment.

"What do you know about her surgery?" Lalana asked.

"Just what I read online, and I know a few people back home who are members of the club I belong to."

Jake understood the basics and had had discussions with other people who'd had sex affirmation surgery. While fascinating, the articles didn't allow general conclusions to be drawn. Each person and doctor had a different individual view and experience with it.

"A club of ladyboys?" Lalana asked, clearly not understanding him at all.

Not really the time or place to discuss this, but in for a penny…. "More of a generic sex club. Some BDSM play, some public displays, and just general kinkiness, but nothing too much."

Lalana scrunched her face as if she was trying to piece together the meaning of his confession. "Probably another reason Boon-nam finds you so irresistible."

Interesting. Ah, he wasn't crazy. He recognized a kindred kinky spirit in her. Damn, with a nurturing partner to help her explore—

She cleared her throat to bring him back to the topic at hand. "Boon-nam's doctor is highly respected and one of the best in the world. But I was terrified for her because so many things could have gone wrong. There's always a risk the surgery won't be successful, but my butterfly didn't have the right body. Did she tell you how she came to Bangkok?"

After his quick headshake, her voice softened as she recalled the past. "Boon was an adorable child. Her father didn't understand why his *son* acted like a girl, and he tried to beat the female out of my precious. Daily."

Jake inhaled sharply, not wanting the mental images her words were giving him.

"I couldn't watch the abuse. I took her out of the village when she turned ten. Once Boon-nam's mother had died, his father, the bastard, was constantly drunk." Lalana bit her lip. "I'm sorry. I mean her father, but at that time little Boon-nam was trying to be the boy his father wanted." She shook her head. "I knew it was kidnapping, but after her father broke Boon-nam's arm, and smashed up Boon-boon's pretty little face, I felt like if I didn't take him, I mean her… she'd have been killed."

"Oh, God." Jake reached out to Lalana, who accepted his hand and gave it a squeeze. He sat down next to her, trying not to cry like a baby at the vision of *their* lovable, sunny, and wonderful Boon-nam tortured for being who she was.

"We got to Bangkok, and I started looking for work. I only had a little bit of money saved, but Illusions & Dreams found us."

"Found you? How?" Jake asked, hoping for something else to wash away the images of an abused little Boon-nam.

"Areva and Tong were shopping. They found us asleep on a side street up against a building." Lalana answered Jake's next question without him asking it. "Sleeping during the day is safer than at nighttime."

She smiled. "Areva and Tong were checking to see if we needed help. Boon-nam woke up and asked them if they were angels."

"I can see that."

She laughed a little as a tear streaked down her face. "Boon said, 'You must be angels, because you are almost as beautiful as Lalana.' Well, Tong and Areva brought us to Illusions & Dreams. They helped us finish school and taught me how to wait tables. When they found out I could sing, they gave me a singing contract. Boon-nam received one for dance and performing later on. We owe them our lives."

It sounded more like Boon-nam owed her life to Lalana. Jake couldn't imagine the pain and trauma Boon-nam had suffered. Most people wouldn't have survived, but Boon-nam had thrived and made a life for herself.

Lalana shook her head as if she could knock out all the bad shit she'd experienced. "I will give you the names of some of the transgender websites, including Boon-nam's doctor."

"Thank you, Lalana." His gratitude went beyond the appreciation he had for her giving him the information that would help him with Boon-nam. Overwhelming gratitude for Lalana poured out of him. Without her, Boon wouldn't have escaped a terrible fate.

"Did she tell you the type of surgery she had?"

The memories she'd shared remained with him, but all too soon, the truce had come to an end. Lalana eyed him as if he were still on trial. "No, we haven't discussed it."

Lalana nodded. "She had penile inversion, which means the penis is skinned and turned inside out to make the vagina. Her scrotum was used to create her labia."

"Did she opt for the sigmoid colon vaginoplasty?" One of his fuck buddies had the extra section of colon installed to allow for deeper penetration and a bit of natural lubrication.

"Someone did their homework." She shook her head. "No, but the sensitive area at the crown of her penis was made into a clitoris, so the sensation she gets from intercourse can create an orgasm. During surgery the location of the prostate becomes altered to the bottom of her vaginal canal, creating something like a G-spot."

"You did your homework as well."

"I don't mean to lecture you. Between exploring this with Boon-nam and having some unwanted pressure from men who thought to push me to have the surgery myself, I have a good understanding of exactly what the procedure entails."

"Okay. Any advice?"

She sighed as if she were unwillingly consorting with the enemy. "Some general advice. The brain is the largest sex organ any of us have. Stimulate her mind, and you're halfway to a satisfying experience. Use lots of lubrication. You're not too big, are you?"

Jake turned away with embarrassment, but he answered, "Just about average."

"Good, otherwise you could rip or tear her. She's been religious about using her stints, but still."

"Stints?"

"To hold the shape of her vagina. Otherwise the walls might shrink."

He couldn't imagine the determination someone had to have to change their body to match their gender. That level of urgency he'd never completely comprehend. No matter how empathetic Jake was, this was something you had to experience for yourself to truly appreciate everything involved.

"So you're not freaked out?" Lalana frowned. Had she wanted to wig him out?

Jake rolled his eyes. "No. I just wish Boon-nam hadn't had to go through all this to be happy with who she is. But I'm glad she lives in a time when it is possible."

Thankfully, Lalana didn't take his statement the wrong way. "Remember sex is shiny to her. She still thinks it's all heated kisses and joyous orgasms... let her keep her beliefs a little longer."

God, he didn't want to disappoint Boon-nam. Jake nodded, ignoring the fear creeping alongside the pressure.

Lalana cleared her throat and changed gears. "So basically make sure you grind into her a bit to hit the right spots, but don't hurt her by going too deep. The rubbing and pressure will stimulate her newly made G-spot. And of course anal sex. She'll like that."

Say what now? Did she and Boon-nam...? His head tilted in silent question.

Lalana was quick to clarify. "Oh, no. I don't know firsthand, of course." She held up her hand and shook it as if to ward off the bad thoughts. "But as I said, she still has her prostate, and, well, I'm sure with your vast sexual prowess you know stimulation there can lead to orgasm. A rather satisfying one." She blushed.

"Indeed." Jake smirked. He was familiar with the type of pleasure the prostate provided. "Anything else?" He couldn't imagine, with how red Lalana's face already had become, this conversation would go much further.

"Do you have any questions?"

He wanted to put her out of her misery. "Nah, I would appreciate the web addresses of those sites, though." He stood up to grab the pad of paper near the phone and the odd-looking, square-shaped pencil next to it. "Here you go."

She took the paper and wrote out the information. "Please be careful with her."

"Lalana, I swear I will." Jake didn't want to say anything more about that. "I can't thank you enough. You're a true friend to Boon-nam. I know she loves you very much."

"She's family. She's all I've ever really had." She stared at him for a long moment. "Please don't shatter her beyond repair."

Jake didn't know how to respond. He pulled Lalana into his arms and gave her a quick hug before she left. He was exhausted, and his new tattoo hurt. But before getting a couple hours of sleep, he needed to check out those sites.

Chapter Nine

"I CAN'T believe it!" Boon-nam slammed into the room she and Lalana shared. "Oh, sorry," she whispered loudly as she realized Lalana had been trying to nap before the show.

"What, baby?" Lalana pulled off her pink satin sleep mask. Reaching out, she pulled Boon-nam down onto her bed.

Boon-nam wiped her face angrily as tears coursed down, destroying her eye makeup. "Jake!"

What the hell could he have done to her, since Boon-nam was at practice all afternoon? "What did he do?"

She'd get Adirake and a few of the boys together to deal with him. Not that she'd need help ripping him apart, but she'd want people to help her deal with his lifeless body.

"Nothing. He did nothing!" Boon-nam sounded brokenhearted before she fell, sobbing her misery into Lalana's arms.

Lalana petted Boon-nam's hair. The action had always calmed her. Cuddling protectively around her, Lalana asked, "What do you mean, Boon-boon?"

If the bastard had hurt Boon-nam, she would castrate him. Boon-nam was too fragile for the American oaf to be careless.

Boon swallowed and sniffled until she cried out words with her tears. "He didn't want me."

"What?" Lalana decided not to cloud Boon-nam's head with the conversation she'd had with Jake. She wouldn't lie about her discussion with him, but at this point she didn't see a reason to bring it up. "Tell Lalana everything, baby."

"I was just replaying it over in my head, and he just doesn't want me."

Boon-nam related every detail. Even though Lalana's own opinion of him had elevated during their conversation that very morning, she kept waiting for the evil Jake did to be revealed. *Farang keenok*, it never happened. She was glad for Boon-nam's sake, but a tad disappointed she couldn't shred him.

"So you two kissed for a long time in bed. Horny little thing that you are, you wanted more, so he licked you to an orgasm. After which he found his own release by taking care of things himself. He held your hand as he walked you back home… the long way after you insisted you wanted to come back home last night. I guess you needed to do your stints?"

After a tearful nod from Boon-nam, Lalana continued, hating that Jake appeared to be romantic and not just after sex. "And he set up another date for tonight. Did I miss anything?"

Boon-nam opened her mouth for a second and closed it. Frowning, she said with no small measure of resentment, "Well, when you say it like that… it sounds like I have nothing to be upset about."

Lalana bit back a smile. She held Boon-nam's hand to stroke the softness. "So how was it?"

"Lalana!" Boon-nam's voice went high, and she blushed an adorable shade of red.

"Spill. Tell me all about your adventures in the land of yum-yum," Lalana demanded, knowing Boon-nam wanted to talk about the experience because her eyes were sparkling with the memory. "Did he know licky licky? Was it good?"

Boon-nam failed to silence her moan at the mere mention of it.

"Excellent." Lalana grinned. At least Jake was good for something.

Boon-nam snorted in an unladylike manner.

"Oh, La-la, Jake is perfect. He made me feel elegant and treated me like a delicate princess. When I actually… you know, the sensation went on and on forever. It was the most amazing thing I've ever experienced. No wonder boys like yum-yum so much."

Lalana knew Boon-nam was innocent but hadn't realized how inexperienced. "I can't believe you really haven't had anyone lick you?"

Boon-nam shrugged. "I couldn't before, but now… oh *now* I loved everything about it. I can't wait to try it again." Boon-nam laughed happily before she pouted. "But that doesn't mean he shouldn't have taken me or at least let me give him yum-yum. If he really found me enticing, he should've wanted to be with me."

Lalana stared at Boon-nam in disbelief. "Jake probably wanted to make sure you were ready." As much as she hated to admit the truth, Lalana did. "He was being considerate and thoughtful." Damn him for being sweet and patient.

"Aw, really? But I am ready. I've been ready."

"Well, maybe he's not. Does he know he would be your first?" Lalana wanted to nudge Boon-nam to come to the right conclusion on her own.

Boon-nam turned away. "I'm an idiot. I blurted it out to him." She shook her head. "But why should my inexperience be a big deal for him?"

Lalana took Boon-nam's head in her hands to make her focus. "Well, that's a lot of pressure." With one hand, Lalana ran her fingers through Boon-nam's silky hair. The other hand held her head against her shoulder. "Being someone's first is a lot to live up to." Her voice went a bit deeper than usual, making her clear her throat.

Boon-nam's little shoulders shrugged, "What's to live up to? Since I've had no one else, I have nothing to compare him to…."

"True, but he does. I have to say I respect him more for not simply jumping on what you offered him." She trailed her gaze up and down Boon-nam as if to assess her infinite worth. "'Cause I have to say, the temptation he passed up, baby girl… well, that's rather impressive."

Boon-nam giggled at Lalana's silliness. "Well, thank you," she said, batting her eyelashes. Inhaling deeply and exhaling slowly, she then said, "I guess I should see it as rather unselfish of him not to… you know. But during practice I kept thinking he'd rejected me because I was a freak."

"Why would you believe that?"

Boon-nam frowned. "I overheard Tong and Areva. Tong said she knew Jaidee never made a pass at her because he doesn't want her. She said men take what they want, and clearly he didn't want her."

"What did Areva say?"

Surely the co-owner of Illusions & Dreams would have set Tong straight. Tong constantly jumped to the wrong conclusions and always assumed the worst of men. Not that Lalana did such a thing—that was completely different. She was sure of it.

"I don't know. I ran out."

Lalana sighed. Of course she did. "Forget about them. I don't think the reason Jake didn't take what you offered was because he didn't want to be with you."

Boon-nam rolled her eyes.

"Or are you admitting Jake's nothing but a player?"

With a quick inhale, Boon-nam made her defense. "No. Jake's a wonderful man."

"So maybe he didn't take things further because he respected you." Lalana probably should tell her about Jake's question-and-answer session, but giving Boon more reason to be head over heels with the man poised to break her heart wasn't advisable.

Lalana switched gears. "Besides, you know never to let anyone's reaction to you change how you view yourself. That's rule one," she said, referring to the ladyboy rulebook Areva had put together over the years to assist the new girls in adjusting to living their dream.

"I know, I know but…."

"But nothing, little girl."

Boon-nam pouted out her pink lips. "But I wanted him to…."

"Yeah, well, just because you wanted something, doesn't mean you automatically get it."

Boon-nam pondered for a moment before she grinned like a naughty child. "Yes, it does." She shrugged. "Usually I get what I want."

Laughter erupted between them. Most people tried to give Boon-nam whatever she wanted. "That's 'cause you're spoiled."

"Am not!" Boon-boon's eyes lit up with mischief.

It was the same as when she'd been little. Other than her abusive father, people needed to make Boon-nam happy because she only seemed to want to make other people happy. She always had a smile and a kind word for everyone. To be bad to Boon-nam was like kicking a bunny. Lalana grabbed her up into a big hug and squeezed her tight.

Boon-nam broke the hug with a kiss on Lalana's cheek. "Enough about me. What about you? What happened with Randy?"

Lalana frowned as the attention turned to her and her drama. "Let's say the same thing happened."

"What?" Boon-nam's face lit up in excited surprise. "But you aren't a… you know."

"Virgin, Boon-boon. If you can't say the word, how are you ready to lose the status?" Another example of why Boon-nam should rethink her hastily made decision to have sex with Jake, but Lalana knew she wouldn't.

Boon-nam swatted at her lightly. "La-la! Spill! You made me talk." Boon-nam's lower lip popped out, making her pout more intense.

"Okay, okay." Lalana sat up farther in her bed.

"So what happened? Tell me," Boon-nam begged.

"No."

"Please." Boon-nam grabbed her hands and squeezed them.

Sighing, Lalana couldn't win against her best friend's persistence. "Well, you know...."

Boon-nam groaned in frustration. "No, I don't know. That's why you're going to tell me!"

"You are a determined little thing, aren't you?" Lalana touched the tip of Boon-nam's nose with her perfectly manicured fingertip.

"La-la! Come on! Spill!"

"Oh, I did, as did Randy." She waited for Boon-nam to take her words in and to translate them into Thai so she could get the double meaning. She held up two fingers and added, "Twice."

"Ahh!" Boon-nam squealed loud enough to break glass as she kicked her feet against the bedframe. She grabbed Lalana's hands and bounced next to her on the bed. "So how did that happen?"

"Well, it isn't polite to suck and tell. Oops, did I say blowjob out loud?" Lalana loved making Boon-nam do her happy, laughing squeal. Boon-nam was her own worst enemy. Her reaction forced Lalana to keep torturing her slowly with details.

"You did yum-yum?" Boon's big eyes got huge, and she bounced with impatience, hungry for the details.

"Yes... this morning."

"You stayed the night? I wish I'd stayed the night." Boon whispered as if she didn't want to let Lalana's secret out. Apparently the prior screaming hadn't alerted every girl and boy in the club that they'd gotten lucky last night.

"I did. Where did you think I was?" After Boon-nam shrugged, Lalana took pity on her and continued with her story. "He's a wonderful kisser. We kissed forever. He was such a gentleman... he never made a move." She paused long enough for Boon-nam to start to bounce. "I did."

Boon-nam's shriek of excitement almost popped her eardrums.

"You are a loose woman!" the giggling Boon accused her.

"What is the saying the English teacher taught us last week?" Lalana pretended to rack her brain. "Something about a pot calling the kettle black, yes, I think that's it."

Boon playfully pouted. "I'm not a loose woman. I'm still a virgin."

"Yeah, not by choice," Lalana teased back. But Boon took the taunt the wrong way and her pretty pretend pout turned real. Lalana quickly added, "And not for long."

Boon clapped rapidly in glee. "I hope!" Appeased, she appeared ready for more details. "So then…."

Lalana sighed as if she were being forced. "After kissing forever I took him out. He's a large man." Boon's eyes went wide, as Lalana held her index fingers apart, demonstrating his size. She added a couple of inches for good measure. "Very large."

"Oh my, La-la. How does that even fit?" Boon-nam swallowed and waved her on before she burst into giggles. "Okay. Okay, go on."

"The first time he came in my hand." Lalana smiled at the memory of how worried Randy had been about releasing too quickly. She decided to leave that fact out. Though a shiver of thrill ran through her at how much she had turned him on. "Then he did the same."

"Thwack, thwack, thwack, ahh?" Boon-nam teased.

"Definitely ahh! But I held out for a little more than thwack, thwack, thwack." She laughed with Boon. "But we did fall asleep holding each other."

"Aw, sweet." Boon sighed deeply. "I should have stayed. Jake wanted me to, but I had to do my dilations." She shrugged, clearly trying to put the regret out of her mind. "So what happened in the morning?"

"Well, we exchanged yum-yum." Lalana felt the flush creep into her cheeks as she remembered the intimate details. "He even swallowed. No one has ever swallowed for me…."

"Oh, La-la!" Boon-nam gave her a big hug.

"I know!" She fell back into the bed with a happy sigh. Boon-nam joined her on the puffy pillow.

"Naptime?" Boon-nam asked hopefully. She yawned like a darling little puppy that wanted nothing more than to curl up and go to sleep.

Lalana loved naps. Naptime meant they would cuddle up and sleep protected in each other's arms. It was the only time she knew Boon-nam was truly safe.

"Yes, Boon-boon." Boon snuggled into her. In the lovely woman in her arms, Lalana could still see traces of the scared little boy who clung to her in the night. "My *phee seuua.*"

Boon-nam opened her big brown eyes to stare at Lalana. "Why do you still call me butterfly?"

"Because you have changed since I have known you and continue to develop. You have grown into a stunning butterfly who is spreading her wings for the first time."

As the sentimental moment choked her up a bit, Lalana held Boon-nam tighter.

"It is all because of you, La-la." Boon-nam kissed her on both cheeks. "You truly saved me."

Lalana admitted, "You saved me too. I might have stayed to live a very unhappy life back home. You made me want more, not only for myself, but for you." Her eyes were misting up. Time for sleep before they got all red and puffy.

Boon-nam sniffled delicately until Lalana handed her a tissue. "Thanks, La-la. As long as we're together, I can get through anything. I will never leave you. No matter what!"

"Me, too, Boon-nam. I promise." She cuddled Boon-nam closer and put her to sleep, eliminating the need for discussion.

Her thoughts drifted to Randy. He was everything she'd ever wanted in a man. He accepted all of her and didn't need her to change.

Hypocrite! Here she'd been telling Boon-nam not to be careless with her heart, and her own traitorous heart had slipped from her grasp.

Boon-nam snuffled in sleep. Lalana brushed a wisp of hair off Boon-nam's cheek. Boon-boon was young, and everything was new to her, but Lalana had no excuse. She should know better. But Randy's tenderness had melted her reserve, and he'd slipped under her guard. Just the notion of him made her happy. He was unlike the men normally interested in her. He had some unidentified quality, which called to her—screamed to her, actually.

Randy wanted to talk to her. He listened to her when she spoke, he held her hand protectively, and when he touched her—well, all of her responded. Maybe she was pathetic, considering her history, but she'd lost her head over this bewitching man.

Chapter Ten

RANDY NOTICED the big billboards for the weekend market. The train was slowing for the Mo Chit BTS station. He almost hated to leave the air-conditioned car.

"Come on, this is the stop for the weekend market." Randy alerted Jake and Boon-nam, who were engaged in a deep conversation about the exotic pet trade. Lalana took his assistance to stand up.

Jake, Boon-nam, Lalana, and Randy exited the Sky Train, which was surprisingly quick and clean.

"Bypassing the traffic below saved about forty minutes," Boon-nam told Randy and Jake.

Trudging down the exit stairs with a number of locals gave Randy a moment to survey the market. "All of this is the weekend market?"

Lalana sidled up close to him. She pointed gracefully at the boundaries.

Randy was amazed. It appeared to cover several square miles of space. "Wow. That's vast, and it's all shops."

Boon-nam bounced up and stopped staring at Jake long enough to answer. "The market has food, home goods, stationery, clothing, shoes, auto parts, furniture, cooking, souvenirs, and art." She swiped a map from the stand as they passed by.

Everyone stopped to study the map.

Lalana spoke up. "If I may make a suggestion? Why not concentrate on the arts and crafts section? It's right next to the souvenirs."

"Great idea. Unless someone else wants to pick anything up?" Randy asked.

The ladies shook their heads. Jake chimed in. "Sounds good to me."

After a ten-minute zigzag path through the other sections, they found the blue placards indicating the group had reached their section. Another look at the map confirmed the rows went for two city blocks—and there appeared to be ten aisles.

Randy suggested the most obvious way to cover the market without backtracking or getting lost. "Let's just go up and down the aisles one at a time."

"Agreed. That way we won't miss anything." Lalana grinned at him as if he were a genius.

Jake led the group with Boon-nam on his heels. He stopped at every leather stall and got a stupid look on his face when Boon-nam inhaled and said, "Ahh."

Jake leaned into Randy. "There's just something hot about a woman who can appreciate the aroma of leather."

"Shut up." Randy did not need to think about his buddy's interests.

With Boon-nam's assistance, Jake negotiated a decent price on a new satchel.

"That's a mighty fine *man bag*, Jake."

"Stop calling it a man bag, Randy. It's a satchel." Jake slung the brown leather strap across his body.

Damn, it was too rare of an event to find something to annoy Jake with. He couldn't stop himself, and Randy continued, "How about manbook? Or man-pocket? No? See? Man bag makes more sense."

Some locals brushed past them.

Boon-nam adjusted a twist in Jake's strap and reassured him, "It's a sharp-looking *satchel*."

"Thank you." Jake smiled at his cheerleader before giving Randy a glare.

Wood chips and varnish assailed their noses as they meandered through the woodcarving section. "Wow, did you make this?" Randy asked one of the stall keepers.

The old man jumped off his little bench. "Yes, I did. Where are you from?"

"New York."

"Ah, the *big* apple."

Ignoring Jake's whispered comments on the way the wooden fruit could be used, Randy asked, "You've been?"

"No, not yet."

"Your work is lovely. The details are done quite well." He studied the intricate carving of an elephant. "How much?"

"Oh, that one took a long time."

Simple questions never seemed to have simple answers. "I can imagine. My grandfather carved."

The man handed him a calculator with a price greater than two tanks of gas. Randy bit back a smile. "I'm sorry. I think you're far out of my price range."

"Half." The stall keeper refused to take back the calculator, but punched in the new number.

Lalana peered over the device and looked over the animal. "These should be about the cost of a liter of milk." She punched in the new figure.

The man balked. "I cannot. That price cuts me."

But the next number he showed Randy was only double the price Lalana had picked. "I'm sorry, sir, but I'm afraid I must pass."

"Okay. Okay. But take more than one."

At that price Randy bought a whole zoo of the tiny animals. Jake laughed at him, but when he heard the price, he bought a couple too.

They moved into the stainless steel section. Maybe he should trade in his hand-me-down dollar-store cutlery. Randy picked up different silverware pieces until he found a knife with an artistic swirl at the end. The decoration served to give the piece perfect weight and maneuverability. He purchased a full set of silverware, including the serving pieces.

He hefted his bag off the counter and realized the weight of his purchase. Shit. "Well, that wasn't smart."

Lalana grinned and pulled out a wheeled bag from her pocketbook. The damned thing folded out to a full size backpack, and the extended handle meant he could pull his purchase behind him.

"Thanks. You're so prepared."

"Always." Lalana touched his hand briefly before Boon-nam called her over to look at the ornately detailed stainless steel hair combs.

They spent the entire morning meandering through the stalls and shops. Jake dragged everyone over to a stall selling juice and foot massages. Five lawn chairs were vacant, so they sat.

Ah, it felt good to sit down. An old woman scurried over to wash Randy's feet in a bucket of warm water before they were dried and put on an ottoman. The old woman who did his reflexology hurt him. Damn, she must have a hell of a handshake! He couldn't even enjoy his fresh-squeezed orange juice because he needed to keep a death grip on the chair arms so that he didn't cry out.

He sneaked a peek at Jake, and he was grimacing as well. The ladies were serene and resting with their eyes closed.

Lalana opened her eyes. "It hurts until you release all the toxins. Once that is complete, you will love it."

Within ten minutes Randy realized she was right. He loved it.

THE WOMEN had gone back to do the evening show. Randy restrained himself from asking if he could go see the show again. He figured Jake would kill him, so they were sitting in their hotel's coffee shop killing time, waiting to pick up the ladies for a late dinner when Jake dropped a bomb on him.

RANDY SEEMED to have trouble processing the words coming out of Jake's mouth. "Say again, please. Slowly and clearly."

Jake thumped his head into the hard back of the bench in the booth. He glared at the fucker across the restaurant table. "I'm just suggesting it makes sense to go slow." He sat back and folded his arms.

Randy almost kept a straight face. "Who are you, and what have you done with my best friend?"

"Fuck you." Jake sipped his lukewarm brew.

"Normally, it's your agenda to get us laid as often as possible. But now all of a sudden you tell me to take it slow. Hell, typically you're in and out of your partner so quickly, they wonder if it happened."

"That is so not true." Jake hesitated under Randy's scrutiny. Fine, on occasion, but he didn't stop his resentful eye roll. "What-the-fuck-ever."

Other patrons turned and gave scathing stares to Jake. He waved them an apology, which was not accepted or appreciated but basically ignored by the mother of three as she ushered her young kids away from their table. Whatever, he'd bet they'd heard worse on the premium channels.

"I'm just saying I think it's good we're getting to know them without the physical stuff. I've never taken the time to do this, and I like spending time with her."

Randy almost spewed his coffee. "Seriously, what's going on, Jake? We've gone to Wat Pho to see the Reclining Buddha."

"Lovely intricately carved feet, right?" He'd suggested it.

"We went to several other temples."

"Didn't you like them?"

"Um, of course. And today we spent all day at the weekend market."

"Boon-nam is a great bargainer. She charmed most of the shop owners." Jake stated it proudly as if he could claim some of her shopping prowess.

"All I'm saying is I'm a tad frustrated, on top of which, my damned feet hurt from all the walking. Lalana wasn't too happy with no alone time."

Boon-nam had been even more disappointed about their lack of privacy, but she'd kept her complaints to herself. She just continued sighing when Jake diligently kept suggesting activities that involved both couples.

"This is our seventh day date. You haven't let any of us have any privacy. Why are you avoiding being alone with Boon-nam? And why does that have anything to do with me and Lalana?" Randy sounded a little tense.

"Isn't it helping to convince Lalana this is more than a vacation fling for you?" Jake reasoned while he tried not to feel like an asshole.

Randy's expression changed to pure anger. Fuck, time to fess up or be murdered by his best friend. Randy wouldn't do well in prison. "Look, Rand, it'll be Boon-nam's first time, and it's got to be special. I can't fuck that up."

"And because you assume Lalana and Boon-nam shared details of all their dates, you don't want what Lalana and I do to put pressure on Boon-nam?"

"Exactly."

"Wow. I can't believe I'm watching the player Jake O'Neil curtail his usual sexual carelessness."

"Hey, fuck you, man. This is serious. I've never been with—" He lowered his voice as if to ward off evil spirits. "—a virgin."

"I'm glad you're using kid gloves on Boon-nam. Her first time should be special."

"I know. That's why I'm wigging out." Jake's head hit the table harder than he wanted. *Damn, that's going to leave a bump.* He supported his head with his hands and hoped Randy had words of wisdom.

"Jake, Boon-nam adores you. Just be careful, and make her know you care about her."

"Like how?"

"Same way you've been doing. Use your shared connection: the little looks, touches, just do things that make her smile. Or in this case, moan."

Did Randy think he was an idiot? "I know, I will, but still—"

"Stop worrying so much. Aren't you supposed to be a god in bed?" Randy asked like it wasn't fact.

"Just give me one more night, okay?" Why did it sound like he was begging?

"This is the last night." Randy sighed with clear irritation.

Jake changed the subject abruptly as he paid their check and stood up. "Let's head over and grab the ladies for a lovely dinner. Then we can part ways. We can say it's to get an early start tomorrow morning for them to tour the Grand Palace with us."

Randy grumbled but agreed, so Jake took it.

AFTER A quick breakfast, the traffic wasn't at a standstill yet, so they grabbed a taxi. On their way to Illusions & Dreams, Randy couldn't contain his glee. "You like her."

"Of course I like her." Jake stared out the window, clearly avoiding meeting Randy's eyes.

"She's sweet." Randy waited, and Jake didn't take long.

"Sweet, ha! She's amazing. Smart too. Did you hear her at dinner last night? She may not have been to college yet, but she's read a helluva lot more than me." He laughed. "And she's becoming a great performer…

and dedicated. You would be shocked to know how many hours a day she practices. And the way she moves her body...."

Randy cleared his throat and arched an eyebrow.

"Oh, shut up. I know...." Jake bit back a smile.

"Am I saying anything?" Randy shrugged and tried to look innocent.

"You don't have to." Jake exhaled loudly. "You?"

"As if you have to ask." Randy chuckled. Enamored by the lovely Lalana and he freely admitted it. Heck, he'd been fixated on her for months, but he'd keep that to himself.

"What the hell are we going to do?" Jake's question went unanswered as they pulled up in front of the brightly lit club.

"Hello!" Boon-nam bounced over to the cab. "Are you guys ready?"

"Yup." Jake tried to pay the driver, but Randy had already taken care of it.

"Come on then." Boon-nam held the taxi door and pulled Jake out.

Lalana held her hand out to Randy.

Baffled, Randy followed, because he'd go wherever Lalana wanted to take him. As they approached the side of the building, the ladies turned and gave them each a small kiss on the lips. Mmm, Lalana's soft lips tasted of her favorite breakfast, strawberries and cream.

Damn. Jake's growl drew Lalana's attention away from Randy. Boon-nam went back in, lips first, for a bit more. Lalana cleared her throat like a schoolmarm. Sighing, Jake stepped back and steadied Boon against the building when she swayed a bit.

Randy rolled his eyes when Jake cocked his eyebrows in an expression of smug satisfaction. He turned to Lalana. "Oh, are we taking a scooter?"

"Of course." Lalana and Boon-nam unlocked their shiny scooters and backed them out. "Hop on."

Grinning, Randy jumped on the back of a purple scooter and off they went. Randy held onto Lalana's waist and enjoyed the sensation of her pert bottom against him. As they hit small bumps in the road, her backside rubbed up and down against him in a most beguiling manner.

Maybe they'd gone slow enough.

At the first light, Boon-nam and Jake caught up with them. Randy shouted a little over the noisy roar of the bike. "Wish I could reach my camera."

Jake glanced down at the pink scooter he was astride and grinned, cuddling up to Boon-nam's back. "Who would have thought it?"

Any further conversation ended as they zipped through the streets. When they hit a wall of traffic, Boon-nam and Lalana turned down a side street without pause. A couple of times, they hopped an uncrowded sidewalk and buzzed down the pedestrian path to avoid the backed-up traffic in the road. When they arrived at the Grand Palace, the ladies found parking for their bikes and locked them securely.

Jake loudly whispered to ensure everyone could hear. "Did you like those strong vibrations between your legs?"

Boon-nam's eyes went wide, and a blush stole up her cheeks, tinting them a dusty pink.

Lalana noticed and chuckled. "Jake, behave yourself. Part of the Grand Palace holds the King's temple. Be good."

Jake smirked. "I always am." He leaned down to purr in Boon-nam's ear. "Very good."

Boon-nam bit her full lower lip before peeking up at Jake. "I wouldn't know." She followed her statement with a bit of a pout that was crushed by a big grin when she realized she'd hit the mark. Playing up more, she shrugged. "I guess I'll have to take your word on it."

Randy snorted and tried to hold back a laugh, but failed. Lalana glared at him before her sparkling eyes indicated Boon-nam's tease tickled her sense of humor. "So hand-holding is bad," Randy clarified, as much to change the subject as to remind Jake of the rules.

Boon-nam piped up. "Hand-holding is fine. Wonderful in fact." She gazed at Jake as if she'd eat him up. "Just not inside the temple." She locked her little hand around Jake's as if she needed to prove the point.

"If your shoes are off, hands off," Lalana said primly. Her wink at Randy tempered her prissiness.

The heat of the day started to encroach, but it wasn't too unpleasant. Lalana opened her sun parasol. "Boon-boon, your umbrella."

When Boon-nam stopped to dig her umbrella out of her bag, Randy read the "Do and Don't" sign. He read the last line out loud. "Do not trust wily strangers."

Jake snickered. "Wily, is he a coyote?"

"Hey, it's underlined. I guess we shouldn't trust the wily strangers." Randy chuckled.

As if on cue, a man in faded uniform-looking attire approached them to announce, "The palace is closed this morning." He waved over to an old vehicle, which appeared as if it would break down if he went over three miles an hour. "But not to worry. I can take you on a tour of the city."

"No, thank you, Mr. Wily Stranger."

"I am Mr. Peter, not Mr. Stranger." The man turned toward Lalana and asked, "Who is Mr. Stranger?"

Lalana stepped up into the man's space, her fists clenched, and she said something in Thai. Randy touched her shoulder in the hope of calming her.

After the man trudged away to find another tourist to prey on, Jake's laughter echoed off the shops they passed. "Do you suppose his first name is Wily or possibly his last?"

Boon-nam's giggling shrug seemed to relax Lalana.

"Imagine that. It's not closed after all." Jake stepped up to the ticket booth to pay the entrance fee.

A real uniformed guard directed them to follow the high wall past the souvenir stalls until they came to the double golden gates. The gates with their ornately swirling patterns stood open.

Wow! The Internet pictures of the complex didn't do the buildings justice. The myriad of structures glistened in the bright sunshine. The architecture was distinctively Thai. Each building had sloping roofs that curved up at the ends, the mythical Garuda guarding them. The creature was the vehicle of Vishnu, and was the symbol of divine power and authority of the king. The buildings were either covered in all gold or in tiny mosaic tiles of blue, silver, green, and red.

"It's like a waking dream of paradise," Jake gasped as he leaned forward and started snapping pictures. He wandered off with Boon-nam close on his heels, pointing out details.

"What do you think?" Lalana asked, staring up with her soulful chocolate eyes.

Randy wished he could take her hands in his. Stepping a bit closer, he held her gaze. "It's like a dream. A dream I never believed I'd have."

Lalana's plump lips parted as if she'd say something, but at the last second, she pressed her lips together. She glanced away and waved her elegant hand. "Taking pictures will be frustrating. You can't capture the grandeur. There's too much."

"I don't think there's nearly enough." Where the hell was this flirting coming from?

Lalana pursed her lips. "Come on."

She gathered Boon-nam and Jake to lead everyone around the stunning complex of gold buildings. Mythical guardians three stories high stood watch and held different weapons. The sunlight sparkled off them, almost hurting their eyes.

"Look at the little shiny, colored mirrors covering the buildings." Randy inspected the tiles. "It sparkles like jewels set in gold."

Jake continued using his digital camera. He took several shots of Boon-nam alone and of her with Lalana, using the golden background to get some magnificent shots with his phone and his digital camera so that he could send them easily.

Strolling around the buildings, most of which were closed, they came to the inner temple. They left their shoes with dozens of others lined up on the ground near the steps. The glittering gold, ornately carved mythical creatures and flowers were almost overwhelming. Hundreds of Garudas circled the perimeter of the building, on the ceiling, and on the three sets of huge gold doors. Symbols mixed with decorative art to please the spiritual as well as the art worshippers in a mind-boggling pattern.

Randy and Jake followed Lalana and Boon-nam to the table in front of the middle door. Pink lotus blossoms were lying on the table next to a big gold pot of water. Boon-nam and Lalana grabbed a flower, dipped the petals in the water, and tapped their heads with it. Dipping again, they turned to Jake and Randy.

Smiling, Lalana tapped Randy's head with the wet flower. "This is a blessing and spiritual cleansing."

The girls hurried up the stairs past the relief, barely sparing the carving a glance. Randy and Jake stopped dead to admire the golden animal carved deep into the wall. After taking some pictures, they followed their dates inside. The opulent beauty of the altar stunned Randy, and he now understood why neither woman had spared the relief a glance.

A guard came up to Jake and put a hand over his camera. "No pictures."

Damn. Randy tried to take in the details of the green Jade Buddha. The statue was dressed in gold, according to the season. All the worshippers were silent. Lalana kneeled on a pillow and simply stared.

Randy knew it wasn't their first time to visit, but Boon-nam froze with her mouth open.

The paintings and carvings were even more elegant than those held in the rest of the complex. Boon-nam and Lalana offered prayers before quietly moving toward the back to rejoin him and Jake.

"Do they really change the Buddha's clothing?" Jake asked. He tapped his lens and pointed at the statue to the younger guard. The man glared at him and shook his head.

"Yes, every season the Buddha is redressed in a different set. You can see the others on the postcards outside," Lalana answered.

After one last look around, Boon-nam said, "The king still prays here. When he's here the temple area is closed off."

They headed outside, and the heat hit Randy. The sun started to beat down, so they meandered over to the covered walkway surrounding the entire complex.

"Is this the Ramayana?" Jake asked.

Boon-nam beamed at him. "Yup. The story of how the great king Rama became exiled for fourteen years with his brother and wife Sita. Sita was kidnapped by the demon Ravana. King Rama and his brother got her back with the help of a supernatural army."

Jake studied the pictures. "But the story is more than a happily ever after. This teaches philosophy. Some believe the answers to the basic questions in life are hidden within the story."

Randy knocked into the show-off. "Someone's been studying."

Jake chuckled and ran a hand through his hair. "Yeah, whatever. Interesting read. I have a copy back in the hotel."

Boon-nam pointed out a piece of the huge painting. "This is where Sita holds auctions for a husband. The guys must string this huge bow." The murals showed Sita sitting prettily while many men failed to even lift the bow.

Boon-nam skipped ahead until the group caught up with her. She stopped at the section of the mural where a strong man picked up the bow and broke it.

Boon-nam pointed to a glowing Sita. "She has picked her husband."

Jake shifted a bit self-consciously as Boon-nam focused on him.

Needing to help out a buddy, Randy said, "Well, that's one way of doing it." He grinned at Lalana. "I'm just a regular guy. I believe dating the person is a terrific start." What the hell, he decided to go for it. "But do you have any bows for me to string?"

Lalana stopped dead and stared at him for a little longer than usual. She decided to laugh off the implication. "Look, here's where the demon takes her."

Damn. Was I shot down? What the hell was I doing proposing marriage? Um….

Thankfully Boon-nam drew his attention by hissing, "Bad Ravana."

Randy studied the appealingly depicted demon for a while before Boon-nam pointed out the guard behind the palace bushes making out with a woman. "The guard appears occupied, which allows chaos to reign."

Randy stifled a chuckle. Boon-nam seemed to be trying to leer at Jake, but her expression suggested she had indigestion. Jake responded to her attempt at sexy anyway.

Lalana derailed the heat when she pointed out, "See, that's what happens when we let sex distract us."

Rolling her eyes, Boon-nam tugged Jake farther around the covered path. A gentle breeze blew through the passageway, cooling the area enough to be a break from the baking heat of Bangkok.

Boon-nam leaned her head on Jake and said, "Is it time to distract me?"

Jake's laughter echoed off the mural. Lalana pushed between them to stand in front of the supernatural army marching off on their rescue mission to save the queen.

"Wow," Randy whistled. The creatures all wore unique expressions as they charged forward on their quest. "Quite an amazing work of art."

They strolled the corridor until they came to a large white monkey turning himself into a bridge over the sea for the others to get to the demon's fortress. "That's Hanuman, the king of the monkeys," Lalana explained.

A bit farther down the mural, Randy asked, "Why is the queen holding her hand in the fire?"

"To prove herself untouched by the demon," Boon-nam answered. "That way the king would take her back."

Jake frowned. "Blame the victim mentality." Lalana stared at him. He shrugged. "She was kidnapped. If something had happened, it would have been rape, but she'd have been blamed for being unfaithful."

Boon-nam opened her mouth as if she was ready to respond but decided to shift focus back on the story. The mural finished with the reunion scene.

Jake wrinkled his nose. "If he needs her to hold her hand over the fire, somehow life with him doesn't seem like such a happily ever after."

Lalana muttered something about foreigners not understanding their culture before pushing past him to brave the sun. She opened her parasol as she cheerfully reminded, "Umbrella, Boon-nam."

The group trudged around the other buildings in the complex before the misery of the afternoon heat forced them to stroll toward the exit.

Lalana extended an invitation. "We'd like to take you for a quick early dinner. Then we have to go prepare for the show."

After a quick bite to eat at a food court, Randy reluctantly parted ways with barely a homm, but with a promise that Lalana would be coming to his hotel after the show.

Randy clutched the paper Lalana had written an address on so that they could do a little souvenir shopping at reasonable prices for made-in-Thailand products. He couldn't wait for the evening to arrive.

Chapter Eleven

HE AND Jake met the ladies in the lobby. When Boon-nam and Lalana arrived, they exchanged quick hugs. Lalana whispered something to Boon-nam, who giggled before she grinned at Randy. Boon-nam took Jake's hand to lead him from the hotel lobby out into the early evening.

Jake and Boon-nam turned to wave to them before they disappeared into the night. Lalana leaned in close to plant a quick kiss on Randy's cheek.

"So would you like to have dessert with me?" Randy asked.

"I would love to have you for dessert," Lalana purred in a husky voice full of promise.

Shit! Randy's heart skipped a beat, but he took her hand and kissed it. "Room service it is."

The wait has ended. Sorry, Jake, but Lalana's the priority. Time to man up and give in to what we both want.

Once they were in the room, Lalana pushed him up against the closed door with unexpected strength. She pinned him to the wall as she kissed his mouth hungrily, like she needed his lips to survive.

She broke the kiss long enough to tell him, "You've got me going out of my mind. I want you."

Randy's mouth fell open, inviting more of the same, and she hurried to accept the offer. Her tongue danced in and teased his with little licks, sending shivers of need racing up and down his body. He couldn't have stopped the moan of pleasure even if he'd tried.

She was in complete control of the kiss, and Randy abandoned his usual reserve. This was the best kiss of his life.

Damn, but her physical power turned him on. The reminder she was more than a fragile little flower set him on fire. Randy's freedom was restricted, but he rubbed against her, seeking an echo of his hardness. Oh, God. No restrictive undergarment tonight—she was every bit as hard as he was.

She gently scratched his scalp with long fingernails as her fingers wound in his hair. She shoved him backward without breaking the kiss. The backs of his knees hit the bed, and she made quick work of his shirt and pants.

Randy sighed when she wrapped her fingers directly around his rampant cock, glad he'd listened to Jake's advice about no underwear. It was cooler, but more importantly, his bold fashion choice seemed to turn on Lalana.

"Mmm, Randy. I like this."

Her sure hands slid over him like she was climbing a rope. Her grip was perfect, and he didn't have to fight off an orgasm immediately. His strong response to her still seemed like a miracle.

Randy glided his mouth away from her demanding lips to kiss her neck. He teased her with his tongue until her head tipped to the side.

"Bite me," she breathlessly begged.

Randy was careful not to leave marks as he bit into the flesh between her throat and shoulder, right at the base of her neck. She cried out and arched toward him.

Groaning in his ear, her voice took on a deeper, masculine quality. "Randy, need you." She squirmed against his thigh.

He traced his hand down her shapely bottom to squeeze a handful of her rump and pull her to him. "How?"

Randy knew, but he wanted to hear her say it.

Lalana pulled the clips out of her hair one at a time and set them aside. She shook out her long dark hair, and the silken waves poured over her shoulders.

His fingers trembled as he helped open her blouse. Her hair protected her modesty and tormented him by giving glimpses of her lacy pink bra. Randy tossed the pink shirt toward the chair and gently pushed the fabric of her skirt down to her feet, so she could step out of it.

"Leave the heels on," Randy requested.

"Hmmm, kinky." Lalana smirked down at him. She held out a leg to display its loveliness to him.

A thrill zinged through Randy as he watched the exquisite stocking-clad leg twist and turn for him. "So sexy."

She definitely had a dancer's legs, and they seemed to go on for miles. He had some quick mental images of all the wishes he had that involved her legs, or more accurately, how he wanted them wrapped around him.

He took his time admiring and running his fingertips over her stockings-and-garter-belt combo, which matched the color of her bra. She mesmerized Randy. Her shaft was visible, pressing out against her frilly pink panties, ruining the line of their satiny lace in the most delicious way imaginable.

Randy didn't know what possessed him, but he leaned forward and licked her hard little clit through the silky material. He did it again, slower this time, because he liked the husky groan of pleasure the action caused. Randy's attention was drawn to where Lalana leaked a sweet spot on her panties. He dropped to his knees and lapped his tongue at the spot, wetting the fabric further.

Randy glanced up at the vision of pure beauty before him with a burning desire to worship her, to possess her anyway he could, give her anything her heart desired.

So Randy asked again, "Tell me how you want me?" He loved how her fingers urgently tugged at his hair to make him continue giving her what she needed.

Realization dawned on him for the first time. He'd always felt a lot of pressure, because he didn't know what the women he'd been with wanted. But with Lalana he knew. She made her desires clear. With her he wouldn't make a major faux pas—not to mention he wouldn't have to wonder if she was faking an orgasm.

"No, Randy. I know you don't do that." She shrugged.

"Say it. Tell me what you want." He would do anything she asked, no matter what she requested. He'd show his devotion to her any way he could.

"Shh, Randy. I don't want to upset you." She groaned as he lavished attention on her with firmer wet licks. Her fingers tightened.

Empowered, he kept licking in between his words, because she clearly wasn't releasing him from licking her needy clit. She held him firmly in place. "You won't. Anything. Just tell me."

She pushed herself, pink panties and all, into his mouth. Randy closed his mouth around her as he sucked on her satiny lace confection. "I don't usually want this but, oh God. Randy, you make me want to be inside you." She peered down at him, biting her lower lip. She seemed to drink him in as he licked her. Her eyes closed.

Sheer excitement ran through Randy at her wanting him as no one had before. "Is that what you want?"

She shuddered. He eased off a little.

"Oh, Randy. Yeah. But I know you don't do that. It's okay." She gasped as he sucked her harder through dripping-wet panties. "Ahh, so good." Panting, she said, "You can fuck me."

Pulling back he stared up at her. "Do you really want to be inside me?"

"Yeah," she grasped. "I have never asked to do it this way, but with you...." Her lips grazed his throat. "We don't have to do that." Lalana's words were laced with gasps.

It wasn't as if Randy had never considered anal sex, because if he was honest with himself, he had. How could he have a best friend advocating every kind of sex and not consider the joy of what Jake referred to as "butt sex"? But he'd never given the notion more attention than to wonder what penetration might feel like.

However, Lalana wanted this connection with him. She wanted to join with him. Randy wanted to give that to her. "Take me," he said, lying back on the bed.

Lalana's eyes heated. With a growl of desire, she followed him up the mattress, stroking his body and spreading fire everywhere her fingers touched. Randy waited and stared. His heart pumped faster. Her assertiveness surprised and excited him as her mouth claimed his. Randy wasn't submissive, but he loved setting this side of Lalana free.

"Do you have...? Oh, not the time to lose my English." She waved her hand, then snapped her fingers. "Condom. A condom and um, what is it called?"

Randy chuckled a little nervously with her. "Everything is in the night stand."

Thanks to Jake, he had the supplies they needed. Though Jake probably hadn't realized Randy would be on the receiving end of the 'ribbed for her pleasure.'

Lalana reached over to pull the items out of the drawer. She sucked Randy's cock into her mouth for a moment, and he cried out in shock as joy coursed through him. He didn't even feel her wet fingers breach him until they were all the way in.

"Does that feel okay?" she asked as she manipulated her fingers in and out.

He tried to decide if the stimulation was uncomfortable or delicious, and then all of a sudden, the decision had been made. "Mmm, I'm starting to really like this," he wheezed.

"Have you ever done this?" Lalana skated her fingers in and out of him.

"No." He rode against her fingers.

Lalana groaned as she bit her lower lip, and she caught his gaze. "Never… not even with a toy?" His headshake made her shift against him restlessly. "So sexy."

Her fingers curled, hitting a spot that made him fuck the air. He'd come if she kept this up. He moaned and told her, "I'm ready, Lalana."

Her eyes flared. She gently pulled her fingers out of his tightness, pushed off her saliva-wet panties, and rolled down the condom. Her breathing turned into moans when she poured more lube on herself, then tugged herself. She panted and positioned herself at his opening.

"You sure?"

Randy croaked. "God. Yeah, Lalana, I'm sure." She'd better hurry.

Randy arched his hips up as she entered him, and he hissed when she remained still.

"I no move until you say," Lalana whispered. Her body quivered as she froze.

After a minute Randy proceeded to test the waters by wiggling his hips. He gasped, grinning up at her. "Oh. That's nice." He gave a strangled cry right before Lalana began to shift.

She pulled out and pushed back in.

Lalana stared down at him, eyes wide. Her breasts rose and fell with her panting breaths. "You're exceptional. Like wet silk on me. So tight." Lalana grabbed under his knees to hold his legs up and started to push into him.

Randy braced himself. He'd endure this act because Lalana wanted it. He'd deal with the slight burning stretch, but when her thrust stimulated his prostate, all thoughts of doing this only for her disappeared. *Holy hell, that's good.*

Not once did Randy worry if he could keep his erection. His cock was like a steel bar. He was afraid he'd come too soon.

Luckily Lalana appeared to be extremely close to climax. Randy pulled her perfect ass toward him harder as she plunged in and out. She reached between them and stroked him off while she fucked him.

"Yeah, like that, Lalana. More."

"Randy!" She went into overdrive and gave him everything he'd never known he wanted.

He leaned up to capture one of her nipples in his mouth. He nipped at the pink tip. When he sucked it into his mouth, she cried out. He released her breast to watch her blissful completion.

She came without inhibitions. Her hand's firm grip sent him into orbit as she continued to pleasure him. Randy grunted loudly as the best orgasm of his life struck. Her pulsing seemed to make his pleasure last much longer as she thrust in and out of him in a sexy rhythm. He came until he was completely empty.

He wrapped his arms around her, and she fell forward into Randy's creamy mess, which had laced both of them. Her head tucked perfectly into his shoulder as their breathing returned back to normal.

"Mmm, it's been a long time. Good," she whispered in his ear before holding tight to the sagging condom on her little cock.

Moving off him, she hurried to the bathroom, leaving Randy grinning like an idiot. She came back and cleaned him off gently, returned to the bathroom, and then joined him in bed.

They stared at each other a bit. Finally breaking the silence, she asked, "Do you hurt?"

"The only thing that hurts is my face. I can't help myself from smiling like a loon."

She laughed with him. "Good."

He pulled her over top of him to kiss her nose. "Is sex like this always that amazing, or is it just you?"

"Oh, no. Sex is usually horrible. You'd hate it with anyone else. It was amazing only because of me. I am the Mistress of Pleasure between the sheets." She maintained her straight face for all of three seconds before cracking up.

He chuckled and ran a finger down her cheek. "I think you are a genius in bed and out." His cock concurred and had already begun hardening again.

Lalana pursed her lips. "Let's see if you are a genius too." She rolled over onto all fours. "I want your dick up my ass." She wiggled her rounded ass as she reached around to fondle his erection. "Oh, you will do nicely. I want you in me. Please, Randy. Take me."

"Oh, you are a wicked one." He gently slapped her ass for her dirty talk. After she moaned in heated approval, he spanked her bottom lightly, not wanting to hurt her.

Glancing over her shoulder, batting her eyes coyly, she asked, "Are you punishing me, Randy? Was I a naughty girl?"

"You are a good girl, but you seem to need your butt smacked."

She giggled as she shoved a pillow under her hips. When his palm met her ass again, Lalana moaned as she fucked down into its softness. He spanked her until her butt cheeks were a dusky pink.

"That's right, keep fucking the pillow like you fucked me." He'd talk dirty too. He reached over to grab a condom and lube.

Randy's history with anal sex could only be described as a disaster of massive proportions. The experience included hysterical crying from his ex-wife and was not something he'd ever wanted to repeat. But now Lalana wanted him. Could he do it?

She peeked over her shoulder. Her chocolate eyes sparkled with playful mischief. "Yeah, I took your tight ass. Now take mine."

As he watched Lalana wiggle and rub against the pillow, all thoughts of his past sexual events fled his mind.

Lalana pleaded, "Come on, Randy. Open me up with your fingers. Mmm, they are long, but your cock is longer." When she spread her cheeks for him, she demanded, "Hurry. Make me ready, because I want to take you inside me." Lalana's voice deepened past her usual pitch, infused with sensual need.

Randy used his fingers to make sure she had enough lubrication, then put on a condom and eased into her entrance. He held her hips as if he was trying to keep a small piece of sanity, but when she shifted around him, all was lost.

He groaned out words even though he'd rarely spoken during sex before. "Oh, God. You're fucking tight, Lalana."

She managed to take him all the way in, his length packed fully inside her compact body. Arching her back, she purred like a kitten.

Randy caressed her back for a moment before he leaned over to kiss her neck.

"Hard! I need you hard!" she pleaded.

Randy kneeled, held her hips tightly, and started moving in and out. Stars flashed before his eyes. Each new experience with Lalana seemed better than the last. His eyes slid shut as he tried to gain some control over his body.

"Randy! More."

He opened his eyes to see her hair swish back and forth as she writhed against the bed. "Randy! Take me. Come on. Use your handsome dick inside me. You're going to make me come without even touching me. You're in me deep. Come on. Yeah. Oh, right there. Yeah. Harder. Oh, that's right."

Her encouragements forced him to thrust like a madman. Sweat dripped down him as he shoved himself deep inside her.

"Almost coming. Almost." Lalana humped into the pillow before she froze.

She cried out, and Randy felt the rhythmic ripples in her channel massage the come right out of him. He grunted as she unfroze to wiggle herself through her own blissful release, which probably soaked the pillow. She took him with her on her ride to heaven. Her body's grip drained him, pulling the orgasm from him.

On a very satisfied sigh, Lalana fell face-first into the bed. Randy chuckled and held onto the condom when he slid from her body. He went into the bathroom and came back with a warm washcloth to wipe her clean.

When he turned her over to get at her front, she smirked. Compelled to know the truth, he asked, "Was everything okay?"

"I definitely believe you are... who is the smart man with crazy hair?" she asked, petting down Randy's hair, which was probably sticking straight up.

"Einstein?"

"Yes, Einstein. You are an Einstein in bed."

He added, "And I have the hair to prove it."

They laughed and laughed. He pulled her to him. "Come here."

"Didn't I just do that? Twice?" She pretended to be outraged that he'd suggest she should come anymore. "I mean, look at your pillow if you need proof."

"You mean *your* pillow."

"What? I came on it, so it's mine? Is that a rule? I believe it's yours." She chucked it to his side of the bed.

Randy chuckled some more. She was a balm for his soul. "I've never laughed so much in my life, let alone in bed. You're amazing, Lalana." He tucked them under the covers.

Lalana didn't speak, and her breathing evened out. It was weird, but he needed to ask. "Is something wrong?"

Lalana cocked her head toward him. Randy could only see the outline of her profile. "I've been trying not to worry about my little butterfly all evening. I hope Boon-nam's okay."

Gathering her even closer to him, Randy hugged her tight. "Jake's a wonderful guy. He'll take care of her."

He hoped.

Her tears leaked onto his shoulder, and Lalana sniffed. "I know. Which makes all of this so much harder." She seemed to want to say more but, instead, snuggled down into Randy's embrace and held him tight.

A long while after Lalana fell asleep, Randy lay awake, lost in what-ifs. He finally came to the conclusion he probably should have accepted the moment he laid eyes on Lalana.

He fell asleep completely content with what he had to do next.

Chapter Twelve

BOON-NAM GIGGLED as she led Jake out of his hotel. "So what do you want to do?"

Jake knew what his best friend would be doing this evening. Normally, he'd be doing the same thing. Hell, he would have nailed someone as angelic as Boon-nam as soon as possible, but could he really take the next step with her? Shit! When had readiness ever been a question in relation to sex?

He didn't want to crush her. If he had sex with her and left, would he break her heart? Hell, he would be breaking his! When had he become an overanalyzing mess?

"What are the options?" He held her hand as they strolled down the busy sidewalk shared by pedestrians, scooters, and people selling souvenirs or food off blankets.

Boon-nam stared straight ahead, but her breathing accelerated. "Well, um, I know of this great club…. A lot of my friends go there…."

"I love clubs." Red flag alert: what kind of club?

She flashed him a smile, and her eyes sparkled. "But it's in Patpong."

"You don't like that area?" He was under the impression most Thai people didn't give that part of town much thought.

"No, I love it, but Lalana doesn't like I go to a club there."

Interesting. He decided to give her a bit of assistance. "Why? She doesn't like to dance?"

"Well, it's not really a *dance* club." The neon from the nearby shops couldn't hide her blush.

Damn. Play it cool. "Oh? What kind of club is it?" Fuck, fuck, fuck, fuck….

"People just sort of hang out and, um, talk…."

Talk? Right. His angel was leading him straight to hell, but it was going to be quite a trip. "So you like this place?"

"Yeah, but I've never been in… *back*." She ended on a whisper that was almost lost in the Bangkok traffic.

Apparently Jake's avoidance pass had expired. He was part thrilled and part freaked out. She'd given him hints before that her thoughts weren't as innocent as her body, but…. "And you want to go in back."

"Only if you'd take me. I've never had anyone I'd want to go back there with… until you."

In the past, Jake had always liked getting fucked carpe diem-style. But Boon-nam's desire to seize the day—or in this case, the night—with him reminded him of their limited time frame. Damn, that stole some excitement, but he'd be her guide into the kinky side.

"Okay."

"Are you sure you're okay doing this with me? I don't want to force you."

"You're an enticing mix of sweet and kinky," Jake mused out loud.

"Is that bad?" Her hand found her hip.

"No, it's not bad, just unusual." When did he become a sexist? She didn't have to fit into the virgin-or-whore category. People were allowed to have different and sometimes conflicting characteristics. Although experiencing the phenomenon in one adorable Boon-nam-sized package was causing a glitch in his program.

"Can't I be both?"

He wasn't sure what he was signing up for, but he'd give his signature on the dotted line for anything she wanted. Damn. He cleared his throat from the warm Bangkok air. "Yes, you can. Take me to your nightlife, my little tiger."

Her steps got a little faster as she tugged him through the chaos of the Bangkok night to the Sky Train station steps. The elevated rail system beat sitting in traffic every time. The train arrived in Patpong within minutes, and Boon-nam was dancing with excitement.

"Come on." She tugged him out of the train and down the station stairs. How could he have been in the "Sin City of Asia" for this long without seeing Bangkok's famed den of sexual treats? He glanced down at Boon-nam's angelic eyes staring up at him and found his answer. He was fucked and not in the way he'd expected Bangkok to have its way with him.

Boon-nam asked for what seemed like the hundredth time, "Are you sure? We don't have to do this for me." The moving crowd swallowed them as everyone on the street headed in the same direction.

"Yes, tiger. I want to do this with you, and I promise I can handle it." Jake chuckled as he wrapped his arm around her. If only she knew about the sex club he belonged to back home. He could handle the "infamous" Patpong, and he'd chaperon Boon-nam through the delights while avoiding the negative parts.

"Good!" She dragged him down the street to show him Patpong.

When they passed a sign indicating they'd arrived, they zigzagged through the night market area. Everything one could possibly need: clothing, shoes, household items, auto products, dry goods, and cheap souvenirs. He stopped at several stalls selling paintings and true Thai handicrafts.

"We should bring Randy here." As Jake said it, he realized the market place was rimmed in girlie bars. "Or maybe not."

Boon-nam pointed out a group of women hassling the men passing by with invitations to do things to their bodies for *cheap-cheap price*. "I try not to think about it, but that could be my life. I could have been one of those girls."

"No." Jake denied the real possibility without wanting to dwell on it. Thank God she'd been lucky enough to be given options. Lalana could hate him forever, but he'd always be grateful to her.

"Unfortunately, yes." She guided them in the opposite direction. "I think that's why Lalana doesn't like Patpong or the clubs. She can only see what could have been."

As if a director cued them, various men began approaching them, holding cards to shout in their faces "Fish show. Ping-pong show. Scarf show. Cigarette-smoking show."

Jake had heard of or seen variations of most of the shows. A ping-pong show involved a woman shooting balls out of herself at the audience. He always wondered what they'd do if he returned the flying ball with a ping-pong paddle.

After the fifth guy accosted them with his pornographic pictures of the best show in Bangkok, Jake had to ask, "What is a scarf show?"

Boon-nam drew him away from the guy holding the flyer to whisper fiercely into his ear. "You know how a clown can pull scarfs out of his mouth?"

"Yeah," Jake said. The dawn of realization came. "Ohhhh. I see, they pull the scarves out of their—"

"Exactly," Boon-nam cut him off. People hustled past them as they stopped off to the side.

There was a definite buzz of sexual excitement in the air as they moved farther into the thick of things. "So Lalana doesn't like it here? But you do?"

Boon-nam's cheeks were an enticing pink, but her eyes were flashing with heat. "I do. But Lalana believes all dirty things are bad."

"And you don't? You enjoy dirty, kinky things in a good way?"

"Yes. I really like it here." Boon-nam giggled as she glanced around and seemed excited by the open sexuality.

"Me too." They were completely compatible.

"Do you know what a fish show is?" Her smile was brighter than all the neon combined.

"Well, the fish is pushed inside." Jake dropped his voice to a pitch he knew she found sexy.

"Yes, and it's sucked right out." Boon-nam wiggled to get closer to Jake.

He snorted. "Well, that's a far cry from someone 'serving fish' back home." It was a silly term his drag queen friends would often trot out when discussing if their "look" could pass for female.

Boon-nam stopped to stare at him as if translating the words before trying to figure out the slang he'd used. She frowned with her lower lip out.

Her eyes flashed with anger, and she planted her hands on her hips. "I don't like that American term. It suggests lady parts smell, and that's not nice."

Damn it, could she be more adorable? Or more right? He'd never purposefully degrade women. "I've never thought about the term, and you're right. I've some friends who use the term, but I promise I won't use it again. I'm sorry."

To his relief, her anger dissolved. "I forgive you. I know some people don't think about the terms they use and insults happen. Lalana usually ignores it, but I can't. Words matter."

"They do, and you shouldn't let something pass. Thank you for correcting me. I get it, and if more people spoke up, the world would change much quicker." He got it, but he wasn't one to focus on his missteps. "What about the other shows?"

Excitement washed over her as she pressed her breasts against his arm. Her delicate rose perfume scented the air he breathed. She peeked up at him coyly. "Which shows?"

He'd never want to disappoint her, so he played into her desire to discuss things of a forbidden nature. "What about the cigarette-smoking show?"

"Well, smoking a cigarette some place other than the girl's mouth," Boon-nam primly told him as if they weren't standing next to a bar with half-clad women spilling out the door.

Cigarette shows always puzzled him. Who decided to try to smoke *that* way? Why would anyone want to? Did these women increase their risk of cervical cancer? Did people find a cigarette smoked in this unorthodox manner sexy?

Ambling farther along the edges, they passed clubs filled with sex workers. Boon-nam didn't say anything, but only scrutinized Jake's reaction when they passed the Alley Cat.

Jake had heard of the Alley Cat, the infamous blowjob bar. For a buck you could get a beer and a blowjob. According to the Internet, the beer tasted like piss, and the girls had seen better days, but they could suck cock to the owner's satisfaction a hundred percent of the time. Jake peered inside and was disappointed to see the legend appeared to be a typical dive bar. No hint of the erotic nature of the establishment, only ripped chairs, dingy wallpaper, and dust.

Boon-nam frowned and answered his unasked question. "Upstairs. There are couches." She shook her hair out of her face. "But you have no privacy."

Jake stopped her for a second when he realized the poor thing worried he wanted to go in. "I'm not interested in going in."

"Really?"

Why did she sound surprised? Jake skimmed a hand down over her pert little ass and gave her butt a squeeze. "Really."

Boon-nam did a happy dance that made his heart twist a bit.

They continued strolling past various bars and clubs offering a variety of services.

"Lalana thinks Patpong is disgusting." Boon-nam watched Jake carefully as if she were waiting for him to judge her.

"I don't find this area disgusting. I guess some of the places are a bit sad. I mean, most of the people here are lonely or don't feel comfortable doing what they enjoy on a daily basis. Or they are doing things to make money. But if you block that out, the eroticism is freeing."

"Exactly." Her eyes sparkled. "And I love Patpong and the sexy atmosphere here. I think people should be free to explore and play."

She guided them into a sex shop. "This is one of the best shops in Bangkok. I used to come here all the time. They can even get special order fetish items."

Jake raised an eyebrow but decided not to ask. He held the door open, allowing her to enter. The shop appeared to have the usual section of vibrators, dildos, cock rings, Fleshlights, blow-up dolls, and DVDs available.

As soon as Boon entered, a short fat man flew over the counter and landed right in front of Boon. "Boon-boon!" He squealed like a stuck pig, pulling Boon-nam into a tight bear hug and shaking her slender body side to side as if she were a martini.

"How is my little Boon?" The man held her at arm's length so he could study her. His eyes stared at her crotch a little too long for Jake's liking. "Ah, the rumors are true."

He glanced around as if seeking privacy in the crowded shop, surrounded by Thailand natives and foreigners alike. "Does everything work, my cherished little Boon-boon?"

What the hell business is it of this guy's if Boon-nam functions fully? Jake wanted to step in to rearrange the guy's face, but Boon-nam and he were friends. Geez, was he turning into a prude? Unable to smack the guy in the teeth, Jake folded his arms and glared at the bastard impatiently, waiting for the asshole to release his girl.

Boon-nam blushed a delightful pink and nodded shyly.

The man peered over Boon-nam and realized Jake wasn't moving. "Ah, is this a *friend*, Boon-nam?"

"Oh, sorry. Yes, this is my friend, Jake. This is Ditaka!" Boon-nam introduced them.

Jake begrudgingly held out his hand. He didn't want to embarrass Boon-nam, but he squeezed the fucker's hand extra tight. "Good to meet you," he mumbled as they shook hands.

Ditaka might have been classically unattractive, but he had a certain charisma. The jackass was a charming old-school Casanova. Jake tried not to be jealous of the guy's familiar way with Boon-nam.

The shop owner turned on his heel and said, "Follow me." He trudged off toward the back of the store. Boon-nam didn't hesitate to follow, and Jake stayed right on her heels.

Ditaka led them into an office, which doubled as a stockroom. Once everyone sat, Ditaka opened one of the marked cabinets lining the room to pull out a box.

He handed Boon-nam the box. "Here, Boon-nam. This has just arrived from America."

Jake examined the box, which read "Rudeboy". The prostate vibrator's box proclaimed to give stunning ass-gasms if the testimonials in bright yellow were believable.

"The doctor recommends this toy. The Rudeboy can help your body remember what to do," Ditaka said, almost religiously. "The curve hits the right place even with everything shifted a bit with surgery."

Boon-nam explained, "Ditaka's lover is a doctor who practices with my doctor."

Ditaka ignored Boon-nam's discomfort to grin at Jake. "This is a wonderful toy. Use a lot of lubrication, but this device will make both your *rides* even better." Ditaka took out the toy to show them. While the toy was out he inserted batteries and cleaned the surface with an antiseptic cloth before carefully replacing it. He stared at Boon-nam for a moment before he asked, "He has ridden you, yes?"

The bluntness of the question bothered Jake, but Boon-nam answered, "Not yet."

Ditaka turned his examining stare to Jake as if he were trying to figure out why they hadn't had intercourse. "Okay. You be careful of pain." He pointed at Jake's lap. "You're not too big, right? Otherwise you could tear Boon-nam."

First Lalana and now a man he'd barely said two words to asked him about his penis size. Holy fuck! It took a helluva lot to say something to shock him, but this did. The little man asked as if Boon's sexual activities were his business. And the man waited for an answer. *What the fuck? Is he going to take measurements?* Jake shrugged.

Ditaka smiled. "Ah, wonderful. Not so big."

He didn't say that. It wasn't like he was tiny. He was average, or maybe, if he were honest, possibly smaller than average. He'd never believed his size to be a problem, but he was conscious of satisfying his partners. Never wanting to be a disappointment due to his lack of endowment had helped to round out his techniques as a lover.

Boon-nam glanced over at him and took his hand. "He looked big to me." She turned bright red and gave Jake a small smile.

"Okay, good." Ditaka stared daggers as he warned Jake, "You be careful with our Boon-boon. She is as fragile as she is lovely and is too inexperienced to understand."

"I intend to be." Jake tried to keep the annoyance out of his voice.

But Ditaka wasn't done giving him advice. "You make sure she is very lubricated. She does not know what she needs yet. You need to protect her. You are okay using a toy?" He indicated the box.

What a nosey bastard! Jake arched his eyebrow at the intrusive question, but Boon-nam's rapt attention made him answer. "I have used this one before."

Ditaka nodded and rubbed his hands together. "Ah, good. Remember, the mind is biggest sex place." Boon-nam turned redder and yelped a bit. Ditaka ignored her and continued with his sex lesson. "Go slowly and not too often until she's more used to it."

"*If* we do that, I will listen to your advice. Thank you." As grateful as Jake was that Boon-nam had people in her corner, he stood up to end this conversation.

Boon-nam jumped up and hugged Ditaka. "Will you let me pay for this, Di?"

Ditaka raised a hand to cup her cheek. "No, my little one. I'm so happy you have a playmate—use the toy and have glorious orgasms with it. Hmm?"

Ditaka slipped the sex-toy box into Boon-nam's suitcase of a purse.

"Thank you, Di. Give my best to your doctor," Boon-nam giggled as she held her hand out to lead Jake out of the shop.

"Wait, wait!" Ditaka came barreling after them. "Here." He grabbed Jake's hand to slip a bottle of lubricant in it. "It's waterproof. Smells like vanilla."

He hustled back into his shop as customers waited impatiently at the register for him.

Boon-nam smiled shyly. "We're near that club I told you about. Do you want to go?"

"Sure." Jake smirked as his little tiger let out a little whoop before anxiously hauling him down the street.

"I know the owners and a lot of the girls who work there. It's a nice place."

"I'm sure it will be fun." Jake tried to hide his amusement as Boon-nam yanked him around so she could have her kinky way with him.

She giggled. "It'll be hot."

God clearly had no intention of saving him. "And you want to go to the *back* booths."

Boon-nam's eyes sparkled with lust as she looked him up and down as if he were on a menu. "We don't have to, but I've always wanted to—"

Jake restrained a growl as possessiveness cascaded over his common sense. He'd follow her anywhere. If his little tiger wanted to go there, he'd make sure she was safe. He'd do whatever she needed him to do, and he'd love it if she did.

This wouldn't be the first time he'd played in public. The risk of getting caught or having other people watch always added a level of excitement and gave him an erotic buzz.

Within a short distance, they came to a gaudy building with way too much neon and too many mirrors. When he opened the door to the club, music throbbed a loud beat into the street as air-conditioned coolness counteracted Bangkok's heat.

As soon as they stepped into the dim room lit by rainbow lighting, *kathoey* swarmed Boon-nam. Some were almost as lovely and feminine as she, while others were absolutely masculine, and several others seemed to embrace the duality of their sexual energy. Nature had denied some their dreams of looking like a fairy princess, but that didn't mean they couldn't be one.

They all spoke rapid Thai to Boon. Even though the words were in Thai, Jake could tell they were asking Boon a lot of questions about him. They kept touching her. Several hommed Boon-nam's neck.

Jake wasn't too happy with the overly friendly way they had their hands on his Boon. Then he realized Boon wasn't his. He started to wonder if he needed to do something about that. But the question was, what could he do?

Before Jake could puzzle out an answer, all eyes turned to him. Damn. These bar workers put him in the spotlight and were apparently judging him to determine if he was worthy. Jake waited for someone to inspect his mouth to check out how many cavities he had. Finally the leader of the group held out her delicate hand for him to shake.

Jake grinned at Boon-nam. They wanted romance? He'd be the suave American they would rub themselves off over tonight. He took the perfectly manicured hand offered to him and stared deeply into the woman's eyes as he bought the hand to his lips.

He'd barely touched her skin when all the ladyboys began to squeal and giggle. Receiving a gaze of appreciation from Boon-nam, he knew he'd won their approval. Every single one of Boon-nam's friends held out their hand for him to chastely kiss as if he were a knight. He took a deep breath and did so.

Within a minute, the beauties all scattered, except the one who acted as a hostess. She led them to the darkly lit back booths. She took their drink order and left.

Jake peered out of their booth to see the club. The seating design mostly blocked the view. There was a lot of room between the table and the surrounding padded-leather enclosure. The cushioned leather bench could allow patrons to lie back… if the need arose.

"So why have you never been here with anyone else?" Not that Jake was jealous or anything, he was just making conversation.

She smiled coyly at him through her long lashes. "I was waiting for you."

It was good Boon-nam thanked the waitress who brought their drinks, because Jake was speechless. Boon-nam had ordered something pink and frothy, while Jake stuck to a Thai beer. Pausing, the waitress ran her eyes up and down Jake. When her perusal finished, she winked at Boon-nam and disappeared.

Jake cocked his head to the side to look at Boon-nam. He couldn't let her hide behind flirtatious lines regardless of how fucking sexy they were. "Tell me why you never come back here, my little tiger?"

Boon-nam leaned toward him so that he could hear. "I didn't want to do this with just anyone and before… I just couldn't."

Jake nodded. He'd be her kinky playmate if that's what she wanted. He pushed past wanting this to be so much more than that.

"And now I can, and you're here… and I really want to be one of the bad girls that come back here."

"Bad girls?" Jake questioned. Confirmation. Boon-nam wants to walk on the wild street where the bad girls play. He didn't know whether he should get down on his knees and thank all that was holy or run. Hmm, he'd like to be on his knees for her. "So are you a bad girl now?"

"Mm, Jake. Stop saying that," Boon-nam whined delectably and wiggled into the seat. She pressed to his side and nuzzled her face against his neck.

This was a game Jake knew how to play. If she wanted to be a "bad girl," Jake could make that happen. "You wanna be a bad girl, don't you?"

Her eyes got incredibly big, and she nodded.

He reached out a hand to cup her breast. Boon-nam gasped and leaned into his palm, offering her body to him. Jake easily found her nipple, the tip erect in demand for attention. He strummed the peak through her top. She squirmed before he pinched it.

"Oh!" Her complaint was more of an invitation.

Seeing they were in relative privacy, Jake slipped his hands under her shirt to find her lacy bra. He plucked the nipple until Boon-nam whimpered. The buttons of the shirt seemed to open on their own, revealing the sheer lacy confection still confining her breasts. Jake's mouth surrounded the visible pinkish brown tip, and he sucked.

Boon-nam groaned and pulled his head against her. He sucked her flesh until she was breathless. Jake nipped the tip before moving to the other side. Boon quickly pulled the fabric down to expose her nipple, and Jake latched his mouth directly onto the sensitive tip. Her head dropped back as he feasted back and forth between them.

Jake would've continued lavishing attention on her buds for hours, but Boon-nam appeared restless with pent-up need for more. She shoved him back and straddled his lap. Damn! Once seated on him, she pulled the bottle of lubrication Ditaka had given her out of her purse. She edged back to give herself room and wiggled her skirt up to reveal her girlie delights. Boon-nam rubbed the lubrication on her sexy pink panties.

"What are you…?" Jake's mouth went dry as he could see the gusset between her legs. She was dazzling in her arousal.

"We girls cannot be unclothed here," she said as she unzipped his pants.

Apparently his cock waving in the breeze was no issue. Jake's unruly cock escaped its confines and sought release. Boon-nam stared into his eyes as if she was daring him to stop, wrapped her lubricated hand around him, and gave him a few experimental tugs.

"My tiger wants to play," Jake purred into her ear as she twisted forward to slide herself against him.

Giggling, Boon-nam kissed him on the lips with a big wet smack. "Yes, please."

Jake cupped her ass in his palms to help guide her over him. "You know what else would be nice, Boon?"

She stopped all motion and tilted her head so that her hair fell to one side, covering one eye. Holy hell, even her innocent curiosity heated his blood.

"What?"

"Would you like if I used your new toy on you?" He made sure his voice stayed low and deep. "Would you like that, my sweet tiger?"

Boon-nam whimpered and circled her lubricated pussy against Jake's naked cock. His little nymph practically creamed her panties. She growled just like a baby tiger and handed him the box.

Boon-nam jumped off his lap to turn and lean over the table, presenting her pert ass to him. She reached up to the waistband of her panties to wiggle them down past her sweet ass.

"You must be quick." She glanced over her shoulder with a grin that said she wasn't completely innocent of what she did to him. "Can't have my panties down for long. This isn't like one of *those* clubs."

Glancing around, Jake decided not to dissuade her from her belief, but this was very much one of *those* clubs. Jake caressed the flawless skin of her ass. He patted her butt several times just to watch her cheeks jiggle.

Focus, man! Jake took the toy. Ditaka had left the batteries in, and Jake lubed up the device quickly. Then he parted her rounded butt cheeks and inserted the toy in one long, slow push. The Rudeboy's angle helped to slowly penetrate her back passage. He'd played with toys in the past. Thank fuck he'd had some experience with this.

Boon-nam tried to stay still but failed. When the toy fit securely in place, Jake shifted her around to face him. "There you go." He patted her bottom.

She pulled up her panties almost prudishly. Boon jumped into his lap to straddle him again. Only the thin scrap of lubricated lace separated her parts from his rampantly hard, leaking dick.

He'd let his tiger play, but he asked, "Are you okay?"

Nodding, she readjusted and started to rub up and down his cock. He reached under her and pressed the button to turn the Rudeboy on.

Her eyes squeezed shut. "Augh!" She took a deep inhale and slowly blew the air out. She reopened her eyes and started sliding over Jake again. Both breasts jutted out of the top of her lacy bra, putting them at the mercy of his fingers and mouth. He showed her he had no sympathy when it came to her pleasure. He licked, sucked, and bit.

The vibrations of the anal device on Jake's cock were getting to him. Even as she ground up and down on his lap, he needed to keep his wits about him. "How does it feel, Boon?"

"Good. So good. The toy inside of me is good, and you are exciting me on the outside," she moaned out the words. She twisted and shifted as she rubbed against him.

Talk got harder, but she wanted his words. A thrill raced through him. "You're getting laid in a club, you naughty girl."

"Oh. Mm, yeah," She writhed her wet pussy over his cock. Breathless and desperate, she clutched Jake's shoulders with her nails.

Jake skimmed his hands over her thighs. Her muscles strained as she chased her orgasm. The tiny wet piece of fabric between them offered no protection, the lips of her pussy barely covered as she glided over his cock, kissing him through the silk.

He loved sliding every inch of his cock along her, but he was careful not to enter her. He could sense the vibrations rocking her world. He fed her mind with filthy words.

"You like being a dirty little girl for me, don't you, Boon?" He guided her body along his to assist her in getting to her destination. The sensation of the wet satin massaging his cock with vibrations was almost too much for him to handle. But he determined to hold on until she was satisfied.

"Mmmm, yes. I am a dirty girl. All for you, Jake." Her hair fanned out around them as she gave him a small kiss. She rode over his cock.

"I like *dirty* girls. You are such a good, *dirty* girl." Jake knew he had tripped her wires, and he got ready to set her off. "You like teasing my cock with your pretty pink panties. You want your wet little panties coated with my come, don't you? Do you want me to come on your pink panties, you naughty girl?"

"Yes, Jake. Yes." Her head tossed back and forth. She trembled in his arms. "Come, I need to come."

Jake cupped her bottom tighter, speeding up her ride. "Yes, that's right—get me off with your sexy pussy. Your pussy sliding across my cock is perfect. I bet I could slip right in and you would let me. You want me to push through your wet heat and pump inside of you until I come? Come in your perfect pussy to satisfy my cock. You want to come on my cock, Boon? You want to be my dirty little tiger?"

"Yes. Yes. Oh, Jake! *Yes*!" She shook. She groaned. "I'm coming in my ass," Boon-nam panted in his ear as she rode the ridge of his cock right into heaven. "I am coming everywhere."

That was all he needed to hear. He let go, sighing with relief as he shot off all over her panties. "Mm, God. Boon. You're making me come with your perfect pussy."

She shuddered in his arms. His cock kept unloading until Boon-nam's charms were completely frosted in his warm cream.

Jake's wild, dirty little tiger collapsed in his arms, completely worn out from her orgasm. He removed the toy from her, shut it off, and slipped it back into the open box in her purse.

Jake held his treasure in his arms and sighed happily. They hadn't had intercourse, but he was absolutely spent. She was a kinky little thing.

After a minute or two, one of her friends poked her head in. She glanced around at the two of them. Giggling, the tiny creature handed Boon-nam a towel and a new pair of panties before popping out.

Boon-nam bit her lip, and her shyness returned. Jake kissed her cheek and said, "They will all be jealous of you, Boon."

His words seem to bolster Boon's confidence. She gave him a kiss on the cheek and a shrug. "They should be!"

Chapter Thirteen

BOON-NAM WOKE up on Jake's bed and smiled. Hearing the shower running, she knew where Jake was, and the image of his naked body danced through her head. She stretched like a cat.

"Mmm." Sighing to herself, she remembered their time at the club and what they'd done when they got back to the room. Sleep hadn't been high on their agenda, but Boon-nam felt fantastic. Glancing over at the red numbers on the hotel's digital clock, she realized, if they hurried, they could be at Wat Arun for the sunrise.

She jumped out of bed and tapped on the bathroom door. "Jake?"

His wet head appeared, followed by a towel wrapped around his delicious body as if he were hiding it from her. "Hey, you up?"

"I can see you are." Boon-nam giggled.

Jake rolled his eyes and grinned at her silliness because she really couldn't see anything, but he looked down just in case. "If we hurry we can get to Wat Arun for the sunrise."

"Aren't you tired?" Jake yawned.

"Nope!" Stretching her body in ways she hoped made Jake drool, Boon-nam brushed past him to steal the bathroom. Since she had already taken a shower after Jake fell asleep, she needed to freshen up and apply some makeup, and maybe do her hair.

WITHIN FIFTEEN minutes the wind had made a mess of her hair as the water taxi sped off up the river to Wat Arun. Boon-nam pulled on her hot pink windbreaker. The boat was empty, so she switched seats to sit behind the driver. Jake joined her. She allowed him to wrap an arm around her shoulder. She couldn't stop herself snuggling into the warmth of his larger body or inhaling the scent of his soap.

She tried to tame her wind-whipped hair but froze when she caught Jake staring at her.

"You look like a goddess." He snapped a picture of her before she could complain.

His heated expression allowed her a glimpse of the divinity he claimed he saw in her.

Arriving at their stop a minute later, Jake took care of the water taxi fare. He jumped out of the boat and extended his hand to guide her. *Aw, he's such a gentleman.*

They ran past the closed ticket office and pushed open the gates to climb the steep steps, which appeared to go straight up. "Come on, the sun's almost up."

Her foot slipped on one of the unevenly worn steps. Jake's large hand on her back steadied her. "Careful, little tiger."

"Thank you." She tried to ignore the fluttery sensation in her stomach. He protected her. Lalana and Tong would certainly be disappointed in her lack of independence, but she liked a man watching out for her. Tong and Lalana needed to know they weren't dependent on anyone. But she found the concept of a dashing American helping her scale the stairs up to the top of Wat Arun romantic.

Five minutes of upward climbing later, Jake released her from his guiding hand. She sighed at the loss, but they were at the top of the temple. "Look." She pointed out over the complex.

The white temple and the smaller ones below them glowed. Tiny mirrors covered the structures and shimmered as the light of the sun dawned.

Boon-nam wanted to kiss him to lock in the memory of this moment and last night, but physical affection was an unacceptable wish to have at a temple. She contented herself with drinking in everything about him.

His muscles rippled under his T-shirt as he confidently roamed around the top of Wat Arun, like a tiger angling for the best pictures. The sun began to glitter off the silver rings he wore in his ear and made his hair sparkle. She lost her breath when he turned his attention on her. In those aviator sunglasses, he could have been a movie star.

The chanting of the monks broke into her thoughts, reminding her how inappropriate they were, being in a temple. Jake pulled her over to the edge of the temple to witness the procession of saffron-clad men chanting their prayers as they headed out to receive alms from the devoted.

Jake glanced up from his phone. "The guide says this Wat was named after the Indian Goddess of the dawn, Aruna."

Intelligence in men always aroused her. "It's a representation of Mount Meru, which is…."

Glancing up from the tourist information on his phone, Jake supplied the information. "Mount Meru is the state of single-mindedness and the center of the universe in some schools of Buddhism."

Purring in delight, Boon said, "That's right."

After Jake snapped a few more enchanting pictures of them together, the sun made itself known. "Do you have your parasol?"

"Oh, um, no." Damn, she always forgot to carry it unless Lalana reminded her. Her bag could have doubled as a suitcase. She wanted to always be prepared, but she didn't have a hat or umbrella. This morning she'd taken the parasol out to lighten her bag.

Jake's mouth turned up. "Don't worry, I won't tell Lalana, but we should get you out of the sun."

Boon-nam hadn't been here in years. She hesitated at the top of the stairs to stare. "That's a long way down." When did heights scare her? One trip or slip, and she'd be broken.

Running his fingers through his hair, Jake surveyed the height and came up with a quick plan. "Okay, we'll do this backward. Just turn and pretend you're coming down from a ladder." He spun around and demonstrated a couple of steps while holding on to the guide rail. "Hold on, and I'll be right beneath you."

She'd be brave. Boon-nam didn't swoon. She glanced over her shoulder, realizing this wasn't the time to be a wimp.

"Just one step a time. And don't dwell on the gorgeous view you'll be giving me."

What view? Oh, her butt would be almost in his face. She snorted in laughter. How could she not fall head over heels in love with him? Before any kind of answer formed, she'd touched the ground.

"Whew."

"You did great." His gaze ran up and down her body until she almost felt it. "And you looked amazing doing it." Jake said outrageously, adjusting the erection in his pants.

Oh, my. She swatted at him playfully but couldn't hide her grin. He was so dirty, and she loved it. Lalana was too uptight to let Boon-nam share her kinky side, even in jokes, where Jake seemed to love her naughty side and even nurtured it.

She drank in his compliments, no matter how laden with lust. She loved that Jake wasn't shy in letting her know how much she turned him on. His admiration gave her a sense of control, and despite her inexperience, he made her feel as if they were on a more even playing field.

They retraced their steps back to the hotel with a few laughs and more than a few hidden touches. Once in the hotel room, Jake ordered them an American pancake breakfast from room service. When the waiter knocked, Boon-nam excused herself to hide in the bathroom.

Hiding was childish, but she didn't want someone making judgments about her relationship with Jake. The waiter would assume she was a prostitute, and she didn't want to be reminded of the temporary nature of their involvement. She washed her hands and tried to push the depressing thought aside.

But the expiration date of Jake's vacation loomed over her. From the first night, she'd been counting down the days. Yesterday when the number of his vacation days left became far too low, she switched to hours. When the door clicked shut, she peeked out.

The waiter had set up the rolling cart by the large picture window overlooking the street. He'd pulled up the leaves and turned the cart into a table. The chairs stood on either side of the table.

After breakfast they would… oh, she *really* wanted to do this with Jake. Their time was running out, and Boon-nam wanted to give herself to him. Better to have everything she could with him and deal with the consequences later.

She stopped bouncing with nervous energy when Jake turned on some soft music before they sat down. Even as a child, Boon-nam could never hide her anxiety or excitement very well. That was probably why Lalana never confided her plan for them to leave their village. She'd sneaked in through the window one night and swept Boon-nam away to Bangkok. No one let her in on surprise parties because she wouldn't be able to hold the secret.

Jake gave her a placid smile to put her at ease, but his handsome face only made her heart race. She pushed around the food on her plate until he raised his glass of mimosa in toast.

"To the most adorable tour guide in all of Bangkok."

He went for humor. She'd be a pleasing girl and giggle. But "tour guide"? Was that all she meant to him? Silly, but hurt ate at her heart.

Sipping at her glass, she realized the orange juice contained alcohol. She downed her glass and went for his in the most unladylike way. She cracked a grin at him and shrugged.

He put his hand on her knee and reminded her, "We don't have to do this, sweetheart."

Argh! Not making love to Jake would kill her, especially after getting so close last night. She'd better let him know she wasn't uncomfortable. "But I want to." She frowned with real concern. "Am I really *only* a tour guide to you?"

He smiled. "Of course not. I love making you smile." Jake traced a finger across her cheek. "You're sweet, wonderful, funny, fierce, and very brave. You're my baby tiger. You're the most perfect woman I've ever met."

Jake dropped his gaze as if he were searching for words. "You make me want things I've never had, never imagined I needed or wanted." He peeked up through the fall of his hair.

The intensity of his stare made her tummy tight. She leaned forward and pressed her lips to his. She needed this, she really did, and she wanted him to make love to her. She didn't care that their relationship was doomed to end before they'd really started. Something drove her to have him. Call it destiny, love at first sight, whatever brought them together, Boon-nam wanted him to be first even if Jake didn't want to be her last.

The alcoholic gulps emboldened her; she didn't have enough to make her drunk, but it gave her courage. Was it hot in there? Restless energy brought her to her feet, and she unbuttoned her top. One button at a time popped open before the garment slid off her shoulders and onto the floor.

Boon-nam hoped she appeared sexy and not like some nervous little ex-*kathoey* trying to entice a man. She longed for Tong's poise or Lalana's beauty. But Jake had said he was interested in her exactly the way she was—maybe she wasn't mucking it up too badly.

She slowly undid the ties on her pedal pushers at her calves and waist to wiggle out of them. Posing in only her lacy things, she stepped over to the bed, hoping he'd follow.

Boon-nam remembered what Tong had taught her about using her hair. She unclipped her bra and let it drop to the floor as she shook her head. Her hair protected some of her modesty. The strands gave Jake only teasing peeks, but gave her a little comfort to prevent the perception of being completely on display in the bright light of the hotel room.

She lay back on the bed like an offering to Jake. Hearing his breath catch as he watched her display turned her on like no sound she had ever heard.

Jake slid between the vee of her legs. His face hovered close to her pussy. Every single inhale and exhale as the air teased across her skin made her crazy.

She needed him to do something. He answered her prayer when he swiped a wet lick across her panties.

"Oh." She moaned and spread her legs wider.

Jake took the hint and tasted her again. This was only the second time she'd experienced such an amazing sensation, and this time the room was lit enough for her to get an excellent view of him. His bad boy persona rolled off him in waves, but he was more: smart, funny, and very dear.

His dark hair moved up and down as he caressed her panties with his mouth. He glanced up. "Is this okay, Boon?"

"Yeah." The word came out strangled.

Every few swipes of his tongue, he stopped to stare up at her with heated eyes and lick his lips. He seemed to want to lick her everywhere down there.

"Maybe I should remove this?" He tugged a little on the wet scrap of lace that stood between them.

It would be the first time a man studied her in the daylight. The last time, she'd had the comfort of shadows. She shivered and gave him permission.

As he pulled off her panties, she closed her eyes. She couldn't bear to see if he found her less than what he expected. She waited. And waited. Finally, after a minute passed, she opened her eyes to find him staring at her in wonder.

"What?" She kicked herself mentally for sounding childish, but she couldn't help it. What had captured his attention? She tried to block his view with her hands.

"No. Oh, please don't hide." Jake stared up at her with a sultry smile. "You're flawless." His said the words with such sincerity, she almost believed him.

She turned her head because she couldn't meet his eyes. She felt like a fake.

He stopped her. "No, don't. You're a ravishing, gorgeous woman."

Boon-nam tried not to sound hopeful when she asked, "Really?"

Jake inspected her. His heated growl reassured her. "Really. I know we just finished breakfast, but you look scrumptious. I want to eat you."

He drew her legs up on his shoulders. She giggled, and her nerves lessened. If she hadn't been in love with him before, she certainly was now.

Once his tongue started licking her folds directly, she no longer laughed. Her hips started pushing up as she tried to hold his questing tongue to her.

"Oh, there," she called out, hoping his tongue would zone in on where she needed it to be. But the sensation darted off in a different direction. She combed her fingers through his hair and pulled him down.

Once again, she breathed a mental sigh of relief that her operation was successful. Those first few months had been hell. She had the body of her dreams, but her parts had been numb. Even though the doctor told her again and again her body would take time, she couldn't stop her panic.

Now her new body trembled in response to Jake's magical tongue. When she had male parts, she'd hated them and couldn't accept pleasure from them, but now.... *Oh, yum, Jake's good at licking.*

She rode his face, and everything in her body tightened up, getting ready for its release. Jake pushed out from between her legs. *What? No! Where is he going?* He needed to get back to where she wanted him. She had to come, damn it.

"Jake, why? Why are you stopping? What's wrong?" She'd been only a few licks away! She shook with unfulfilled desire.

He slid up her body in a way that dragged his cock along her soft thighs and teased her feminine parts a little. Whispering to her softly, he asked, "Do you want me to be inside of you?"

Oh. Groaning, she thrust against him. "Yes. Please. Be my first."

"I don't know how to tell you how honored I am."

Geez, why did I remind him of my inexperience? But at least he was taking off his shirt. What did he have on his chest? "Is that new?"

"Yeah. I wanted my little tiger to know she's my first. No one's ever been in my heart before."

Tears sprung to her eyes. Boon-nam reached out to trace the colored lines etched over his heart. The skin was a little red, but she could see the picture. "It's a tiger."

"Yeah." He captured her fingers and squeezed a little of the healing ointment the tattoo parlor gave him onto them.

She carefully traced the ointment over the picture on his skin. "Did it hurt?"

He smiled. "Probably. But it was worth it."

She wasn't even going to try to figure out what he was saying. She'd never have imagined anyone doing such a gesture for her. Pushing away the sorrow, she focused on the man over her.

"Take me."

Jake lowered his mouth back to her. He gave her teasing little licks until he'd reheated her to the point of boiling. She begged.

Jake opened the nightstand drawer, pulled out a bottle, and squeezed—a reminder that she needed lubrication.

"I'm sorry we have to use… ohhhhh."

Her apology was lost as his wet finger slid into her. He rubbed wetness into her gently. She arched off the bed. "Never apologize for giving me a reason to touch you."

Swallowing, she nodded as he added another wet finger. As it stroked into her, she realized he was talking. "What?"

"Are you sure you want to do this? 'Cause we can do something else," Jake asked as his fingers teased her.

Boon-nam had never been so sure of anything before. "I want you." She thrust onto his fingers, trying to get enough friction to come. Again, as soon as she was close to coming, he pulled away. Boon-nam whined and probably sounded like a wanton trollop.

"Shhh, I will be right there." He sheathed himself in a condom.

"Hurry," she said in a breathy voice unlike her own.

Jake hovered over her and settled his lower half between her legs, teasing her with his condom-covered cock. Brushing her long hair out of the way, Jake surrounded one of her nipples with his lips. He sucked on her breasts until she was sure she'd die if he didn't take her.

He backed away to line himself up with her. She reached out to touch the tiger over his heart. Slowly, very slowly, he slid inside her tightness.

Jake's low, quiet "Ahh" filled the room.

"*Dtem!*" He was inside her. Inside her body, she was complete. Relieved there was no pain, she stared up at her very own god of sex. His eyes were studying her carefully as if he were protecting her from everything bad in the world.

The total connection between them made this perfect. Physically she understood the act, but she hadn't anticipated how much tighter their entwinement would be after sharing their bodies with each other. Still it wasn't enough. She dug her nails into his ass to get him as deep inside her as he could go.

"No need to rush, tiger. I'm right here."

He gave her another inch as she purred her approval. Incredible. Jake pulled out farther only to push back into her deeper.

"*Di!*" She loved his body in hers. This was fabulous, and she pleaded for more. "Come on, Jake. *Khun!*" She pushed up into him in case he didn't understand her words.

Jake's bad boy grin of victory made her tingle. Soon he found a teasing rhythm that made her pant. "You're heaven, Boon. Just like heaven."

She squeezed his butt as he thrust into her. But when Jake started swiveling his hips for her pleasure, she was certain she'd lose her mind. Her body didn't seem to know what it needed beyond "more" and "now." But based on their last two experiences, she trusted Jake to know how to satisfy her. She just lay back and enjoyed everything he did to her.

He leaned down to press affectionate kisses over all her face. "You okay, tiger?" Jake asked between kisses.

She opened her eyes. "*Khaa*, Jake." She giggled at herself when she realized she'd told him yes in Thai. She answered again, "I'm more than okay."

"Good. Your body fits mine perfectly." He seemed to vibrate as he thrust in and out of her. "You're really okay?"

"Oh, Jake, I love… it." She almost admitted something that would ruin everything. Hopefully he didn't catch it.

He paused in his thrusting to stare deep into her eyes. He didn't say anything, but in that moment no doubt existed. He was aware of what she'd almost let slip. Jake took her hands, touching them to the tiger tattoo directly over his heart before he kissed them.

She didn't speak because in the next moment her mouth captured his.

He touched all the parts inside her that craved his touch. There was no air in the room. *Close.* Her body built toward orgasm.

"Jake?" Boon-nam didn't even know what she was asking. She prayed he knew what she needed. She writhed against the sheets, trying to reach her peak. The soft cotton rubbing against her back grew damp as Jake labored over her like a sexy dream.

She held her breath right before she cried out his name. She had no words. Her body started trembling and wonderful waves of pleasure washed over her. Again and again her insides shivered around Jake as she shattered into blissful pieces of mindless delight.

Distantly she felt Jake stiffen and grunt as he melted into her satisfied body.

"I didn't hurt you, did I?"

"Mm-mm. No." She stretched after he separated from her to deal with the condom.

"As beautiful as you are on the outside, nothing compares to what shines from your inside."

He tenderly kissed her face and murmured sugary words of praise in her ear. She didn't know how much of his candied words to believe, but she didn't care.

"It was good for you?"

She giggled. Was he not there? "You made my first time everything I ever hoped it would be and more."

Jake settled down, and tension she hadn't realized he was carrying seemed to leave his body. "It won't always work like that because timing can be a bitch sometimes. But you should always tell me if you need something else. Okay? 'Cause I know you have toys, and you know I know how to use them."

As sexy as Jake was, he talked too much after sex. Giggling, she told the worrywart, "Shh, sleep." She pressed her lips to Jake's heart, then fell asleep within his strong, protective arms.

Chapter Fourteen

HOURS FLEW by as the days ticked down on the big vacation clock that everyone tried to ignore. No one wanted to talk about the big multicolored, shiny-with-bright-lights, Thai elephant in the room.

Randy couldn't believe they only had a few days of vacation left.

Lalana was more subdued and laughed less. Randy's heart broke with the distance his Lalana put between them. Without a fight, Lalana seemed braced for the end of their time, but she didn't try to stop the ticking clock. Her acceptance of the pain hurt him. Randy mourned the loss of Lalana, and he hadn't even left her yet.

So much had happened in the last two weeks, he could hardly believe his good fortune. True, his relationship with Lalana had occurred quickly, but he couldn't deny how right he felt being with her. He'd found answers to questions he wasn't aware he'd asked. With Lalana, pieces of his life fell into place and made sense. His entire world changed.

And he wanted to make the change permanent.

Randy cringed at telling Jake what he planned on doing. But he'd put it off as long as he could. Lalana and Boon-nam had to go to an early-morning practice, so it was just him and Jake for breakfast.

"You okay?" Randy was almost afraid, lest Jake jump down his throat.

"No. Goddammit, I feel like shit. For the last few nights, Boon-nam has cried herself to sleep." Jake rubbed a hand over his heart.

Last night's dinner had been a soul-crushing affair. Poor little Boon-nam could barely hold back her tears. Every time her gaze landed on Jake, she misted up. Several times she'd rushed off to "fix her face" with Lalana not far behind her. However, her red-rimmed eyes told everyone she'd been weeping her heart out in the ladies' room, and if there were any doubts, the daggers Lalana tossed at Jake removed them.

Jake ran a hand through his hair and stopped midway to pull it. He shook his head. "I don't ask her what's wrong, because I know what's wrong...."

Randy cleared his throat before saying, "I'm sorry, man."

He ate a bit of his ham-and-cheese omelet, wishing he could taste it. His timing was for shit, but if he didn't tell someone, he'd go crazy. Randy hoped Jake would handle what he needed to say better than he expected.

"Can I talk to you about something?"

"Course, bud. What's up?" Jake shoveled another spoonful of cereal into his mouth. How he ate dry cereal without milk was anyone's guess. He sat up straighter while trying to mute his loud crunching noises.

"I want to marry Lalana," Randy blurted out the words as if they burnt his tongue.

"What the fuck?"

He'd steeled himself for this response. "I love her. I can't imagine my life without her."

"But you haven't known her very long."

"Jake, I'm the happiest I've ever been in my life. She's amazing, and I want to spend my life with her." Randy could only hope, in time, Jake would understand.

Jake's eyes widened, and he gawked at Randy for a long moment. Then Jake jumped up so fast the chair he sat on almost tipped over. Other people in the hotel restaurant looked at them in mild alarm. Jake dashed around the table and grabbed Randy up into a big man-hug.

He shook his head. "Rand, I am happy for you. I certainly have no right to judge. But Boon-nam didn't mention it. When did you ask Lalana?" Jake slapped Randy on the back and returned to his seat.

Randy sighed and took a sip of coffee before admitting, "I haven't yet."

Jake nodded as if the movement helped him digest the information. "Okay. When are you going to ask her?"

"The girls have practice all day today. I'm heading off to go to the Office of Immigration and see what's what. I need to understand what's even possible."

"Well, with the Defense of Marriage Act struck down, you can get her a green card." Jake high-fived him.

Jesus, would Lalana even allow herself to be considered male to get a green card? One step at a time, but he needed to get information first. Randy forced himself to eat some more of his omelet.

"You want to tag along?" He would appreciate the moral support.

"Course," Jake mumbled around more cereal.

Randy shrugged and gave him a grateful smile. "Thanks for not questioning me and thinking I'm crazy."

"Didn't say you weren't crazy." Jake snorted. But before Randy got his nose out of joint, he added, "But not for wanting to marry Lalana. She doesn't like me much, but I can tell she cares about you a whole lot."

Randy was a little embarrassed, but his smile returned. "She's warming up to you." He grinned over at his best friend. "You're like a fungus. You'll grow on her."

"I'd rather consider myself an STD."

"You're an idiot." Randy inhaled and exhaled. "We're okay?" After Jake's nod, he continued, "I don't know. There's the fact she's still...."

Jake rolled his eyes. "She still has her boy equipment. Please! You know my cock has always been about equal opportunity. I don't believe in gender boundaries—way too limiting—you know that."

"No, you idiot. I mean her papers will say she's male even though she's not, and I don't think there's a way around that here in Thailand."

Jake grinned. "Yeah, the Thai government only accepts the genetics of birth. It's ass backward, but whatever, it's a fucking piece of paper."

"I hope she feels that way." Randy could only cross his fingers and pray to all the deities it wouldn't stop them from being together if that's what she wanted—and that was a big if.

Jake leaned over the table with a lecherous grin. "So tell me, you liked the sex, huh?"

Jesus, Jake was a jerk. Randy felt his face heat up as he admitted, "Well, yeah." He shrugged. "I never thought I would... like having sex that way." Or sex anyway, if he were honest with himself.

Jake tilted his head and surveyed him as if he were an alien. "What? Ass sex? Or having another cock?" His voice was a bit too loud, causing several people to glare at them.

"She doesn't have a cock," Randy snapped.

"Fine. I'm sorry. Don't tell Boon-nam, 'cause she'll kick my ass. You know the girls down at the club back home thumb their noses at anything politically correct."

"This isn't about politically correct, it's about respect."

Jake nodded. "True."

Still flustered and needing to drive home his point on respect, Randy added, "Do you know that the Thai government won't even acknowledge Boon-nam as a female? If she commits a crime, she'd go to a male penitentiary."

"Are you shitting me?" Randy was able to see all the fancy dental work Jake's dentist had done in the past few years.

"No, that's why it's important to speak mindfully. At least in the USA, they're beginning to make changes to the laws and evolving their processes so they can catch up."

Jake sat there for a moment, appearing rather unhappy. He shook his head and brought them back to his second-favorite subject. "So the sex...."

"Shh, quiet down. Jesus, you're loud." Randy laughed in spite of himself.

Jake rolled his eyes and mocked a whisper, "Which way?" One didn't have to struggle to imagine what Jake was referring to. He was like a curious seventh grader, although Randy was positive he had less tact.

Randy chuckled at Jake's persistence. "Either. Both. Jesus, why do you want to know?"

"Just wondering. Dude, you liking...." Jake stopped. "You enjoying anything sexual is rather impressive and a tribute to Lalana. 'Cause I questioned if you ever enjoyed your wife."

"Hey, she's still a friend. And I like sex just fine."

"So what about your *issue*?"

Jake tried to diplomatically refer to Randy's erectile dysfunction. However, Randy could have done without Jake's limp index finger dangling in front of his face.

"This is what I get from drinking too much with you," Randy laughed. He barely remembered his drunken confession to Jake, wondering if he had been asexual because he had very little interest in sex with his wife.

Jake's grin got bigger as he leaned back in his chair. "No more issues?" His finger popped up straight.

"None." He almost felt proud when his hand swept out to knock away Jake's finger, because the problem had disappeared.

"I'm happy for you, man." Jake surveyed the restaurant and lowered his voice. "But seriously, you like… um, everything?"

Randy covered his eyes for a moment, but his wish of Jake disappearing didn't happen, so he leaned over the table a bit. "Don't know if I like *everything,* but I love Lalana."

"You love *all* of her?"

Why does this need to be clarified? Jesus, Jake can be a pain in the ass. Randy closed his eyes for a moment, and the vision of Lalana spread out on his bed with her erect clit pushing against her satin panties was enough to make him hard.

"Love every inch of her."

Jake got serious for a moment. "Do you love her or love the sex?"

Wow. Is Jake going there? Does he think I'm into Lalana as a fetish? His anger calmed a little because he'd asked himself the same question. Was he just enamored by someone who could get him off in such a satisfying way? Hell, no. Even if they never had sex again—perish the thought—he would still want to spend every day of the rest of his life with her.

He wanted to hold her hand and share his life with her, just as he wanted to share hers as they grew old together. "Her. The sex is just an amazing benefit."

Jake folded his arms and appeared rather amused. "You do remember I took you to several male strip clubs, drag clubs, and tried to get you to go to the BDSM club," he bragged as if he should be given extra credit.

Is he hoping for something to counterbalance the points taken off for being a dick on the friendship test?

Laughing, Randy said, "How could I forget? You collected a ton of numbers. I expected the strippers to start handing you dollar bills."

Jake snorted. "Whatever! I'm trying to understand you. Why Lalana?"

Randy's cheeks were hot. "In terms of sexual attraction, if you must be a nosy bastard, I find her unique dual energy very alluring. Lalana is very feminine, but there's a strong undercurrent, which comes out sometimes. That's just who she is, you know?" Randy wasn't willing to tell Jake he relished the times when she went all aggressive and possessive on him. "She's sexy as hell."

Jake smirked at him. "Adjust your pants there, buddy."

He cursed himself when he glanced down.

"Made you look."

"Ass."

"All joking aside, I am happy for you. I truly am. As long as she's good to you, and you're good to her. You feel me?" Jake chewed the last bites of his cereal.

"No, I don't feel you because doing that would upset Boon-nam," Randy teased. Jake's face lit up when he mentioned her name. "So you and Lalana talked. I never did ask you how your conversation went." Jake whirled his head up from his empty bowl to stare at him. "No worries. She didn't tell me what you two talked about, only that you seemed like a nice guy."

"Really?" Jake probably found Lalana not hating him hard to believe, but he clearly hoped it was true. "Yeah, I asked her about Boon-nam's surgery and stuff."

Randy nodded and waited to see if Jake would continue. He hadn't asked Lalana what they'd talked about, but he figured the only thing they had in common would be the topic of discussion: the subject of Boon-nam.

Shrugging, Jake played with his coffee cup. "Didn't want to hurt her, you know?"

"But haven't you been with other women who went through the surgery?" Randy knew Jake had several friends-with-benefits relationships with various women, including one who'd shared that she'd had surgery.

Jake shrugged and nodded. "But Boon was—" He appeared to be having trouble picking the right word. He finally settled on: "—innocent."

"As in virgin?" Boon-nam did appear sweet and naïve, but complete innocence seemed astonishing.

"As in yes." Jake laughed. "I've been with a couple of ladies who had surgery, but never anyone who was... *pure* in that sense of the word. I did some research online, but I wanted to make sure I covered all the bases. I wanted Boon-nam to enjoy... everything, you know?"

"And she did?" Randy asked, realizing it wasn't any of his business. But since Jake usually shared the details of his sex life freely, he didn't take the question back.

"Yeah." Jake glanced away. "Thank fuck. I was dying. You always remember your first time."

"Or try like hell to forget it." Randy tamped down the unwanted memory of a pretty redhead and the back of his father's SUV. Trying to seduce Mindy Stubbins into sexual ecstasy was the first in a long list of sexual disasters.

Jake didn't notice Randy's trip down the memory lane of inadequacies that lined the corners of his mind, so he caught up to what his friend shared.

"It was never like this for me before. Being with Boon-nam made me feel like it was more than *just* sex, you know?" Jake sounded embarrassed by his emotions. He cleared his throat and stared at Randy as if waiting for judgment.

"Love?"

Jake didn't comment, but also didn't give him an eye roll or a sound of disgust. *Hm, interesting.* Jake pulled up his T-shirt.

"What are you—" Randy shut up when he saw the tiger tattooed over his best friend's heart. *Damn.* Jake yanked down his T-shirt.

"So, um, yeah… I used all of Lalana's advice, which helped. The websites she gave me were much better than the ones I'd found. They were from local doctors who specialize in affirmation surgery."

Randy watched him. He'd known Jake was into Boon-nam, but hadn't been aware his boy was head over butt in love.

"It was the best ever. She's angelic. And I don't know how to say this without sounding stupid, but being with her was important… magical. You know, the experience meant something. It wasn't just sex. I can't imagine my life without her."

"Really?" *Wow.*

"I keep thinking about all the places I want to share with her. I want to see her hold a panda, watch her cuddle a koala and go on a safari with her. I want… my little tiger."

A thousand emotions chased across his best friend's face before Randy could catalog them all. He had to ask, "So, you're coming to immigration for more than just to keep me company?"

Jake set his coffee cup down and gaped at Randy. His smile went big. "Well, fuck! I guess I am." He seemed to process everything for a minute before slapping his palms on the table and standing up. "Yeah. Yeah, I want the information."

Randy patted him on the back. "Come on. Let's get a taxi card from the front desk to the Office of Immigration."

FINALLY THEIR number was called. A bitter little man with a pinched face waited for them impatiently behind his counter. "Bride male or female? Or do you even know?" His attitude screamed, *I hate tourists!*

Jake opened his mouth, but Randy stopped him with a small kick and spoke up. "Transgender female who's had surgery and one female, um, *kathoey*." He didn't know, based on the government stance, how to state the gender.

"Two men can't get married here in Thailand." The nasty little clerk started pulling papers together in two stacks as he glared at them.

Jake watched Randy's patient smile. "I don't even know if she has a passport."

The twerp behind the counter snorted. "Typical. What are you planning to do?"

"I hoped to get married and return to the United States."

"Any biological kids?" the snarky man asked, knowing pregnancy would be a medical impossibility.

"Er, no."

Jake chimed in. "Not yet. But they're going to keep trying." He slapped Randy on the back as the little man turned purple. Jesus, Jake was an ass, but a funny one.

"Your intendeds will need to fill these out." His voice took on a monotone as he described the process. "You won't be able to get married here. You need to marry in America, where same-sex marriage is legal in some of your states." He held up his finger. "They should fill out an H-1B for special worker permit or tourist visas to visit the country."

"So we could get married once we return?" The man shrugged, sending the message that their lives were of no consequence to him. Jake continued to write down all the information. "So they can work or go to school if they want to?"

The little man cocked his head and peered closely at Jake. "Yes." He pulled some more forms and added them to the stack. "You want a school visa too?" he asked, like he didn't quite believe the question was necessary.

"Yeah, we don't know whether they want to work or go to school yet." He shrugged at Randy. "Boon-nam said Lalana was really smart and always wanted to go to college."

Randy beamed. "She is." Turning back to the man giving them the evil eye, he smiled. "Sir, please make sure we have information for the student visas. Would that be separate from the K-3?"

"The K-3 is a student application." The clerk pointed out with irritation.

"Yes, I know."

Apparently the student visa application gave him pause. He studied Randy before he eyed Jake. "You would send her to school?" The man had disbelief in his voice.

Jake shrugged. "If she wants to go, of course he would. Why?"

The man's face no longer appeared angry and disgust morphed into a surprisingly happy and helpful man. He spoke low to them as if he were telling them state secrets, "Sometimes *farang* make big promises and take our young people back to their country. They're put in bad places and made to work too much or do bad things." His eyes went to the crowd waiting to be seen.

Jake and Randy followed his gaze to look at the people filling the waiting room. Some of them looked like they would steal your eyeteeth if you opened your mouth too long. Maybe it didn't excuse the clerk's rude behavior, but at least Randy understood it.

"Look, if our girls say yes to us, we'll treat them like princesses," Jake stated.

The man nodded his approval. "Okay, sirs." He added a couple of forms that had been missing from their pile. "Here are all the papers you need. Return them to my attention, and I'll help speed your processing time." He clipped his personal card on the top of each stack. "Here's my card."

"I've been so excited, I didn't even consider the timing of everything." He stared at Jake before addressing the man behind the desk. "How long does the process take?"

"Usually a month or two." The little man smiled with the immense power his position allowed. "But if you put your packet to my attention, I can process everything in less than two weeks."

Two weeks! Randy and Jake smiled at the guy. "Thank you very much." Randy stuck out his hand to shake hands. Jake did the same.

Hailing a taxi, Randy asked, "Do you think Lalana will want to go to school?"

"Not sure. Boon-nam told me she loved studying when she and Lalana moved into Illusions & Dreams. Maybe they will both go. We can be married to sexy coeds." Chuckling, Jake gave the taxi driver their hotel card for the address, before he added, "Now all we have to do is ask."

This was a huge step. Randy'd already crashed and burned once. While Jake sidestepped relationships, let alone commitment, this was what he wanted more than anything else in the world.

He took a deep breath. "There are literally hundreds of reasons Lalana could say no. We haven't known each other for very long, but the connection between us is undeniable. I love her."

"You're just scared, man. Have some faith and stop spinning yourself into circles."

"I can't help it. There's so many reasons she could say no." He pointed out the obvious, even if Jake didn't want to acknowledge it. Randy had crashed and burned too many times.

"She loves you, man. Just relax."

Randy sighed. "Easier said than done."

Chapter Fifteen

ILLUSIONS & Dreams was dark, so the girls had the night off. Jake and Randy planned romantic dinners in order to pop the question. Jake took Boon-nam to the Four Seasons for their special Thai dinner show.

"Randy's taking Lalana to a fancy new restaurant that recently opened. But I thought we'd have more fun here," Jake rambled, trying to use Lalana as a subject to get Boon-nam to speak.

Once Boon-nam settled into her seat, Jake couldn't stop complimenting her. "You look charming in your white sundress." As he stared at her, he realized he loved everything about her. "I love... your sandals. They make your bare feet sexy."

His rambling compliments broke through her sadness. "Are you okay, Jake?"

No. "Yes, fine." He was insane with the need to wipe the pain off her face but decided to stick to his plan. He'd ordered champagne and flowers to be sent to his room for after dinner, where he'd propose. It was an excellent plan. He wanted them to be able to enjoy complete privacy as they started their life together.

They sat outside, but the Four Seasons denied Mother Nature her propensity for making people perspire by cooling the area with misting fans. Jake glanced around the hotel grounds, which appeared to be a Thai village—or at least what his tourist's mind envisioned as a perfect Thai village. Tiny thatched-roofed huts littered the expanse of green grass, and the staff wore traditional Thai garb.

"Shall we check out the food stations?" Each station set up in a little hut had a different specialty of Thailand.

"Yes." Boon-nam stood before Jake could hold her chair for her. They strolled to the next station. "I know you need to skip the raw vegetables here in Thailand, so let's go directly for the meat."

Jake prepared to make a joke about Boon-nam liking Jake's meat, but Boon-nam's somber mood made the funny die on Jake's tongue. He wanted to shout to the heavens for her to marry him. He didn't want her to dwell on the fact that this was supposed to be their last night together. He needed to stick to the plan.

She explained each of the dishes and which part of Thailand they originated from. Each sounded delicious. Even though he wasn't hungry, Jake took some of each type of meat. Boon-nam barely had anything on her plate.

They wandered through the remaining food huts. Jake added food to his without even hearing what he'd not be eating. *Damn it,* Boon-nam appeared to have come unglued.

He was relieved when the show started, but wished they had sneaked out. Their table happened to be front and center. Slipping out now would be an insult to the performing troupe. He endured the traditional and modern Thai dances. Boon kept dabbing at her eyes, and Jake counted the minutes until he could get her alone.

"It's not as good as your show," Jake whispered when the last song came to its conclusion.

Only a ghost of a smile graced her lovely face to acknowledge the compliment. After the applause she bolted to the ladies' room. When she trudged back to his side, her red-rimmed eyes told him what she'd been up to in the restroom.

Anxiously he took her back to the hotel to end their pain. He'd been crazy to follow the original plan. Waiting to implement his damned idea started to seem cruel, but he'd wanted his proposal to be special.

He gave up on trying to make conversation. Boon-nam's words came out as a sob. Finally, as he shut the door to his room, Boon-nam flittered over to smell the big arrangement of flowers.

Jake hoped she liked them. "Those are for you."

"Thank you." Her voice held none of her usual zest or glee.

He needed to propose. Jake opened the bottle of champagne and poured two glasses. He raised his up in a toast. A tear slid down Boon-nam's face as she raised the delicate crystal flute to join his.

Jake toasted, "To the most wonderful woman I've ever met." They clinked and drank.

Since Boon-nam gulped her drink, Jake bit back a smile and poured another glass of bubbly. She raised it to her lips, but he stopped her from throwing the champagne back like a shot. He cleared his throat and held his glass back up, entwined their arms together, and drank.

The romantic gesture seemed to choke Boon-nam up further. He was dying here. More tears ran down her face as she bravely tried to smile.

Jesus, the time was now or never. Jake took their glasses and set them aside on the desk. He had a whole big speech planned about how she'd become the most important person in the world to him, how much he loved her, and how he needed her in his life, but those sentiments could wait.

The deep need to wipe the misery off her face overwhelmed him. He pulled a box out of his pocket and dropped to one knee. "Boon-nam, will you marry me?"

Jake was glad she'd positioned herself near the couch, because when her knees buckled, he was barely able to guide her back onto it. She plopped down and stared at him as if he were the oddest thing she'd ever seen. Many emotions raced across her expressive face: shock, happiness, sadness, and now—*fuck*—resignation?

She sniffed wetly and swallowed hard. "Thank you, Jake. But I can't leave." Her voice was bleak like her gaze.

Is she a prisoner? "Of course you can." Nothing could be simpler. She'd fill out a ton of paperwork, they'd board a plane, fill out more paperwork, get married, and live happily ever after. It was a good plan.

"No, I can't." She was adamant in her claim.

Fuck. "You can't?" Jake clarified. How could he have been wrong? Didn't she love him? He'd never given his heart away. Pain stabbed his guts. Maybe this was the reason he'd never let himself fall in love. 'Cause only stupid fucks get caught out in the open like this. "I thought...."

"I am sorry."

"Sorry?" He was drowning, and the only thing keeping him afloat was repeating her words. His brain rebelled against processing them. Had he misread her? What the fuck did he know about love? Obviously not a single goddamned thing!

Why? Why? He wanted to know why, but *why* didn't really matter when she said no.

Boon-nam unsuccessfully tried to sniff back tears as she rose. Positive she'd vanish right out the door, Jake was surprised when she hesitated at the foot of the bed. As if she'd come to some decision, she unzipped her dress and slid the fabric down her body. She stepped out of the light material and toed off her sandals as if she hadn't just broken his heart.

What was she doing? She'd rejected him, but she undressed as if everything remained copacetic. Boon-nam lay back on the bed, her slender form positioned perfectly as if she were sacrificing herself for his final meal.

She whispered to him, "One last time, Jake. Please, just one more time." Tears rolled down her face.

He wanted to rail against her cruelty, but she was his Thai goddess. Boon-nam offered him one more fix before she'd force him to live without his drug of choice. She'd show him what he'd forever miss. This would be their last night together before he returned to his empty, meaningless life. He wanted to hide from her rejection, but he couldn't take his eyes off her.

He should turn away from her. His sanity depended on it, or maybe the preservation of whatever was left of his pride. Even before he decided, he knew he'd never pass up the opportunity to have her one more time. He'd never deny her.

A tiny spark of hope ignited in his broken heart. Perhaps he could convince her with his body she'd made a mistake. Maybe he'd make her reconsider after she remembered how exceptional they were together. He'd use his body to worship her and prove she craved him the same way. His brain told him he'd gone crazy, but the smashed bits of his heart forced him to try.

Jake ripped off his shirt, destroying the fabric in the process. He kicked off his bamboo sandals, and his linen pants found the floor as he climbed onto the soft mattress next to her. She reached over to pull out their stash of supplies and tossed them next to the pillow. Reaching over, she turned off the lamp, plunging the room into darkness.

Jake's body and mind separated as his hands ran over her silky smoothness. He didn't understand how his body could be in heaven and his mind in the depths of hell. With his soul in tatters, he found solace in focusing on her pleasure, which was slow in coming tonight.

Boon-nam's soft sobs and little sniffs kept his mind on the solution to this problem as if one of his programs had a glitch. This wasn't an error in the code, no easy fix, not for this. She'd said no. The rejection rang in his ears.

He shoved the harsh reality away and traced his mouth in wet trails of worship up and down her body, licking and sucking, letting her moans of appreciation be his guide. He wiggled between her legs to kiss and love her with his mouth and fingers. On and on he licked until she cried out in the surrender of a shuddering orgasm.

He slid up her sated body to hold her close, the physical contact almost blocking the confusion eating his brain. Why couldn't she understand they were meant to be together?

Jake had never fallen in love before, and now he almost wished he never had. Whoever said "It is better to have loved and lost than never to have loved at all" must have been on acid.

This hurt like a motherfucker, but she was still in his arms. His guts were ripped out and stepped on while still attached. Jake didn't want to contemplate the vision of emptiness his life would be without her.

She grabbed a tissue and blew her nose wetly. Tossing the used tissue across the room in the general direction of the trash basket, Boon-nam swung her leg over him to straddle his lap. Without the light he saw only shadows of her in the moonlight.

Boon-nam was the picture of feminine beauty as she sat up on him, cupping her breasts. He reached up to caress the nipples she offered, giving her more aftershocks of pleasure. She took the lubrication and prepped her opening for him. Tears still glistened as they slowly tracked down her face.

Jake should stop her, but he couldn't. He froze as he watched her roll a condom down to his base. She hovered over him and guided him to her entrance, crying out as her body opened up for him.

When he was fully inside her, she leaned forward to kiss his face with what could only be love and said, *"Chan rak khoon maak leeuy!"*

More tears and more Thai words he could never hope to know the meaning of came out of her as she rode his erection, slowly, lovingly, as if she were trying to make it last forever.

Forever. He'd allowed himself the fantasy of forever, but now the dream slipped through his fingers—the things he yearned for and the things he'd be denied. Maybe the white picket fence and growing old together were too clichéd to ever have a place in the real world. He wanted to be angry, but as he watched her writhe above him, he'd give her up without a fight if only to make her happy. He'd learn to go back to his reality without her.

She pressed kisses all over his face twice before capturing his mouth in a heavenly kiss. He'd never appreciated kissing as much as he had in the last couple of weeks. Maybe it was her lack of experience combined with her eagerness to please him, but right then, their fading connection forced him to savor every second. Each touch, kiss, and thrust was a miracle making him hope for the impossible.

She broke the kiss when the need turned too frantic to dance above him to a song in her head. Her rhythm faltered as his hands skated back up to her breasts to caress and fondle their fullness. She collapsed onto him again so that her mouth could capture his in a kiss tasting of desperation and sadness. Immediately he wanted to erase the pain in her kiss as their tongues entwined.

Their movements began to pull out whimpers of pleasure, overriding the tears spilling down her face. She required more from him.

Jake knew instinctively what she lacked. He twisted, flipped, and braced himself over the top of her. He took control. She melted into the bed with a grateful sigh as he thrust into her.

"More," she cried out, tossing her head back and forth on the pillow. Her hair fanned out in a dark silken spill against the white pillowcase. Her hand rested over his heart.

Jake pushed himself deeply inside her again and again, hoping he could outlast what she needed to come. Her tight body clung to his as he pushed them closer to the edge. He wanted to stop and hold on to the moment, but he couldn't.

Seconds later she shattered in his arms, and he joined her in incredible physical pleasure even as his heart broke.

They clung together as they drifted down from the heights no lover was ever allowed to stay at for very long. Boon-nam tried to swallow down her broken sobs and wet breaths but continued to cry as if she'd been the one who'd been rejected. With one hand he took care of the condom but didn't let her go for fear she would slip out of his life.

Jake tightened his arms around her. His heart swelled, wishing he could beg her not to say no, but he wouldn't make this any harder on her. A pathetic part of him wanted to keep her in bed, because he knew as soon as she left, she'd never return.

She cuddled in his arms as he watched the digital clock and tried not to contemplate that this was the end.

Neither one spoke as the silence grew louder. If Jake opened his mouth, he'd beg her to stay. Beg her to marry him. He wanted to tell her he loved her and he would make her happy, but he didn't. He loved her enough to shut the fuck up.

Boon-nam kissed his tattoo and got dressed. Jake tried not to watch but couldn't help himself. In the dark silence of the room before she left, he said, "Thank you… for showing me Bangkok."

On a choked cry, she ran out of his room. The door slammed shut behind her, crushing his hope of happiness.

Chapter Sixteen

LALANA WAS determined to make the best of their time together. Randy had one more night. Tomorrow would be soon enough to wake from this fairy tale and return to her real life, devoid of happily ever after.

She had Boon-nam and her friends at Illusions & Dreams. Some even considered her a star. Lalana did what she loved, with people who loved her. She had been foolish to allow herself to fall in love with an American tourist. What had she expected would happen?

Granted, he was truly the most wonderful man she'd ever met. She'd miss his smart and funny conversations. He always treated her like a lady, but when her more aggressive side reared its head, Randy reveled in it. Lalana had never had a lover accept all of her before, and now she could never settle for less.

If genies were real, she'd have many wishes. She wished she had more time with him, wished she and Boon-nam could have a romance-novel happily ever after, but she didn't wish she hadn't fallen in love with him. She'd be grateful for the time they did have together. The last two weeks had been some of the best moments in her life. As much pain as she would endure, she would never regret a moment.

Her heart would eventually heal. Lalana bit her lip to avoid crying and ruining her makeup as she admitted she would probably never be able to love anyone this deeply again. Not the way she loved Randy—she just couldn't. She'd known the risk, but still lost control of her emotions. Randy was everything she wanted. But she'd survive, as she always had.

Seated in a lovely French restaurant, she smiled at a joke Randy made while ordering for them but couldn't bring herself to laugh. Lalana swallowed a taste of the wine. She glanced around at the fancy restaurant he'd chosen for their last meal together. The chef, a transplant from France, had gotten nothing but rave reviews since the restaurant opened earlier in the year. Too bad she wouldn't be able to taste any of it.

Randy reached across the table and took her hand. She couldn't help but survey the other diners' reaction to his bold display of affection. The pricey restaurant tables were filled with foreigners, which prevented anyone from being offended and casting judgment on their hand-holding.

"Lalana, I know I should wait for dessert, but I can't." Randy grinned like a little boy. "I can't wait."

He brought her hand to his lips, pressing a kiss to her knuckles. Randy had this way of treating her like a princess that made her believe it. Pain skated through every part of her; she'd be devastated without him. She blinked back tears and tried to smile.

"I went to the Office of Immigration today. We can't get married in Thailand, but you could come to America on an H-1B visa. As you know, I live in New York. To me you are all woman, but the man at the Immigration Office said Thailand wouldn't change your passport to reflect your actual gender. But not to worry, even our genetics won't stop us. We can be married in New York. Once we're married, I think you must take a class. I'm not sure, I didn't get a chance to research that, but whatever. You'll be my wife and a citizen as soon as possible. We can figure out how the evolving laws on transgender people will allow your information to be properly recorded on your new United States passport."

Randy spoke so quickly. Was he saying he wanted to marry her? All she could say in response was "What?"

Pulling a black box out of his pocket, Randy opened the top to reveal a big sparkler.

"Will you marry me?"

"What?" she asked again, positive her English translation must be off.

Randy glanced around sheepishly. "Will you marry me?" His face got a little red.

"I don't understand." He couldn't possibly be asking her to *marry* him.

Frowning, Randy squeezed her hand. "I want you to get an H-1B visa, so they will let you come back to America with me. Once we're home and settled, we can get married. It's legal in New York for us to get married."

Quicksand sucked her under. "You want to marry me?"

"Yes." Randy smiled at her, but he appeared not to realize what he was asking her.

Oh my God! He wants to marry me.

She wanted to sing out in complete and utter joy. Lalana wanted to love him every single day of his life, and as his wife, it would be her right to do so. How badly she wanted to say yes. It was everything she wanted, but… everything she could never have.

She couldn't leave Boon-nam. Her Boon-boon needed Lalana as desperately as she needed Boon. It had been the two of them versus the world for the last twelve years. The idea of separating from her was simply unthinkable. Even to live the happily ever after she'd always fantasized about with the man of her dreams, Lalana couldn't leave her sweet little butterfly. Lalana wouldn't abandon Boon-nam even if her heart broke into a million pieces.

Boon-nam would need her more than ever after Jake devastated her. Lalana would have to pick up the pieces of her broken heart so that she could help it mend. Her own heart didn't matter when she focused on how much Boon-nam had suffered. Her little butterfly would be destroyed when Jake went home. Lalana couldn't leave her too.

"Lalana?" Randy asked, his upset spilling over into his voice.

She tried frantically not to disgrace herself by letting the tears gathering in her eyes fall, because if they started, she didn't know if they would stop.

Taking a deep breath, Lalana broke their hearts in a single word: "Can't."

She shook her head and repeated to stop Randy's protests, "Can't."

Abruptly she jumped up and hurried for the door even as her heart screamed for her to stay with Randy. Lalana made it out of the door before Randy had a chance to stop her. Luck must have been on her side, as a cab instantly freed up. She jumped in and gave her address.

As the vehicle pulled away, she couldn't resist one last vision of the man who'd stolen her heart. Randy stood at the top of the restaurant steps, reaching out a hand to her. She turned away but heard him call out her name.

"Can't," she whispered to herself. She could no longer deny the tears, and they started to roll down her face.

TONG WAS first person to see Lalana as she hurried toward her room, wanting desperately to crawl underneath the covers and fall apart.

"Oh, fuck!" Tong put an arm around her shoulders and dragged her into her private room. "Tell me what the fuck happened. Whose ass am I kicking? Because I've got lots of different kinds of shoes to do the job properly."

Lalana sniffled and tried to calm Tong down. "'*Fuck.*' Is that a new word I missed last class?"

Tong ignored her poor attempt at a joke and pushed Lalana toward a little chair and made her sit. Tong stepped over to her small kitchen area and made some tea in her hot pot. She didn't have a roommate because she was the manager of the club, and she'd decorated her room in gold, accented with jewel tones.

A glance in the mirror explained Tong's concern. Lalana had fixed her face a bit, but she couldn't do much. She braced herself for Tong's grilling.

Tong's delicate teacup clinked against the saucer as she stomped over to Lalana. "Here's some lavender tea. I find this particular brew quite relaxing, but only after I add this." She held up a bottle of whiskey and poured a generous amount into Lalana's teacup and then tipped some into her own.

Once she sat on her bed, Tong asked, "So what happened?"

Lalana stalled for time by taking a slow sip of the mostly whiskey 'tea.' Warmth licked down her throat. When she had herself under control, she tried to tell Tong what happened, but she had to stop to hold in the sobs that silently racked her.

Lalana didn't know Tong's history, but she knew it was ugly. Tong was never one for physical displays of affection, so Tong's bear hug shocked her. The unexpected tight squeeze broke the fragile dam she'd built around her tears. A coughing fit finally helped her calm down, along with finishing Tong's special tea.

Tong held her quietly, petting her back as she mourned the loss of Randy and tried to bury her silly dreams. Time slipped away. How much, Lalana wasn't sure.

A shriek in the hallway forced her to pull herself together. *Boon-nam?*

She opened the door. Boon-nam darted past her and begged in Thai for someone to stop Jake.

Jake barreled down the hallway after Lalana's little butterfly. She and Tong stepped in the way, forcing him to stop. When Boon-nam shut and locked the door, Tong called for Jaidee.

"Lalana, please, I only want to talk to her." Jake appeared distraught, and none of his usual bad boy self was present. "I have to talk to her."

Before sympathy could give her bad judgment, she asked him to leave. "Go. She obviously doesn't want to see you."

She sounded bitchy, but she couldn't make herself care. Her own pain twisted in her heart, and she didn't have the patience to be delicate with Jake. He'd obviously broken her little butterfly's heart, so he'd gotten what he deserved.

A scowl marred Jaidee's handsome face when he entered the hallway. He wisely brought a couple of the other boys who could help him assist Jake to find the door if need be.

"Please, Lalana. Please help me." Jake sounded desperate.

When he got no sympathy from her, Jake allowed himself to be escorted downstairs and out the front door.

Lalana sighed. There was no help for any of them.

Tong came and stood by her side. "If you need more special tea or need to talk, you know where I am."

No more talking. Spiked tea held a lot of appeal, but Boon-nam needed her. "Thank you, Tong." Lalana grabbed her hand to squeeze it. "You are a true friend."

"Always." Tong smiled sadly and tightened her hand around Lalana's. "Go see to Boon-nam. The poor little girl needs you. Fucking foreign assholes… I hate men."

As Lalana passed the stairs, she watched Jaidee turn abruptly and sneak quietly down the staircase. She turned to tell Tong that Jaidee might have misinterpreted what she said, but Lalana could hear Boon-nam's weeping. She'd tell Tong later.

Their door was locked. Lalana's bag was probably on Tong's bed, so she didn't have the key. She gently tapped on the door. "It's me, Boon-boon. Open up."

Boon-nam scuffled over to the door and unlocked it.

Before Lalana shut the door, Boon scurried back to her bed and wailed into her pillow. Inhaling deeply, Lalana closed her eyes for a moment to find strength, because she wanted to do the same thing.

She pushed her pain away to focus on her little butterfly. Boon's bed shifted under her weight as she sat down to stroke her back. "It will be okay, Boon-boon."

No answer came, only more tears. Eventually Boon-nam stopped to blow her nose. Lalana held out her arms, and the younger woman flew right into them to hug her close. Lalana hoped Boon-nam hadn't noticed she'd been crying too.

She let her own tears fall while the two of them held onto each other as if the world depended on them being together.

And their world did.

Chapter Seventeen

IT WAS an hour or two after Randy's illusions and dreams had imploded. He was sitting in the hotel bar, halfway to drunk, when Jake plopped down next to him.

Jake waved the bartender over. "I'll have what he's having."

Once the bartender delivered Jake's drink, Randy muttered, "What? You've developed a taste for heartbreak and despair?"

"Fuck. I'm sorry, man, but I'm already there, my friend." Jake played with the napkin under his drink.

"What? Boon-nam said no?"

"She ran out of the room crying. As fucked up as I am, I even chased her through the fucking streets of Bangkok." He lifted the drink to his lips and sipped the golden liquid.

"I only need a couple of dozen of these for the numbness to kick in. Hopefully the humiliation of chasing her back to her apartment will be erased."

"What happened?"

Jake sipped his drink before continuing. "Lalana and the hostess we met our first night here, they blocked me while Boon locked herself in her room. Some of the guys *walked* me out."

Jake signaled the bartender for more. "Glad they serve alcohol for breakfast." He took a swig of the scotch the bartender had put in front of him.

Randy needed to know. "You saw Lalana? How was she?"

"Buddy, you're drinking to forget her, or have you forgotten that?" Jake threw back the drink and gestured for another. He put his hands on his face and took so long to answer, Randy wondered if he'd fallen asleep. "Lalana looked like she'd been crying."

"Crying?" Randy asked with a frown. He hated that he'd upset her.

"Yeah, she was a mess. Her eyes were all puffy, and she kept sniffling. Though she was totally ready to kick my ass. She wouldn't let me past her to get to Boon. Protective as ever."

Randy nodded. "Yeah." He bowed his head and tried not to imagine how he'd go home without her.

"Why did Lalana say no?"

Randy shook his head in confusion. "I don't know. When I first asked her, she seemed ecstatic, like I'd had the best idea ever. And thirty seconds later, she told me couldn't marry me." He shrugged. "All I can figure out is I guess she loves singing and performing more than me."

He took another drink, but his half-pickled mind couldn't figure it out. "Why'd Boon-nam say no?" Randy had concluded Jake had a sure thing.

Jake patted him on the shoulder. "I have no clue. She smiled happily right after I asked her. Then she burst into tears and started sobbing in Thai. She claimed she couldn't leave Bangkok. Maybe you're right. Maybe they love performing more than us."

"You really chased her back to the club?" Randy tried to imagine the scene.

"Yeah, I chased her down like a freaking crazy man. That's when Lalana stood in my way, and a bunch of the guys helped me out the door."

Randy winced. "You get hurt?"

"Nah, just kicked in the teeth by a pair of high heels. I can't believe it." He drank the new drink. "She had the most delectable tiny feet, with sparkling toenail polish. I don't get it. I thought we had something."

"Me too." Randy sighed. "She looked at you like you were a god." Randy elbowed him and tried to make a joke. "Granted she didn't know you very well."

"I really believed she loved me, Rand." Jake sounded lost.

She *did* love Jake. Randy had been sure of Boon-nam's feelings for him, and he'd been confident she would jump at the chance of a happily ever after. Something wasn't making sense. "She does. I know she does. Maybe the offer overwhelmed her. Maybe—"

"Maybe you're grasping at straws," Jake said skeptically.

Misery kept Randy quiet for a while, then, "I think we should go to the club tonight."

"What kind of masochistic bastard are you?" Jake was annoyed by the suggestion. "Are you insane? That's simply begging to get rejected again. Wasn't once enough for you?"

"Look, maybe they'll change their minds." Randy put his hand up to stop the flood of reasons why showing up at their place of work could be a bad idea. "Maybe they won't, but I want Lalana to have my contact information, you know, just in case."

Jake snorted. "Fine, but we do this now."

Randy would take it. It would be the closest thing he'd get for confirmation. "I'll meet you at the lobby door in a half an hour."

Jake shook his head. "Don't get your hopes up."

Randy nodded. "It probably won't change a thing, but I want to make sure I did everything I could. No regrets!"

"Sure, what's one more kick in the balls? No regrets." Jake shook his head. "Why do I think I'm going to regret this?"

Randy chuckled. "Shut up and go shower. If nothing else, we can give them our contact information."

THE HEAT was brutal as they pounded on the side door of Illusions & Dreams.

"Illusions & Dreams is dark tonight, and the bar closed a half hour ago." The man called Jaidee waved them off.

"We don't want to drink. We want to give Adirake something." Randy said loud enough to be heard through the closed glass door.

A click of recognition passed across Jaidee's face, and he unlocked the door. He shouted something in Thai and then growled to them, "Get the fuck out of here."

The muscle-bound guy clearly had the power to kick the shit out of one if not both of them. But then several other hulking performers stood behind him as backup. Fuck, he and Randy were going to get their asses handed to them.

"We need to see Adirake." Jake pushed past Jaidee, but the performers grabbed him and escorted them directly to Adirake's office. Randy followed.

Jaidee knocked on the door and opened the ornate carved wood as Adirake called out, "Enter."

"Hey, Jaidee. Remind me not to fill in as a bartender on Island night." His voice changed dramatically when he noticed Jake and Randy. "What the hell are you two doing here?"

Adirake reared up from his chair to stomp around his desk piled full of papers. He was dressed much like when they'd first entered Illusions & Dreams almost two weeks ago. Maybe the skirt was a different color, and he didn't wear his coconut bikini, but his face and hair were done up for paradise night at the bar. His outfit appeared feminine, but his stance and attitude befit an aggressive male.

Jake stared at him. *Who the fuck does this asshole think he is by asking such a question? I don't answer to him or anyone, damn it.*

Randy brushed past him to hand the asshole the sheet of paper—with their addresses, e-mails, and cell phone numbers, as well as their landlines—like a peace offering, but Randy hesitated. "Hey, maybe I should put my parents' number on the list, just in case one of us moves or something."

Randy, God love him, peered up at Adirake and asked, "Do you have a pen?"

"What the hell is this?" Adirake inspected the paper filled with their information.

"Just in case Boon-nam or Lalana ever want to contact us, you know," Randy answered him quietly.

Frowning, the jerk handed Randy a pen and the paper while giving Jake the evil eye. Jake broke the stare. If he didn't, he might try to beat the fucker senseless. He'd never win, so he ignored the asshole's smirk and focused on Randy as he added another number and address to the list.

Fuck. Jake was leaving the woman he loved. This was why he avoided pointless endeavors like love. He watched Randy, who appeared to be as miserable as he felt. All the anger and attitude left Jake.

Randy handed back the paper to Adirake, who tossed the slip on his desk and returned to his rolling desk chair.

"Oh, right, you guys are leaving." Adirake appeared irritated and a tad disgusted. "Had your little *kathoey* fantasies fulfilled, and now you go home without looking back."

"Without looking back?" Randy choked on his words, making Jake's temper flare.

Jake wanted to see how long it would take for the bastard to turn a nice shade of purple while his hands got a workout on his neck. Call it an experiment or call it fun, his fingers were itchy.

"I don't know what the two of you did to those girls, but they've been crying since your dates." Adirake glanced over at Jaidee, who was still taking up space in the door, appearing like he would love an excuse to punch them in the face. "Jaidee, could you get Areva and Tong. I'd bet Areva is with Boon-nam, and Tong is with Lalana."

"Sure, Adirake," Jaidee glared at them, seeming annoyed that they hadn't given him a reason to do some damage.

Jake shrugged and rolled his eyes at Randy. "Look, we're not here for any trouble."

"Yeah, well, playing with our girls' hearts is pretty fucked up." Adirake shook his head.

"Dude, we didn't play with their hearts," Jake defended. Fuck, his and Randy's hearts were the ones broken.

Randy rested a hand on Jake's shoulder and squeezed as if asking him to take it down a notch.

Adirake sat back in his chair and folded his arms over his bare chest. "So explain. Why are they crying like they got their hearts shattered?"

Sighing, Randy said again, "Look, we don't want trouble. We aren't here to push ourselves on them. They said no, so... we'll accept that, but—"

Randy's voice wasn't heard over Adirake's bellow.

"You're damned right you aren't going to push yourselves on them! What the hell is wrong with you fucking Americans? Coming here—"

Jake jumped in. "Fuck you!"

"No, fuck you!" Adirake jumped up and shouted in Jake's face. Jake inhaled the sandalwood that rose off Adirake's skin.

The door opened, and a soft feminine voice said, "I thought you only fucked me, Adirake?" The elegant Areva sashayed toward her lover in a traditional long Thai dress in bright eye-hurting red.

"Oh, only you, Areva." Adirake breathed out her name like it was a prayer he reflected on daily.

She sidled over to stand between the two of them. Areva kissed her lover on the cheek as she melted into his side.

Tong stood next to Adirake and Areva and rolled her eyes at them. "Look, no one is fucking anyone. It's late. So fuck tomorrow, you two."

Jaidee arrived at the door and stopped dead. His eyes seemed to rove over Tong's stocking-clad legs to her ass and back again. But Jaidee snapped himself out of his lust fest to refocus his attention back on Adirake.

Turning to Randy and Jake, Tong waved her finger. "Well, I warned them. But Lalana and Boon-nam fell in love. They let themselves believe in love, and what did you two do? You crushed their dreams and proved love is just an illusion. Proud of yourselves?"

What the fuck? Jake watched Randy open his mouth and close it twice, before he opened it again. "Look, we understand they don't want us. We want them happy. All we wanted was to give them our contact information in case they need us, or if they ever change their minds."

"Change their minds?" Adirake demanded with a growl.

Areva gasped at what she must have gotten from Randy's hurried speech. "Don't want you?"

Tong appeared annoyed with everyone. She clapped her hands like they were unruly school children and she was the teacher. Her tone suggested her job was to take charge of chaos.

She stepped toward the middle of the room. "Okay, horny foreigners, one question at a time. Let me understand this."

She pointed her elegantly manicured finger at them. "You two believe *they* don't want *you*?"

Jake grimaced. *What the fuck? Why do they seem to relish torturing us? If Tong wasn't a girl, I'd smack her in the teeth.*

Jaidee had to be a mind reader, or maybe a tell crossed Jake's face, because he stepped toward Jake with a growl.

Jake ignored him. Clearly the guy had anger management issues. "Look, Randy and I know they don't want us."

Each person's mouth dropped open except Randy's.

"This is so good, wish I had some popcorn." Adirake dragged Areva back to his desk chair and took a seat, pulling her onto his lap. After shifting her into an appropriate cuddle position, he chuckled in Jake and Randy's general direction. "I need to ask. What do you think they might change their mind about?"

"Marrying us," Randy admitted barely above a whisper, but everyone heard him.

Adirake started to laugh. Areva frowned before she jumped off his lap to stalk over to Tong. The two women started speaking rapidly in Thai to each other.

Jaidee's eyebrow rose as a slow smile crossed his face. He glanced over at Adirake. Jaidee did the mind-read thing again, because he slipped out of the room, shutting the door behind him.

Adirake's deep laughter grated on Jake's nerves.

"Don't laugh at us! We're aware we've become the typical Bangkok tourist clichés. We're just two stupid Americans falling in love with dazzling Thai women. Whatever."

His humiliation was complete, and "pissed" didn't even begin to describe his mood.

"Come on, Jake." Randy turned toward the door, probably hoping to avoid the fight. Jake was spoiling to knock someone in the mouth, even if he'd have his ass handed to him. He'd had all the humiliation he could suffer in this lifetime. "Just see they get the information."

The door opened, and Jaidee marched in with Boon-nam and Lalana. Boon-nam wore the white sparkly nightgown and feathered cape she'd had on during the show as a robe. Lalana pulled her peach robe around her tighter. Neither one of them would pull their gazes off the ground.

Adirake asked several questions in Thai, which Lalana answered, presumably for both of them. Apparently, it was Areva's turn to ramble a bit.

Jake had no fucking clue what Areva said in Thai, but her words resulted in astonished expressions on the faces of their tightly knit group.

Tong shook her head, still appearing displeased, though she smiled in spite of herself when her eyes landed on Jaidee's big-assed grin.

Adirake chuckled again, probably at their expense.

Jake knew Randy wouldn't leave, not when this would be the last chance to catch a glimpse of Lalana. Randy wouldn't miss a second of breathing the same air Lalana exhaled even if the price was being laughed at by the jackass behind the desk.

Boon-nam listened intently to what Areva said. She started to squeal happily and bounced up and down. Lalana's mouth dropped open before a giant grin of pure happiness changed her face from shocked to thrilled as she hugged Boon-nam in her arms. They talked in Thai briefly with happy shouts and giggles and a big hug.

Jake leaned over to Randy. "What the fuck, dude?"

"Lalana's happy at least. So is Boon-nam." He stated the obvious, not understanding the dynamics of the conversation either.

Boon-nam's squeals got louder right before she launched herself at Jake. He opened his arms in time to catch her. *God, this is where she belongs.* He spit out an escaped feather from her flying cape. He wasn't letting her go ever again. She belonged with him. Didn't she know that?

His hair fell into his face, forcing him to peek through the strands as he tried to put together what the fuck had just happened. Boon hommed him—mm-mm—and started to kiss his face.

Fuck, it didn't even matter. Jake didn't need an instruction manual, just a little privacy. Realizing he'd find none, he settled for a tight squeeze to kiss her back.

Out of the corner of his eye, he watched; Lalana was in front of Randy. She took his face in her hands and stared into his eyes. She held it for a moment and planted a big kiss on his mouth.

Jake still didn't have a clue as to what the hell had changed, but he liked the direction things were taking.

He noticed Adirake ushering everyone else out of the room and heard Tong say, "I don't care what anyone says, love still sucks."

Areva snappily replied, "Only if you're lucky, dear." She skipped out of the office, blowing a kiss to Adirake. He caught the invisible affection and put the imaginary smooch on his cheeks before blowing one back. He hurried after her.

Once they were alone, the girls finally unwrapped themselves but stayed close. Jake was thrilled that Boon-nam remained within touching distance as if she needed to be held.

He stared down at the delectable Thai woman happily dancing in place next to him. "Boon-nam?"

She giggled musically and peeked up at him. "I couldn't leave Lalana. She's been everything to me." To Jake's possessive growl, she smiled and added, "Not that." She held a hand out to Lalana as if she needed the connection with her as well. "She saved me. Without Lalana, I can't be happy." Boon-nam touched Jake's chest above his heart. "Just like I can't be happy without you."

Lalana rested her head on Randy's shoulder. "I've always taken care of my Boon-boon, ever since she was little. I couldn't abandon her."

Smiling sadly, she added, "She's the only family I have ever really had. Please forgive me."

"Nothing to forgive. We should have talked more," Randy said. "Boon-nam is like your sister, best friend, and child all rolled into one. I can't be upset at you for not being able to desert her. But I do feel like an idiot I didn't figure that out."

"Can I still marry you?" Boon-nam grinned at Jake. "Please?" she added, batting her long eyelashes.

Jake tried to frown at her but failed. He ignored his best friend, who laughed at him. Jake had been a goner when she kissed his tattoo. "I accept your proposal, Ms. Rattanawong."

Boon-nam squealed and leapt into his arms. She called out, "Lalana! I'm getting married."

Lalana turned to Randy. She took his hand and kissed it. "Mr. Randy Camster, will you marry me?"

Boon-nam's giggles pealed out from her, even past Jake's hand covering her mouth.

Randy didn't hesitate. "Why of course, Ms. Dulyarat. I'd be honored."

"Boon-boon, I'm getting married too." Lalana fell into Randy's arms.

Jake wasn't sure what happened with them because his arms were full of Boon-nam, and just when they started to get into it, a sharp knock sounded on the door. Damn!

Adirake opened the door and clapped his hands. "Are congratulations in order?" The bastard had the worst timing.

Boon-nam shouted happily, "Yes, I'm getting married, and so is Lala!" She slid down Jake's body slowly, rubbing over his hard erection.

Damn, that was painfully good.

"Wonderful. Wonderful." Adirake kissed both ladies on the cheeks. He shook Randy's and Jake's hands. "We will celebrate soon. But for now it's late, and I have to finish this paperwork. So get the hell out of my office." His smile tempered his words, letting them know he'd been glad the bedlam of their love life had all worked out. "And the visa process can take a while."

"Two weeks," Jake said, enjoying Adirake's reaction.

"Friend at the visa office?" Adirake smiled when Jake nodded. "Good. Will you two be staying?"

"I'm not leaving without my bride," Jake said firmly, to which Boon-nam squealed happily and jumped up and down. He kissed her right on the mouth, not caring if he smudged her lipstick.

"You too?" Adirake asked Randy. When he got a nod, he went on. "Well, since Jaidee and Tong are going on an errand for me, one of the couples can borrow Tong's room."

Through the shut door, Tong shouted, "What errand?"

"We'll talk in the morning," Adirake said to her. He turned back toward Lalana and Boon-nam, "Since you will be here for a couple of weeks, you two ladies can pick and train your replacements for the show. I don't know what you guys do for work, but we have Wi-Fi if that helps."

Randy grinned. "Wi-Fi would help, and thank you for everything."

"Hey, when I figured out your tangled drama, I couldn't let it go. Areva says my need to fix things is one of my many strengths as well as one of my flaws... as if I have flaws." Shrugging, Adirake went off mumbling about how he had a club to run.

Randy wrapped his arms back around Lalana. "Are you really sure?"

"Very sure. Never so sure of anything in my life." She sighed as she tucked herself into Randy's arms.

Boon-nam giggled at Jake. "I'm not even asking," she said as she pushed eagerly against Jake's erection. "I can *feel* that you are sure, very sure. But I think I should get down on my knees and propose properly." She gave a dirty little giggle.

"Hmmm, you are a naughty little tiger, aren't you?" Jake whispered hotly in her ear. "But only if I can get down on mine."

"Oh, Jake." She glanced at the clock before doing what appeared like dibs on their room. "Lalana, I am going to need you to disappear."

Lalana grinned. "Really? Disappear?" She pretended to yawn. "Hmm, I don't think I can. I have nowhere to go. I think I'll go to bed."

"Go to Randy's hotel room," Boon cried out as if it would be a tragedy to have Lalana in their room.

Grinning, Lalana turned to Randy, "Are you tired, Rand?" She let her peach robe slip to the floor, revealing a lacy peach dress with a plunging neckline. Randy's mouth dropped open.

He arched an eyebrow. "Not even a little. Let's go." He grabbed her robe and tossed it over her shoulder. "Let's get you into some clothing." He left with Lalana in a hurry.

Boon-nam squealed and grabbed Jake's hand to drag him up to her room.

Epilogue

Happily Ever After

IT TOOK a little longer than expected to get all their paperwork and passports in order. They made do with the rooms Adirake offered above Illusions & Dreams. Randy and Jake didn't mind the tight quarters, especially since they had their ladies back. Their work could be completed via the fast Internet connection Adirake had installed. Luckily Lalana and Boon-nam's visas were approved.

Once all their paperwork was in order, Boon-nam and Lalana wanted a double ceremony. Jake and Randy realized their two ladies would take America by storm when Boon-nam charmed the airline check-in agent and they'd been bumped up, not to business class, but first class.

The ladies settled into their new lives quite easily. Jake's and Randy's houses were within shouting distance of each other, so Lalana and Boon visited every day. They talked or texted nonstop on their cell phones when they weren't together.

Lalana had already found a job singing on the weekends at the pub Jake and Randy often visited. In the fall, she and Boon-nam were going to attend a local community college to see how they liked school in America. Meanwhile Boon-nam studied to take placement tests to opt out of various 101-level coursework.

Jake didn't have family beyond his sister, Julia. As kids they'd been close, but as adults they had grown apart. Jake always regretted their distance. However, Boon-nam seemed to bridge the gap and eliminated the void that had grown between them.

Hell, within the first week, Jake's sister agreed to weekly family dinners just because her adopted little sister wanted her to visit. She confessed to always wanting a younger sister, and didn't blink an eyelash when Boon-nam admitted she had been born a male. Julia shrugged as if she'd learned an interesting fact about the weather and started telling her the best places to shop for designer clothing at discount.

Randy's family had been more standoffish. They were a bit worried at first with a foreign bride. They assumed Lalana must be after Randy's money until she proved them wrong by paying for most of the wedding. Once they let down their guard and got to know her, they realized how wrong they'd been about her. Randy's mother insisted Lalana wear her wedding dress—something she hadn't done with Randy's first wife.

Maybe the initial guilt of not accepting Randy's bride right away made them put together such a delightful day for the two couples in their lovely family home in Upstate New York. Whatever the reason, Jake was grateful for Randy's family.

The whole day had been the fairy-tale wedding Lalana and Boon-nam deserved. Randy's family went all-out, decorating their backyard with a big white tent, white ribbons, and white flowers. At dusk, tiny sparkling lights lit the backyard, casting a magical spell over the expanse as the brides walked each other down the aisle arm in arm.

Randy's bride was elegant in an off-the-shoulder body-skimming floor-length gown with white button-up gloves. But Boon-nam took Jake's breath away as she bounced toward him in her confection of spun white lace and flowers. Her dress was above her knees in the front. Damn, Jake couldn't help but notice how easily the dress would give him complete access, and those long ruffles cascading to the ground could easily bind her hands.

Shit, these tux pants just got tighter.

"Do you, Randy Camster, take Lalana Dulyarat to respect, love, and adore?"

His buddy's smile was the biggest Jake'd ever seen.

"Absolutely."

"Do you, Jake O'Neil, take Boon-nam Rattanawong to be your lawfully wedded wife, to love, honor, and cherish?"

When he looked into Boon-nam's gorgeous eyes, he had no doubts. "Oh, hell, yes!"

"Do you, Lalana Dulyarat, take Randy Camster as your husband, to respect, love, and adore?"

"Yes." Tears glistened in Lalana's eyes, and her voice broke.

"Boon-nam Rattanawong, do you—"

"*Yes! Yes! Yes!*" And she launched herself at Jake's mouth.

Ow.... Mmm, that's my girl. He returned her eager kiss.

The officiant grinned but wasn't going to be lax in her duties, so she continued on. "Take Jake O'Neil as your lawfully wedded husband, to love, honor, and cherish?"

Boon-nam stopped the bruising kiss to answer again. "Yes. I promise to love, honor, and cherish Jake O'Neil every day of my life."

"By the power vested in me, I pronounce the happy couples married. It looks like I don't have to encourage either couple to kiss. My job here is done."

The crowd chuckled and applauded as she backed up and let the kissing continue.

Lalana's throat clearing finally forced Boon-nam to stop the rocking kiss. "Do you need a cough drop, La-la?"

"Time for the toss." Lalana grinned and hugged Boon-nam.

Thankfully they'd decided to skip the traditional reception line for a nontraditional wedding-bouquet toss.

During practice, Jake had determined Boon-nam needed a stool to stand on so her toss could reach the same distance as Lalana's height allowed her. From under a chair, Jake grabbed a stepstool decorated with white ribbons and bows.

"Here you go, my little tiger." He helped her step up and accepted her kiss as a thank-you. He kept his hands at her waist. She might not have needed him to steady her, but he wanted to hold her. Damn, his little tiger glowed with happiness.

"Okay, on three. One... two... three!" Boon-nam shouted.

Lalana and Boon-nam each tossed their bouquet of rainbow roses, which separated into single stems. Rainbow roses rained down on the crowd.

"We're going to make sure everyone has a blossom." Boon-nam kissed Jake before dragging Lalana with her to fetch the baskets of roses on either side of the aisle.

Jake strolled over to the table where Randy sat and flopped down next to him. "What a day."

Randy grinned. "Yeah. God, look at them." He pointed over to Boon-nam and Lalana animatedly chatting with two of his aunts and Jake's sister. "Boon-nam and Lalana enchant everyone they meet."

Jake nodded in agreement. "I really can't believe we've been back for two months."

"Oh, I can. My mother drove me crazy about the wedding plans." Randy smiled warmly. "I was relieved when Lalana and Boon-nam took over the planning."

"Come on, wasn't the cake tasting fun?" Jake referred to sitting at a bakery and feasting on cake and milk until he got nauseous.

"It was… after." Randy smirked and elbowed Jake. "I followed your suggestion with what to do with the excess cake."

"Lalana made an acceptable plate, huh?" Jake barked out a laugh. The blush on Randy's face told him his buddy might have been the dish. "I'm telling you, you guys should come to the club. It isn't all sex." Randy stared at him. "Okay, there is a lot of sex. But Boon-nam loves the eroticism of the club. And we get a lot of interesting ideas…."

Randy made a snorting noise. "As if you need ideas."

"Point taken. But seriously, you could come hang out with us, and you two can leave before anything starts up."

Randy grinned. "Maybe in a few weeks. We'll see." He shook his head in disbelief. "So much has changed. Pretty mind-blowing, you know? I can't believe we're married and happily settled."

"Happily married but never settled," Jake teased. "Oh, I forgot to tell you." He laughed, "Do you know your grandmother asked if Boon-nam and I were planning to have children?"

Randy whipped his head around. "Are you?"

Jake laughed for a second but gave serious consideration to the concept of children. "We'll see. Boon-nam is certainly a nurturer." He pointed over in the general direction of Boon-nam assisting Randy's elderly uncle out of his chair, taking his arm to guide him toward the house while chattering the entire way. "But we want to travel too. There are lots of animals to play with before we have our own zoo. How about you?"

"My grandmother asked me too. She obliviously doesn't realize Lalana can't have children naturally."

"Actually she can. Lalana just can't carry to term or deliver them, but she can provide the semen."

Randy pondered Lalana's little ones for a moment. "That's true. But I don't know. Maybe after Lalana is done with school."

"How are your parents?"

Randy shrugged. "My parents let me know again today they're thrilled I found my other half."

"I am too, buddy. You deserve to be happy."

"Thanks, Jake. So do you." Randy appeared a bit choked up. "Where would I be without you? You're a great best friend for dragging my sorry ass to Thailand."

"Hell, buddy, if you hadn't insisted on giving them our contact information, we would have been in our very own sitcom minus the laugh track. I don't even want to imagine where we would be right now." Jake gave him an emotional man hug.

Lalana beelined over to him and slipped an arm around Randy. "Hello, husband."

Boon-nam raced over and did the same to Jake. She leaned up to get a kiss. Boon-nam loved the fact that America had no stigma attached to kissing in public.

Jake gave her a kiss before he said, "You're vibrating, my little tiger."

Boon-nam giggled, teasing, "Later, honey."

Randy laughed out loud. Lalana shook her head with pursed lips.

Jake smirked. "No, I mean your bag. But if you want to play with some vibrators, I think you'll love a couple of your wedding presents from me."

"Ee!" Boon-nam squealed and giggled.

Everyone nearby stopped to smile at the excited bride before continuing on with their conversations.

"Definitely, I want to play with anything you want to give me." She batted her eyes at Jake before she pulled her cell phone out of her white sequined bag. She read the message and jumped up and down. "Happy Wedding wishes from Illusions & Dreams." She turned the phone so they could all see the picture they'd attached.

"Aww, look at them."

Jake grabbed Boon-nam into his arms and hugged her. "Do you miss them?"

"Of course, but we'll visit, and they will visit." Boon-nam giggled. She pressed a kiss over his heart. "Now do we have time to play with my gifts before dinner is served?"

"There's always time to play, my Boon-boon."

Lalana laughed. "I don't have any vibrating gifts, but I would like a *nap* before dinner."

Randy glanced around at his contented guests with a big grin on his face and decided on the best route to sneak his bride upstairs. "Sounds good... I'm not tired at all."

Z. ALLORA thinks everyone deserves a happy ending, and she makes sure they get one. Her stories are about love and romance and are tied together with erotic sex. She utilizes her time overseas and travels to bring you to places you've yet to visit. She introduces you to cultures you've yet to explore. But with every word she writes, she tries to convey love is love. She welcomes contact and looks forward to hearing from her "pretties"!

Contact Z.:
z.allora@yahoo.com
https://www.facebook.com/Z.Allora
http://zallora.blogspot.com

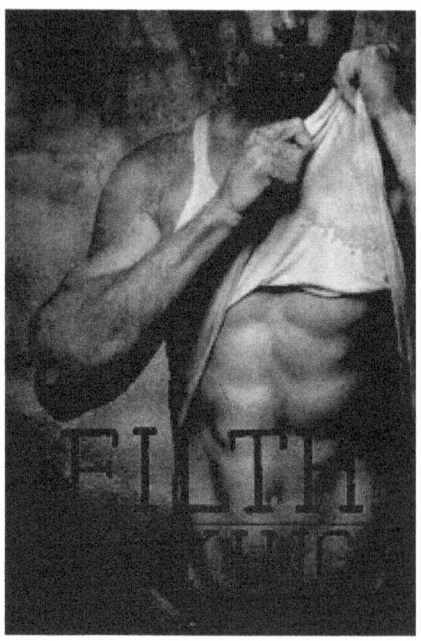

Don't miss

Sensible Commitments

By Susan Laine

A SENSES AND SENSATIONS STORY

Sensible Commitments

Susan Laine

After their troubled pasts and their rocky road to "happily ever after," the time has come for Jordan Waters and Sebastian Sumner to officially declare their love for each other. With the wedding two days before Christmas, the happy couple can't put off addressing their tenuous relationships with their birth families. Between supportive friends like Jack Waters, Kevin Thompson, Bro Sumner, and Lacey Adair, they've had a taste of what a happy home means, regardless of blood ties. As the wedding approaches, all three couples must make peace with their pasts as they prepare to celebrate friendship, brotherhood, and true love.

http://www.dreamspinnerpress.com

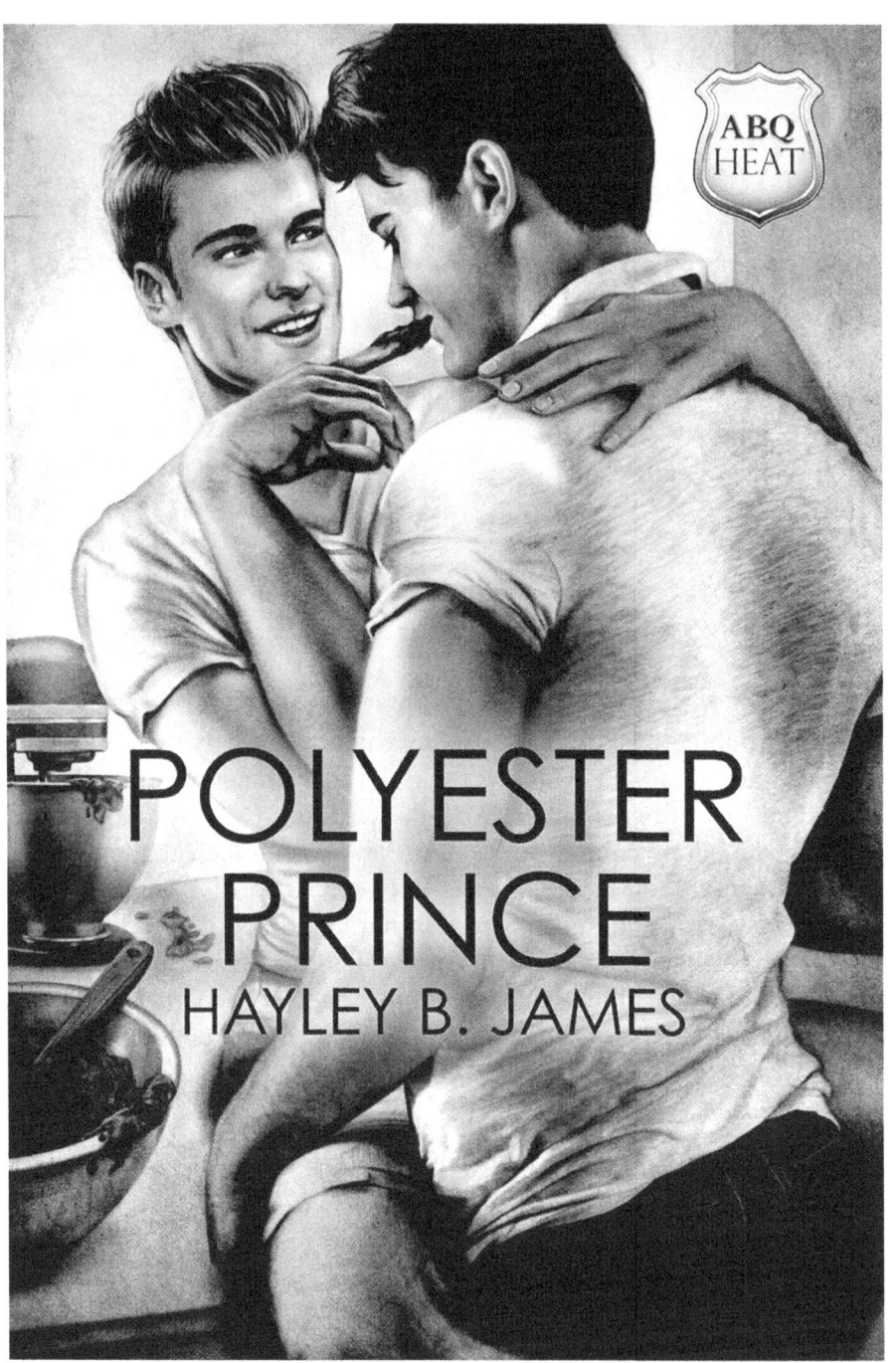

POLYESTER PRINCE

HAYLEY B. JAMES

http://www.dreamspinnerpress.com

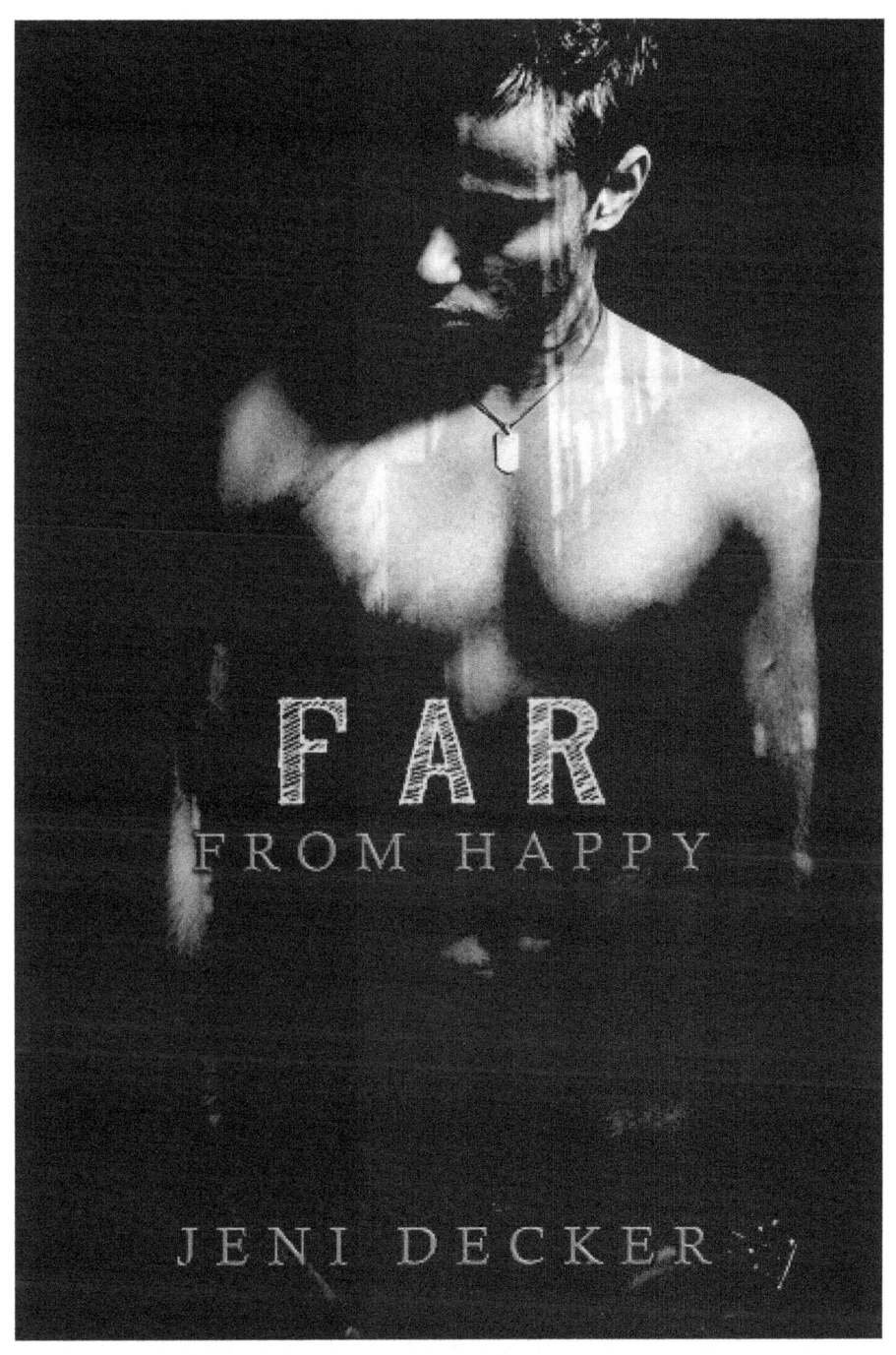

http://www.dreamspinnerpress.com

FOR **MORE** OF THE **BEST GAY ROMANCE**

Dreamspinner Press

DREAMSPINNERPRESS.COM